Readers' advance praise

for *The Emperor's Golden Carp and Other Stories*:

"...enjoyable, creative, and wonderfully surprising!" KJ

"I did not want it to end." TK

"I really loved it." CH

Also by J.K. Stephens

The Ibis Door, Dreamers Book 1

Readers say:

"I loved this story. It was a perfect read." GCH

"Hard to put down." PG

The Singer, Dreamers Book 2

Readers say:

"Whimsical, challenging, and a whole lot of fun." JM

"It has everything a good book needs." C

In the Ring, Dreamers Book 3

Readers say:

"A great story with a perfect ending!" VS

"You know you have found a good read when you finish the first book in a series and find yourself looking forward to the next, and the same for the third...I am looking forward to reading more..." JC

the emperor's golden carp

and other stories

J.K. Stephens

Daybreak Publications

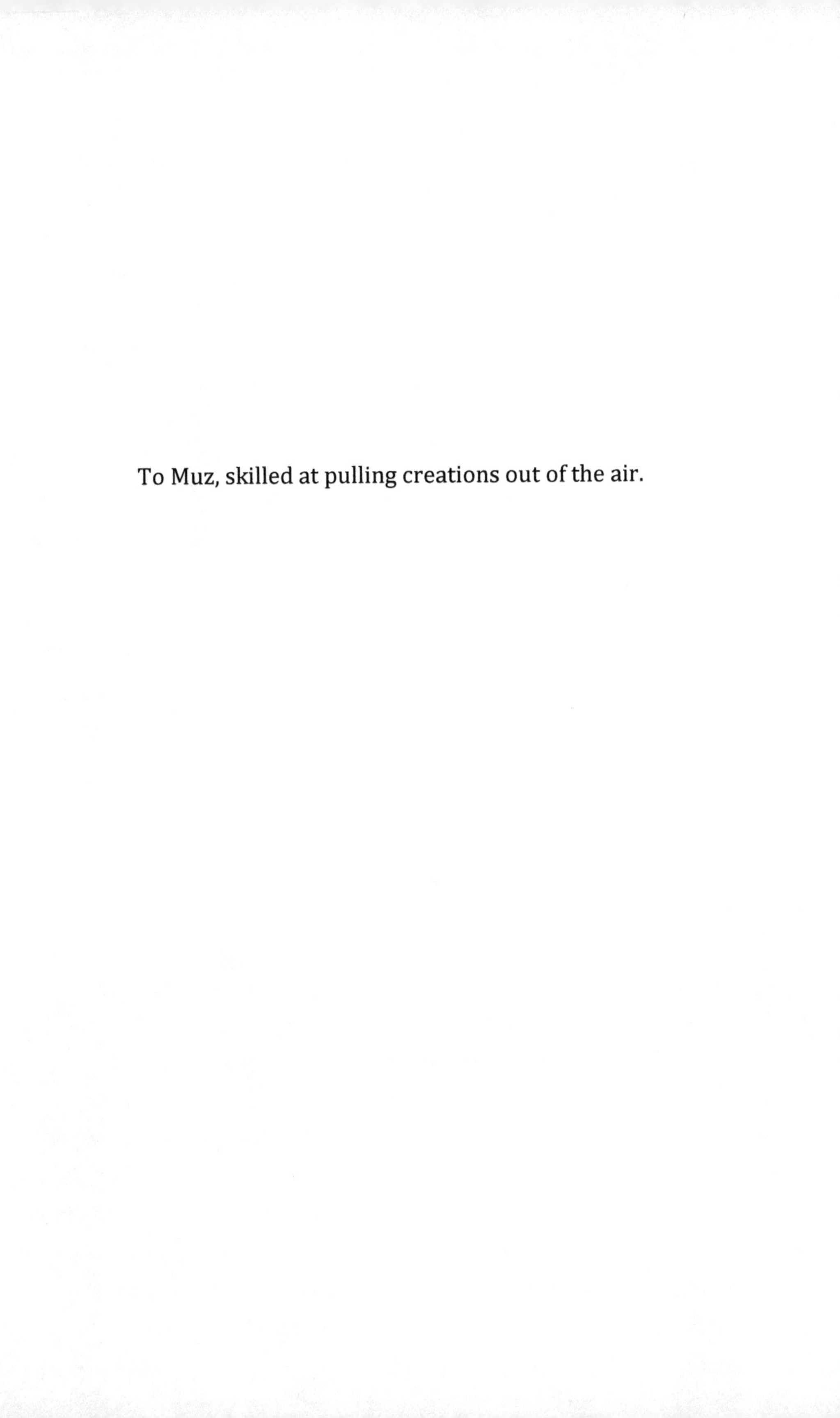

To Muz, skilled at pulling creations out of the air.

Contents

The Emperor's Golden Carp 1

Chameleon 15

The Cure for the Sleeping Woman 23

Digging on the Dark Side 30

Found 42

Silver Alert 53

Kokopelli 62

Slaves 75

Fun City, Callis 94

Dark Chocolate 107

Shale 120

Sister of a Crocodile 140

Escape Route 155

One Basket 165

The Knife-Thrower's Assistant 176

Red Planet Blues 184

Martian Crepes 194

The Trade 206

Bracelet 222

It Might Be Today 232

the emperor's golden carp

and other stories

J.K. Stephens

The Emperor's Golden Carp

AT THE ENTRY GATE to the enormous palace, Lena slid from the blanket on the zakrin's back and held its tether, wanting to be ready when they called her forward. The line of waiting vendors in front of her, all on foot, was short. She repeated the words silently. Hearing herself say them. Karn had warned that the accent had to sound authentic to stave off trouble with the entry guards. She felt the pulsing of the coinlike disk against her own pulse, there in her left sleeve.

Around her earth-colored buildings rose to enclose the broad square, swarming with people, that fronted the palace. Many of these buildings had scrawny plants trailing from tiered gardens, and on their roofs sickly trees stood. These must be the famed hanging gardens and fruit trees of the ancient city.

The near buildings were mostly three or four stories tall, but behind them others towered ten and twenty stories above her, their metal-and-glass angles flashing in the sunlight.

The square smelled of cooking herbs. And dust. Despite the crowds, the place was possessed by strangled quiet.

Her long-legged beast sighed a little and cast its neck around, looking for a bunch of grass. When it found one growing against the palace wall, the rented zakrin stretched to uproot the tuft of dry hills-grass and stuffed it in its mouth, dirt and all, letting a muddy mixture of dirt and mouth-juices ooze down the whiskers on its chin. Lena patted the curls on the creature's sweaty left flank, realizing too late that it was going to make her hand stink. She wiped the hand on her woven coveralls and pulled her face-scarf up against the dry wind.

She had more story ready if it was needed. But she just had to get in, place the coin, and get out, then back to the cart Karn had loaned her and off. The cart was under some brush in the little boxed-in valley he had mapped for her, a fair distance outside the city: wings folded now, perching compact as a raptor ready to unfold into the sky.

This isn't what I do. Not my calling.

"But sometimes we do what we have to," Karn had said soberly.

She had no answer then, and didn't now.

Karn was a fellow student, or so she thought until one day when they became romantically involved. Then he was her lover, mentor, director. And one against whom she fought to understand things.

The emperor would expect her delivery, Karn said. She had to hope this improbable statement was true.

The guard's bark echoed against the stone wall a second time. She hastened forward, tugging the zakrin's lead. Her water-flask had been empty for hours. Her throat was dry.

In a local dialect she said the memorized words that meant, "For the emperor's carp. I have the order here." Her accent was good but the official looked at her skeptically.

She knew what he saw: a dusty-faced, blue-eyed female in a dust-colored coverall, with curly dark hair escaping from her headscarf. Traveling alone. She handed over the wrinkled piece of computer-printed government paper with the bill of lading printed on it, and waved her hand at the beast beside her to show the bundles on its back. Most of them were stuffed with her clothes; but the vials of medicine for the Emperor's golden carp were in there too.

"Will you spend the night here in the city?" he asked. From reading news transmissions she understood this dialect well enough, although she spoke it poorly.

She had been prepared for this question. Not if I can help it. "No," she answered. It was one of the 10 or so words she had learned to speak properly in the dialect. If he refused her admission, she would have to turn back, leave the city by the West gate, and cross the wasteland again, without water unless she could beg some. But with her flask filled, she would be gone tonight.

He inspected the stamp carefully, then her face again. "You may enter," he said, his eyes half-lidded, and turned his hand over to display his palm. She had been warned about this; she opened a flap on a side-bag carried by the zakrin, and pulled out a crumpled piece of paper money.

"Ten only?" he warned her.

"Orders of the Emperor," she said in dialect, pointing to small print on the bill of lading. It said clearly, in the government-approved written language that his job required him to know: "Gratuity limited to 10.000."

He sniffed and waved her through the gateway in the thick palace wall, where a temporary stable awaited the zakrin.

**

Inside, beyond the entry stable, the palace grounds were as rich with life and sound as the threadbare city was dry and quiet outside. She had been admitted to a walled garden that must serve as a waiting room for visitors. In here lush plants were fed by fountains and pools, splashing lavishly, and from somewhere she heard music.

She lowered her bags to the ground, pulled down her face-scarf, and stopped to drink a little from a pool with a cupped hand. She washed the dust from her face and mopped it dry with the cotton scarf. All the while she looked around for a location for the coin, the palm-sized silver and copper disk tucked into the knit sleeve of the field shirt she wore.

Strolling toward a fountain, she stretched the cuff of the sleeve with a curled finger to let the coin slide down into her left palm; she thumbed it between two fingers as she had practiced, depressing the timer button. She rested that hand on a mossy wall beside the fountain pool and leaned over the water as if to view something in it, pushing the coin through the moss between two stones, deep between, while she stirred the surface of the water with the other hand as a curious child would. She saw no carp.

"The Emperor awaits you." The quiet voice just behind her made her heart stop.

**

The Emperor's eyes were not cruel. Karn had said His Imperial Majesty was heartless, a foe of his people. But here was a small, fat, bald old man with deep crow's-feet at the outer corners of his eyes, not very imposing-looking because it seemed as if his face customarily wore a smile.

Only at this moment he was not smiling.

He sat in a dark-blue brocaded robe at the other end of the thin carpet. She kneeled at her end as she had been instructed.

This audience chamber was not large, but carved and gilded ornamentation curved ceilingward on each side, on ribs that traveled up to meet in pointed arches at the peak of the roof. A very large Stones board sat on a heavy table beside the Emperor's chair, with carved large and small game-pieces, some the size of her fists, positioned on the board in what looked like a mid-game strategy. Faint smells of incense and old cloth mingled with stringed music and fountain sounds from a courtyard outside, and she could almost taste the grain-and-spice aroma of a meal cooking, far off.

She had not expected to meet him. She was only the courier of medicine for the golden carp, which any lackey could have taken from her, and checked against the bill of lading. And then allowed her to fill her flask with water. And maybe given her a small piece of money in return for her speedy delivery, to show the graciousness of His Imperial Majesty to underlings.

"But if you do see him, kneel immediately," Karn had said.

So here she kneeled. Now she recited carefully in dialect the all-purpose greeting she had learned: "Greetings, Honored One." And repeated her memorized message about the medicine, displaying the bill of lading, waving a hand at her saddle packs.

The Emperor gazed at her without speaking.

"You have not eaten," he said finally, in dialect.

She stared.

"Not for some time," he said. "Unpack your delivery. Then you will join me."

He waved to the servant who had brought her. The man exited and returned almost immediately with others carrying a low table, cushions and trays of food. The smell made her weak with hunger.

She rose to unpack the flasks of medicine from her leather side-packs, grateful for the motion that would cover her confusion and give her a moment to think.

Refusing his invitation would be ill-mannered, unheard of. But she couldn't say more than a few things in the dialect that she was pretending was hers. How long could she be here before she said or did something that would expose her as a fraud? Karn had arranged this delivery only as a cover, to get her inside with the coin.

As soon as he saw the bottles of medicine and bill of lading handed to one of the servants, His Imperial Majesty seated himself lightly on a floor-cushion and held out an open hand to indicate the cushion opposite him, across the table.

She was hot. She could hardly breathe. She bowed her head politely and sank sweating onto the heavy pillow, noticing that all three servants now stood by in various quarters of the room, each about twenty feet away, one behind her. One wore some kind of quiver and carried the traditional ceremonial bow. Probably all of them were armed, actually.

Again the Emperor held out his palm, this time toward her full water-bowl. She was in their hands; if they meant to kill her it would not require the expense of poison, she knew. She bowed her head with gratitude she couldn't help, and drank it to the bottom. A servant was at her elbow as she put it down, filling it again from a flask. She hesitated, and His Imperial Majesty nodded gravely. She drank again.

Only then did her host turn to look at the food. He served it family-style, lifting the lid from each serving dish and filling a plate for her with some of everything: a scoop of grain, another of greens, one of spicy-looking meat, some fermented vegetables, a little fish, a clot of cheese, a prongful of noodles. And a ladle of soup into her bowl.

He lifted her plate and bowl to the servant, who had arrived silently to take them and settle them before her. Then he filled his own. The smells tormented her. Her stomach was more frightened than hungry, but it was very hungry.

Silently he nodded and began to eat. She followed his lead, starting off slowly to keep this abrupt breaking of her fast from making her sick. Her eyes snagged now and then on the Stones board, much like her father's. Also like Zarn's much smaller one.

Mercifully he said nothing until they had eaten all that was served and tea was coming. "My carp are like old friends," he said then. "Very valuable to me."

Conversation? Her eyes rose to meet his, then fled to her teabowl. She raised it to her lips and nodded politely.

"They have lived for fifty years, through everything, and they are as healthy as I am." He smiled slightly, with satisfaction.

So why the medicine? She sipped the tea. It was very good.

"Perhaps you have heard that I am a prisoner here," he said.

Lena struggled to keep the astonishment out of her eyes. Prisoner? Karn had not said. The Tyrant of Bindare a prisoner? She sipped again, as an excuse to look away.

"Since last new year. It was a quiet coup." In his voice there was a microscopic thread of sadness. "So, you did not know."

She shook her head, unable to keep herself from answering honestly to his unhappiness. Her mind raced with questions.

"There have been countless attempts on my life since then, during the last year. My servants and family, my people in this city, are loyal and have protected me, but life would be easier for my captors if I were to die. You may be wondering, now: why would a healthy man, with healthy fish" — he smiled ironically — "who is subject to plots against him, invite danger by asking for a delivery of medicine he does not need?"

She looked into his eyes and almost smiled. As a student she enjoyed other students with this kind of mind: nimble and fond of truth. She too was a student of truth.

Or had been. She saw the coin, buried in the moss of the wall next to the courtyard fountain. She took another sip, a long one, looking into the cup. She was a student of truth before her abandoned studies were replaced by Karn's political discussions, meetings, plotting and planning. She saw her anxious father, sickened and failing last winter, urging her to get wiser before she solved problems she knew so little of.

When she raised her head she found that he continued to look at her, unwavering. Her eyes met his and she nodded, regretting how transparent her mind might be to him, behind her eyes. It felt transparent to her. Yes, she nodded in answer. I wonder.

In fact, her mind raced with many more questions besides: If he was loved enough to be protected by his people, why was he a prisoner? If he was already imprisoned, unable to fight or muster troops, why did Karn and others need for him to die?

She nodded again. This time she waited, and watched his eyes. Why *would* the Emperor ask for a delivery he did not need?

— Of course.

"Of course," he said. "It's because I need your help."

Yes, of course. Her mind fled to the coin, and came back hastily. He gazed at her. She felt as if he could see her too well; she could only hide by saying something.

And at that moment she wanted to help the man.

"What help do you need?" she asked. She watched, a dawning horror choking her, as his eyes lit with recognition. He had not asked for her help in dialect. He had asked in the language of the realm, the language of educated people. And she had answered in the same without noticing. She had spoken in the patrician tongue.

Now he knew she was no merchant's servant or small trader or delivery-hire. The danger almost overwhelmed her.

Now he knew what she also knew, right now: she was just the latest of many attempts on his life.

Her heart thudded with fright. What had been done to the others who attempted?

And how many of them had been sent by Karn? Bitterness flooded into her panic. Bitterness and truth: she was a small piece on a Stones board, Karn's stone. Just a stone, and she was trapped.

"There's enough explosive in that coin to destroy the entire palace," Karn had said, his dark eyes smiling. And later, as he kissed her and sent her off on a dark road toward the ancient capital, "Remember: if you have not signaled within 3 hours the explosive will blow."

To her eyes this emperor was not as evil as Karn had assured her he was. Not a man who deserved to die. But she had just been revealed as the Emperor's enemy, as a probable murderer. It didn't change things that she herself had been tricked as well. Or that he had just fed her with his own hands as a father feeds a daughter. Or that she had wished, just now, to help him.

She lifted her chin and raised her eyes again to meet the Emperor's. His gaze was even. She met his gaze as one who meets a deadly foe, unwilling to die begging. She was certain to die soon, bravely or not.

The sudden sound of engines roaring seemed to be the noise of her death surrounding her. The noise rose to a painful pitch. But then it resolved into large machine noises from outside the palace.

The sound came from out near the thoroughfare, from vehicles that must be much larger than the vehicles she had seen as she entered the city. The Emperor rose and gave quick orders in dialect to his servants. He left the room.

**

She stared, unseeing at first, for many minutes. When it was clear that death had been postponed she came back to the present and began to shiver, too hard to control it.

She looked behind her. The servant with the bow was the only one who remained in sight, standing at attention in an archway in the nearest wall.

"Can I talk to you?" she addressed him in the educated tongue. She had to tell someone about the coin.

The servant scowled and said nothing.

She rose and turned her cushion, reseating herself on it to face him. She didn't want to sit with him at her back.

There was another clamor of engine noises outside, still in the distance but nearer. And coming from many directions at once, now. As the imminence of her own death moved a little farther away her mind began to race.

By now most of the time left on the timer of the coin-bomb was gone. Where was the Emperor?

People ran scuffling through hallways nearby in the palace, echoing in the passageways, giving and passing orders in bits of clipped dialect. There were some cries of fright, but they were few: children's voices. These people must be used to attacks.

The Emperor seemed to know how to defend his fortified palace.

But not if the coin went off.

It was wrong. She was sure Karn was wrong. All she wished to do now was to disable the coin. But Karn hadn't told her of any way to do that.

At the entry to the palace proper, the electronic weapon detectors had shown she wasn't armed with a personal weapon, but the Emperor might have guessed that she brought another kind of threat.

He had invited her to ask for her help. What help could she possibly have given him?

There were more scufflings in the hallway. Someone called. Her lone guard disappeared from view.

Wide-eyed at the opportunity, she leaped up. She dove and rolled sidewards to make her body a difficult target, then ran to the opposite doorway.

Through the doorway the empty corridor astonished her. She ran down it on her toes for quiet, retracing her steps to the entryway door, flung it back, darted into the entry garden. But she heard sounds behind her.

She didn't dare to look back and risk the paralysis of fright. Dodging among fountains and pools, she made it to the mossy wall where she had rested her hand.

She panted hopefully as she stuck her little finger between the stones, where inserting the coin had plowed a slot through the moss, to pry it out. She could fling it over the wall. Find a direction that would do least harm.

Between the cool stones was only empty space. The coin was gone.

Hopes sunk, she turned to face the arrows of the guard.

The Emperor stood before her: twice as far away as he was tall. Against the splashing fountains and the green leaves he seemed taller than before. His blue brocaded robes were undisturbed, his face only slightly damp with sweat. His gaze at her was calm as before but sharply focused.

"I have to warn you —" she began.

He silenced her with a commanding slash of his hand. "You will want to come with me," he said loudly, over the din outside the walls. "Quickly." Then he turned and swept away.

Her shame was deep as she followed him. If it could be possible to be shamed before everyone and everything, she was that. To herself she was a fool. To Karn, she would be a failure. To the Emperor, treasonous. To his family and his people, a murderer.

As she brushed hastily by a potted tree near the entry door, a fruit blossom fell at her feet. The bruised thing seemed to lay yet another claim against her.

**

Lena stood near the Emperor on the flagstone floor of the battlements, looking out past a hip-high wall onto confusion. A stiff wind, mercifully cooling, curled back the brocade on the front of his robe. It dried the damp curls at her temples.

He didn't speak, so she only looked out across the haze of dust and exploding ammunition. The public market that ringed the palace was empty of traders, filled instead with armed people facing outward in every direction. Some of the buildings encircling the palace showed damage — a few more toppled fruit trees.

Extending outward from the palace like the points of an eight-pointed star were the ancient trade roads, which also seemed to be filled with people, armed and moving outward in all directions, gouts of fire spurting from their weapons now and then.

At every point of the star, at the farthest end, was a small clutch of war machines facing outward. Lena marveled: somehow the imprisoned Emperor had acquired some sophisticated weapons and war equipment.

Beyond, the broad thoroughfare that travelled past and arced around the center of the city was lit with explosive fire and filled with giant war machinery. Its roaring was so loud it put the grinding noises right in her face and ears, the burned-fuel smell right in her nose. There was no distance or escape.

Everywhere she looked around her the huge machines encircled this old part of the city, face-to-face at each point of the star with the older, smaller machines belonging to the Emperor's supporters.

She had begun to decide she saw the game-board of this fight — how the forces were placed — when a voice sounded in her ears as if it surrounded her. Horrified, she recognized Karn. Amplified. Karn, here. And declaring the terms of surrender, like someone's lieutenant.

In fact, he probably was.

Involuntarily she turned to look at the Emperor and found his eyes on her face. He nodded soberly at her.

That was Karn, out at the thoroughfare, at the forefront of the attacking machinery, and now she knew him completely: offering clemency for surrender, knowing that there would be no clemency because the palace would go skyward into fragments soon and none of his terms would ever have to be honored. Knowing too, without regret, that Lena probably would never get out alive.

"Please!" she said. "We have to —"

The Emperor turned away from her, reached down to the flagstones at his left and raised the cage of a large carrier bird up onto the parapet. The creature's feathers stirred drily within it.

Lena staggered backward when the Emperor pulled from the inside of his robe the metal coin-bomb. She stared as he checked the flat display window on its face and his clever-looking fingers pressed locations that were unknown to her on top and sides.

Then he opened the cage and laced the coin to the bird's feet. He eased the creature through the cage door by its legs, held it facing him eye to eye while he stroked its wings and bent his head toward it. Then he raised it slowly at arm's length and threw it high up into the air. With a cry the bird dipped, turned and rose again on powerful wings.

The bird would die. And the Emperor seemed to be showing her that not only the bird would die today.

She stood facing this game of power and death, watching as the bird shrank to a speck in the distance and became indistinguishable somewhere near the center of the enemy's machinery of war.

Her breath paused.

Enormous fire shot skyward, obliterating machines and earth, carrying waves of rock and the remains of bodies high into the air.

She could only stare. But relief landed around her as the terrible wreckage of the bomb was landing, out there in the distance: the coin had failed to hurt the Emperor. He and his family, and his allies, seemed to be safe.

The Emperor turned toward her. She turned to him too now, with dread.

To her surprise he was smiling, his eyes crinkled deeply at the corners. "Thus we acquire new weapons of war," he told her happily. At the star-points far to left and right, his machines were shooting to provide cover as his skirmishing troops captured the large new war machines that faced them. "Thank you for coming to help me with this."

Stunned but recovering, she thought to save herself. Maybe he would believe: "I was deceived," she said. "I —"

"Yes, I deceived you. And that one" — he waved a disgusted hand toward the site of the explosion — "deceived you too. You have been a fool," he smiled warmly at her. "It's how we all learn."

He turned amiably from the wall toward the stairway downward.

"Before you go," he said, "will you join me for some tea and a game of Stones?"

Chameleon

AT ONE SIDE OF THE LONG STRIPE OF ROAD Lem stood with its hand out, one digit up like the last local person it had seen. The heat of the sun was burning its skin where the clothing didn't cover, and that was worrisome, but the hat protected its eyes and face. A huge noisy truck roared by, surrounded by swirling dust, and was gone. The lingering dust smelled of minerals and machinery.

Lem was a student, newly arrived at this place.

All the signals for help had gone unanswered. Lem was uncertain how long it might take to get to the place called "Roswell," where the rest and repair cellar was, to order a mechanic who could return here to retrieve the malfunctioning craft. But the surrounding terrain was interesting, in a stark way, and the small creatures that came by to observe Lem were friendly enough, the ones with legs and without. The chameleons seemed almost like brother creatures.

This morning while Lem had hidden the disabled craft and covered it with sand, and while the yellow dwarf sun rose toward the zenith, its chameleon-like body had gradually assumed the correct anatomic structure and cellular structure, modifying the foundations of its Basic Form for this locale.

It had walked on the hot sand, protected from view by round mounds of large dry vegetation, to a structure along the roadside where local sentients and their surface-craft seemed to be gathered. It had watched them from the shade of some more of the dry vegetation, mimicking their appearance until it had assumed a form and structure that would seem to belong to a generic local sentient.

Lem was careful. To shock or disturb the locals would violate all the rules, of course.

As Lem's body structure shifted, it swiftly removed and buried its foreign-looking boots and suit, leaving only a heat-resistant short undergarment that was much like something a few of the male sentients were wearing. The sun was hot without the protection of clothing, but it was better to be scantily clad if that was appropriate garb for this place. He put the tracker, a small silver disk, into the internal pocket of the undergarment.

A few hours of leisure spent looking at the objects inside the structure, and going in and out listening to the sentients, was all it took for Lem to absorb some of the language and customs of these locals. They were called "people," or "guys," or other flattering and unflattering names, besides the proper name of each. They drank water or beer or other liquids in containers. Lem drank thirstily from a water container on a wall.

By that time he was able to talk briefly with one or two people, and ask about some of the small creatures outside the "gas station," and observe that they felt his silvery undergarment was, maybe not shocking, but a little unusual. Lem borrowed some replacement garments from a shelf inside the place — long bi-legged dirt-colored things and a black shirt that said BEER on the front for viewers to read, with small flimsy footwear someone called "flip-flops" — and struggled into them in the shade behind the structure.

Now a passing truck skidded to a stop some distance past Lem. Sprinting down the gravel shoulder after it, Lem grabbed the door handle and hoisted up into the cab.

"Where you going to?" the driver said, as the door closed. He driver looked Lem up and down. Lem was glad to find that the driver was male. Because they had similar appearances the guy might be friendlier to Lem's purpose. But the person's eyes rested lingeringly on Lem's pink flowered flip-flops.

Lem was not only chameleonlike by nature — one whose race understood things by becoming and mimicking them — but like most of the sentients in the home system, Lem was a hermaphroditic entity, able to be male or female or some combination at choice. Outside the gas station there were two main types visible, and he had adopted the most numerous type that he saw there, in a medium sort of color, hoping it would be acceptable enough to get him a ride. It had worked. Or seemed to.

But he had also learned from his hours in the gas station that male, female or other was an important feature of life here. Whether you were one or another mattered. And not knowing how to change at will — that seemed to make it even more important to these people.

The driver gazed at him skeptically. Lem's vision focused on a large hairy creature on the seat between him and the driver — Lem's first sighting of such a thing. It raised its head and growled menacingly.

Lem considered briefly: If the driver liked this growling being well enough to keep it near, maybe it would be more suitable to take the form of this sort of creature, more likely to elicit friendliness. But then, the thing didn't seem to be able to speak. Not sentient enough.

The driver spoke to Lem again. "If my dog doesn't like you, I can't give you a lift. What's yer name?" he asked.

Lem murmured an answer, eyes fixed on the dog's bared teeth.

"Lemma?" the driver said, giving Lem another up-and-down look that sparked a flash of inspiration.

Lem displayed the facial expression he had learned in the gas station. It was something sentients did in that place that seemed to result in improved relations. While he smiled persistently at the driver, Lem hastily rearranged form and structure more, then a little more.

Then she answered, "Yes! Lemma. You can call me Lem."

And she pulled off the hat and shook out sun-streaked curls. And she smiled again brightly, full lips parted as if the smile itself were delicious to wear.

She saw the moment reflected in the driver's eyes: all around him the day had just dawned again and it was all like sweet food, ready for the eating. The dog ceased growling. The driver smiled a lopsided smile back at her, pushed up the brim of his hat and gazed appreciatively, then pushed a lever forward. "Well, then, Lem. I'm Jared. Where you headed?"

**

As opposites, male and female, they seemed to get along very well, Lem noticed. Jared told her about his cargo, hundreds of sleeping birds destined to be food someday. They watched a "movie" on the dashboard screen while they went.

At sunset, going east on Route 40, they stopped at a gas station Jared called a "truck stop." Lem slid into her flip-flops and got out of the cab.

"Hey, Jared, where'd you hook up with that pretty little thing?" a voice boomed from behind them. — A friend of the driver's, clearly, and the biggest person Lem had seen so far: a large red-faced man with red hair on head and face.

"Why thank you!" she boomed back at him. But she noticed the surprised looks she had just drawn from both males; clearly she had just committed an interpersonal blunder. Some violation of local custom?

While the males exchanged destination intel, she looked around for more females so she could study proper local behavior. One, far off, she could barely permeate for one long moment...

"From the Mohave Desert to Roswell? That's a long way to hitch," the large male boomed at Lem again. "Going to visit the extraterrestrials there?" he grinned down at her, coming rather close for a stranger.

Jared edged between them, possessively. She looked up at him then, and tested an idea. She delivered him a richly promising smile, filled with waving grass, warm wind and desert starlight. Now, that was acceptable behavior; she could tell.

He took her elbow, with just a hint of victory in his motion, and steered her away from the booming male into the truck stop, toward smells that made her internal functions eager for replenishment.

**

"Time to rest for the night," Jared said. They had turned off the road at a small truck stop called MOTEL.

They had talked long and Lem had learned a lot. Now Jared had a look in his eye. She felt energy from him so strongly that her body answered his, even without her willing it.

But she also felt the tracker pulsing in the side pocket of her undergarment. "I'll be in soon," she said.

The tracker had Lem's coordinates. Why hadn't they answered her call before this? She put in the code for Disabled Vehicle again. A message was returned: Lem must arrive at the "Roswell New Mexico" rest and repair cellar by sunrise tomorrow or miss entry and shelter, as well as repair crew, for another week. Lem knew the downed craft ought to be towed soon — before it could be uncovered by wind, discovered and stolen or destroyed. She re-sent the craft's coordinates. But, the response reminded her, Lem's presence was legally necessary to re-key and move the vehicle.

Inside that structure over there, the tired driver was sleeping.

How could she get Jared to drive all night and get her to Roswell by sunrise?

She twirled the unaccustomed curls around her small pretty Earth-female fingers as she considered for a long while, permeating the darkness around her. Life is usually ready to assist life, she knew. Maybe she could seek the help of the sleeping birds in the back of the truck.

She woke them, all fifteen hundred of them, as gently as possible and showed them her problem. They seemed to quickly align their life force with her need, or maybe her life force aligned somehow with their need: they all began to screech and cry and crow at high volume.

When the owner of the MOTEL truck stop had finished telling the trucker loudly about the bird noises, it was time to go. The trucker climbed sleepily back into the cab of the truck and started the engine.

"But look, I wasn't really going *to* Roswell. The processing plant is out further on 40, past the turnoff. I just couldn't resist your sweet smile." He was almost as abashed as he was sleepy.

She gazed at him. Not go to Roswell: this was not good.

"Look, I get it about getting your vehicle into the shop. I'll take you there! But I got to get these chickens where they're headed — now especially since they've woke. Can't go straight to Roswell, Lem. You understand?"

Lem understood, but she saw her chameleon self broiling in the heat, hiding under that large round vegetation for a week until the repair and rest cellar could open again. There might be dogs around there too. Beside her the dog began to whine and twitch.

She looked at Jared's earnest face, and was surprised to find that she couldn't help the smile this time. She reached over and patted his arm gently, wanting to comfort him — this one who wished to assist her. "You will think of something," she said soothingly.

She saw his eyes go liquid and moons rising in them. What forces moved the males and females of this place! Lem had never seen such a thing. Jared nodded, and began to sing a little tuneless song as he stared earnestly at the road vanishing under the hood of the cab. She watched the road vanish with him.

"I know!" he said, brightly, in a while. "At Cline's Corners I can get you a ride with Robbins, a guy who goes back and forth from there to Roswell. You can make your deal with the tow and repair people there, since you like them guys so much, and I can pick you up tomorrow night, take you back to your vehicle again! Goin' back to Mojave anyways. I'll get Rollins now." He hit the buttons on his dash phone.

**

As they pulled onto the dark turnoff at Cline's Corners he smiled at her. "See, over there's Rollins' truck. A good guy. He'll take you to Roswell before sunrise. Take good care of you. Then, I promise, I'll come get you on my way back, so just stay at the town park there till I do."

Lem felt the happiness radiating from him. She hoped the courageous birds in the back of the truck got free somehow without damaging his happiness. But take her to her vehicle? The thought made her breath stop. Forbidden, impossible.

He must have seen it in her face. He said, "Hey, girl, I want to see you again. You are the best woman I've ever met — don't know how to say it — you're the most woman I've ever been around."

She patted his arm. His eyes melted again, this time with longing. She leaned over and kissed him, like in the movie, to be friendly. And then, with her body going wild, did it again a long time. No wonder Earth people acted the way they did.

Fortunately, the tapping at his window was Rollins. Gratefully she slid her feet into her flip-flops, catching her breath again.

She kissed her hand and blew it to him, also like in the movie: Goodbye.

It would have to be goodbye.

Still, when Lem closed the door, a sorrow entered the belly of its chameleon body that was larger than any it had ever felt before.

A Cure for the Sleeping Woman

YOU WOULDN'T IMAGINE that I'd have any kind of cure up my sleeve. I don't cure things. I make things. But there she was and the neighbors all insisted, for no reason I could see, that I was the one who would know how to do something about her.

She had long, coarse hair let loose in the kind of wriggly blonde curls that Botticelli's Venus on the Half Shell wore (not really the name, but you know), with a sky-blue embroidered overblouse and a long retro skirt that covered all but these pretty plump feet she had. There was a toe-ring on one of her ten perfect toes. Her toes were staggeringly perfect.

Somehow she had carelessly left herself, unconscious, on the old maroon couch in Larry's living room, in his stale-smelling apartment two floors directly below mine, on the second floor. Several of us had gathered there in answer to his urgent call for help. He wasn't eager to talk about how she got there, but he was willing, in exchange for help and sympathy from all of his neighbors, to say that he had tried to wake her without success for twelve hours, and now he was panicky about getting blamed for whatever had come over her.

Shapeless, sacklike Mrs. Fogel from the third floor stood there, alternately shaking her white topknot at Larry for this disreputable scene and reaching to nudge the pretty woman gently, again and again. That seemed to be Mrs. F's natural right, as the only other woman in the room, and no one else competed with her for it.

Raymond, the graying violist from Mrs. Fogel's floor, kneaded his long-fingered hands anxiously and frowned, asking questions in a scratchy voice now and then: What is her name? Does she have anyone who can be notified? What have you tried? and although they were all sensible questions, Larry answered them all in the negative.

How he got her into his apartment without ever learning her name or anything about her was a marvel to me, because Larry isn't that magnetic a guy. And the fact that he hadn't tried anything except asking her to Wake UP didn't say that much for his imagination either.

John, the building's trust fund boy from the top floor, had been the only other person available for this emergency, mid-afternoon on a Tuesday. Besides me, Charlie Friehoffer, that is — and I was there because I'm a studio painter and John demanded that they all seek my help. I'm usually around during the day, at my home and place of work in a studio apartment on the fourth floor, which smells of oil paint and wine and garlic, I am told. Nice smells, I think; and this ring-toed woman would go much better with my aqua blue thrift-store couch.

"This is awful!" John was insisting. Called away from the romance novels he was always binge-reading, he had the free head space to entertain dramatic notions on a Tuesday afternoon. "She could die here!"

Larry cringed. They all looked toward me. "What do you think we should do?" Raymond asked.

"She doesn't feel injured," Mrs. F testified scientifically. "And she's warm." Her chest rose and fell peacefully. Her cheeks were rosy. I thought about what color I would use to paint them.

Now, as I said I know nothing about curing people. But it seemed to me that anyone who wasn't dead or ill but didn't seem to want to wake was probably just not in the right place to wake up in.

I was really taken by how much I'd like to paint her portrait, reclining on my couch in the garlic and linseed smells of my studio, with her ten perfect toes showing.

"I think she needs to be moved to a new location," I said. "Let's move her to my couch." When Mrs. F. looked at me skeptically, I said, "There's more light and fresh air up there."

**

That night I ate my dinner at the little table in my kitchen, which sort of faced the tiny living room, watching her body lift a fraction and fall as she breathed, like a moored boat afloat on the small waves of a quiet harbor. The smell of my sizzling stir-fry hadn't seemed to affect her at all, and my watching her didn't either.

As I fell asleep on my bed, opposite the kitchen and living room, I heard her quiet breathing, in and out, and thought briefly how odd it was to have a roommate.

**

The next day while I was finishing up a commission for a bank branch vice president's office, she sighed. When I turned to look, she shifted slightly on my aqua velvet couch. She tucked her feet under the skirt and settled into dreamland again.

**

That afternoon I noticed that her toes had re-emerged from the skirt. While the commission was drying — a boat on the waves painted from a photo of the guy's rented Bermuda vacation-of-a-lifetime — I shifted my easel and paint table so I could look past them at her as I painted her.

"Going to do your picture now," I said to her. It seemed polite to let her know in case she objected. She didn't seem to.

Really, I couldn't stand to wait any longer to paint her. I put a freshly-stretched canvas up on the easel and began to brush on the earth-brown underpainting, drawing her in with shadows and loving the rhythm of head and shoulders, the curves of her body, the shadows her eyelashes cast, her small plump hands tucked under her chin. Much more engaging than a sailboat, although I like painting boats just fine.

I was lost in curve and line and color, until I came out of it to find that I had finished the underpainting and had put the basic color into her clothes and hair, skin, the couch, and it was 2 a.m. Past Charlie's bedtime.

**

A sound woke me. When I opened my eyes moonlight poured in through the uncurtained studio windows, silhouetting her against the city lights. Her silhouette stretched its hands ceilingward, let the stretch extend downward to its toes like a cat's stretch does, then subsided to a flat-footed stance and was still. She seemed to be gazing out into the jewelled depths of the city.

I waited, holding my breath. Her ripply hair was lit at the edges, like the penumbra of an eclipse.

She turned. Now she would see me. I should say something to prevent her from being frightened.

"Hi there," I said quietly.

She strolled toward the couch and sat on it.

"Are you wondering why you're here?" I said.

She lay sideward, curling to tuck her toes under her skirt. I could see them disappear under the cloth.

She seemed to be ignoring me. On the street I'm not often chased by drooling women, but they don't usually ignore me either.

"Don't be afraid," I said.

In a minute her steady breathing said she was asleep.

**

The sun was well up when I woke again. And she didn't seem to have moved an inch since I saw her lie down hours before, except that her toes were out. I noticed that half the glass of water I'd left beside her on an end-table was gone. Unless it was being tippled by a mouse, at least she must have drunk something. I guessed she wouldn't die of dehydration. She hadn't eaten for at least three days.

But I was mystified. She'd finally woken last night, and she didn't pay any attention to me.

I pictured her sitting in the bar with Larry, and going home with him, without ever noticing him. I've already said Larry wasn't too exciting, but it was a disturbing thought.

I couldn't figure it out. But I wasn't hungry and I wanted to paint before she woke all the way; just wanted to finish her toes before she moved them, capture her curled there like a beautiful piece of fruit in a bowl.

While I painted, enjoying the glossy strokes of color, loving the curve of her shoulder, the hint of freckles across her nose, I was struck by one thing: my eyes were straining to see her.

Why? The light was OK, nice northern light, no glare to it. I should be able to see her with no trouble. But now she was back. Then she faded again. And she bloomed back.

My eyes must be tired.

A little more, a few last fine-brush strokes, and it was good. I smiled, breathed, and began to wipe off my brushes.

**

I was hungry. But for no really good reason, today I had to eat in a perfectly clean place. To celebrate my finished painting, I guess. Sleeping Beauty was soundlessly dreaming and she didn't stir when I swept the place up and made my bed, so I dusted, washed all of the dishes — including the coffee mugs and wineglasses — and took out the trash.

I returned with an armload of castoff flowers from the alleyway bin beside the flower shop downstairs, one door over. Lucky find: the armload was enough to put fat bouquets in my two vases on the table and scatter little clumps of them in bowls and dishes around the place. I stuffed some daisies in a teapot on the end-table next to the couch where Miz Beauty still slept. I had to squint a little to see her now and then, but when I walked nearer or turned my head to change the light she was there for sure, plain as day. Should I shake her and try to wake her up?

Not yet. I was having too much fun boiling water and chopping the garlic for some shrimp scampi.

She sighed, suddenly and deeply. She rolled over and turned her toes toward the back of the sofa. It was then that I realized I wanted more shrimp than the six sorry specimens left in the freezer. Those would cook down to nothing.

I called up Mrs. Fogel.

**

"I've been wondering how she is!" Mrs. Fogel said in a loud whisper, standing in her slippers on the faded rug in my living room. She had agreed to come be the babysitter while I ran to the store. "The garlic fumes in here are so strong I can taste them, Charlie!"

She gazed wonderingly at Miz Beauty. "She looks a little pale! Is she eating?"

**

At Gibson's Deli, down the block, I tucked a bottle of vino under my arm and looked over the jumbo shrimp in the glass display case of meats and seafood at the back of the store. I was the only one in the store, not surprising on a Friday midmorning, but now the little bell over the door jangled.

While I bent and concentrated on the shrimp down there in the case the new customer arrived next to me: a pair of female legs in jeans, a pair of feet in sneakers, positioned to look into the case beside me. "Do those shrimp look fresh to you?" she asked. It was a strikingly fruity voice.

I turned my gaze from the shrimp to the face: a plump, rosy face with crinkly blonde hair pulled up in a loose clip and falling back out of it to frame her cheeks.

I stared. It's not my usual approach to women, but I did.

**

Sleeping Beauty's babysitter met us at the door. "Sorry to be so slow, Mrs. Fogel. We had to...This is Venus Martin—"

But I saw that Mrs. F shook all over with agitation. Something was clearly wrong.

"I'm sorry!" she said. "I waited here to tell you! She got so pale and she wouldn't wake to eat, even when I shook her! Then she was gone! I didn't mean to — I don't know what to —

"Venus?" She caught up to what I was saying and stared at the blue-jeaned, sneakered person beside me. Whose hair was now loosed from the clip, falling in long wiggly strands over her shoulders, down to her waist.

"Mrs. Fogel," I introduced the babysitter to Venus.

We all looked at each other. No one seemed to be able to say anything.

Over Mrs. F's shoulders I couldn't help noticing how cheery my place looked, with the flowers and the new painting on the easel. Venus was smiling, looking around her now and breathing deeply like someone waking on a perfect day. The place smelled of paints and butter, garlic and flowers. And Mrs. Fogel was right: the couch was empty.

Well, I make things. In my life, half the time I don't understand most things — and I certainly can't cure them. But let it never be said that Charlie can't invent something to serve the purpose when he has to. "Dinner will be ready soon," I announced. "Would either of you ladies like a glass of wine first?"

Digging on the Dark Side

IF I CHOOSE TO GROW MUSHROOMS in my side-garden for food, even if it is on company time, it ain't nobody's business but my own. Not everything grows here on the Terran moon, in fact almost nothing does, and sometimes I have to get out there in the spacesuit and hoe, pronto.

This morning I do. I oversleep because I had shell-duty go long last night and then the mushroom starts had to be tucked into the compost under the water blanket before noon to get them going on their growing curve soon enough. Two weeks is all I have if I don't want to eat nothing but disgusting packaged food all the time.

My station is belowground on the "dark" side of the moon, which is really only dark half the time. This morning a transmission had to go out, but I let it delay for an hour while I hoed up the compost out there and tossed in the germinated spores for the next batch. They have little enough time to grow as it is.

That's when the complaint call comes in. Those can get nasty.

I get the transmission out right after that. So who has a right to complain about me, Kodor? My scrambler is a fast one, and I have the mobile locations of all orbiting Terran surveillance satellites tracked. I send the bolt from yours truly, the man in the moon, and those puppies go limp and fail within minutes. All that budget money blown, so sad, and more budget will be needed to get them going again, although probably no one tells the taxpayers. The satellites interfere with my centuries-long strategic work, so they have to go dark to make way for what's important.

My garden is visible where I work from my desk, through a periscope I've set up. The mushroom garden and the periscope aren't things any Terran scientist could see. And I like to be able to look out there now and then to keep an eye on the area and see the mushrooms grow.

It's absurd to get a complaint call from Central. I have a lot to do every day here and I only have four hands.

Like there's shell duty once a week. Causes of things on Terra are designed to be something other than you'd think, to keep their scientists tied in knots and unable to progress much.

So of course they are ignorant about the shells: the fact that sea mollusks, univalves and bivalves both, are actually what perform the function of generating human emotions. They operate by emitting electronic waves and wavelets, probably more complex ones than anyone with half a brain would want to waste time hearing about, that create emotional patterns.

The dying conchs broadcast fear. Expiring oysters emit aesthetics. Don't let appearances fool you: the humble quarterdeck shells emit lust and the moon shells put out greed. The shells washed up on beaches all over Terra are indications of the waves that have been transmitted to confuse those poor idiots, the Terran people.

And let's not get into conspiracy theories. This is outright — just plain deliberate — messing with their heads.

Here's another task I have, one to do whenever we are in the light: sit for hours and pot-shot drones that are located anywhere within the moving shadowy edge of the interface between dark and light on Earth, which is right in the way of my transmissions.

That's the window my genetic transmissions have to go through — transmissions of DNA mutations, via electronics, into traveling sperm to introduce such anomalies as Big Foots and cancerous man-boobs. Anomalies that produce confused scientific studies and theory wars.

So I shoot drones out of the air from here with a scope, and it doesn't matter whether they're somebody taking aerial shots of a family reunion or government spy drones — the things all fizzle in midflight and drift to the ground somewhere with their insides mysteriously shorted out.

It's a political strategy I guess. They don't tell me. It's the usual in one of these organizations: the slogan is "Ours is but to do and die."

I've worked faithfully, day in and day out, for four hundred years with no objections for almost a century before this Complaint comes in. No need to send threats to get me to work. But the Complaint says there is new management and "any further delays for gardening on the company clock will result in repercussions." How did they know? Were they surveilling me?

**

Complaint Filed Record first quarter 41,645:

Inmate Eldn Kodor

Praetorian Lunar correctional facility Station 12,

24 degrees 45' 11.5 South

95 degrees 14' 12.6 East

Event: Inmate Kodor allowed a scrambler transmission to Earth to be delayed.

Background note: Inmate Kodor was a notoriously clever galactic criminal operating near Draco 2. Caused the Breng insurrection of G.D. 40,991, escaped capture until shot out of his ship in 41,233 and survived only partly intact mentally and physically. Inmate at this facility for 400 local years. Occupied with make-work tasks to keep him focused; for example sample collection, mollusk manipulation, air production, and DNA alteration in semi-sentient inhabitants of Terra.

Surveillance: screen images show Kodor busy at tasks assigned, but beginning to invent own tasks, like mushroom growing and creating periscope.

Recommendation: file complaint on any violation to keep him under control. *Do not parole.*

**

Originally I sent Lily Freel a message via canister gun. There was an old one in the half-buried tool quonset I discovered 40 local-standard kilometers east of here. I got to the quonset by tunneling horizontally for a few decades and finally digging straight up underneath the thing like in the old bank-breakin flat films. The place is loaded with useful stuff.

I didn't know her name then, of course. How I knew she existed I don't remember, but I found that her station is about 20 kilometers north of here, located like mine in the libration belt that's sometimes visible, sometimes invisible, from Earth. How I located her: sent a small seismic ping using my pulse tool and there was her station, showing up on the view screen that I pillaged from the tool quonset and made over for the purpose.

Lily's so hot she makes my skin quiver. Her hair is crazy red and she wears knee-high shiny black boots, always. Her eyes are always spaced-out looking, but I don't mind — because she doesn't mind, either, that I'm missing a quarter of my torso.

I'm guessing she was a chem-sniffing techie here in this galaxy; fried her own brilliant brains with the chemicals she cooked. I remember some old story that a bunch of them joined to blast holes in The Pretorian's conquering war-machines and buildings.

In spite of that, she still knows how to do fancy calculations. She sent back my canister somehow, containing a drawing that showed me how to be the other end of a surveying beam and once the angle was calculated we dug toward each other for about five local years, including detours around buried meteors. It was a great day when we met for the first card game.

**

Complaint Filed Record first quarter 41,645:

Inmate Lily Freel

Praetorian Lunar correctional facility Station 13,

23 degrees 36' 25.9 South

95 degrees 14' 15.6 East

Event: Inmate Freel was found to be absent when a call rang in from the Guidance Supervisor.

Background note: Inmate Freel spent many Terran years as a brilliant research scientist for Earth Space Forces, but abruptly defected and aided a rebellion, creating the chemistry for an explosion that destroyed 50 Pretorian structures, blacked out power and caused Pretorian government shutdown for a month, Terran time. Chemicals used for explosion destroyed her brain. Inmate at this facility for 420 local years. Occupied with make-work tasks for mental balance; for example, long-distance structural disintegration, natural disaster production, air filtration, sample collection, and arrangement of chemtrails into characters readable by Terran inhabitants.

Surveillance: screen images show Freel performing assigned tasks, but at times off-camera, unreachable and unresponsive.

Recommendation: file complaint on any violation, to get her to answer up when called. *Do not parole.*

**

Lily and I have set up a halfway meeting spot in the tunnel so we can split the kilometers, with a vintage atomic air cleaner we leave there for better breathing. She's there when I arrive, kicked back on the slabs of foam I brought from the quonset. She leaps up. "Hi babe,"

I say, patting her bottom while I wrap the rest of my arms around her. She pats me back.

"Avast me hearties," she says to greet me, thinking that makes sense. We've both brought some party food we made from the air-drop packaged crap: hers is rehydrated fish balls in some kind of sweet, shiny dark-brown crust. Not my kind of thing, but I eat some while I deal out the cards.

"Let's play ball!" she crows. "And they're off!" she announces as she plays a card. I never know what she'll say. When she plays the card that beats me on the first hand she says, "No holds barred, my good man."

We play more hands, laughing till I almost choke, while the games get faster and faster.

**

"Hey, Lil," I say later as we lean back together on the foam things and relax. "How do you think they are surveilling me? Maybe that last food drop contained some kind of hidden equipment?" It still bothers me. No one likes to have someone peeking at them. A person has some right to privacy.

She pulls a screwdriver from the tool belt that lies beside the foam pile, smoothes the layer of fine dust that covers the floor of the tunnel near her booted feet, and begins to draw things in it. At first they're impossible to make sense of, just big loopy scribbles. But she knows my face by now; she can tell when I'm not tracking. She smiles at me sweetly, wipes that layer away, and replaces it with something a little more like a drawing. We both gaze at it, she shrugs sweetly at me again, and wipes it out to replace it with more lines. After six tries she has something I can make sense of.

Neither of us know where Central is — At least, I know I don't, up to that moment, except that I know it's where the Complaint came from. But the drawing seems to be a map with lots of electronic symbols, showing our stations with the tunnel between, like a barbell, and what look like power channels, signal corridors and relays to the east and west of us. With a symbol that seems to show Central at the hub of all these channels, probably submerged, somewhere out there to the west beneath the surface of the light side of the moon.

She points to one line that runs from Central eastward onto the dark side, toward our little tiny barbell. The line branches out there so lines run to her station and mine and at least a few hundred others. I didn't think Lily's station and mine were the only ones, but I didn't know there were so many others. Startling.

She hashes the screwdriver around in the line she drew just before it branches, scrambling up the sandy layer. She grins proudly at me. She has some idea of how to cut the surveillance transmission line and stop the snoopers! At least for a while, while they figure out how to fix it. Hope she knows how to keep the cause of the cut line secret.

We slap hands, something she likes to do. I think it means "that's good." And she says, "Yeah, Kemosabe!" Her wild hair flames around her head. Her eyes crinkle.

"How do we start?" I try not to ask her too many questions, but that was another one. I also try to memorize the map quick because she's already wiping it out.

"First and ten, do it again!" she explains. She begins to draw more big crazy loops.

**

Complaint Filed Record second quarter 41,645:

Inmate Eldn Kodor

Praetorian Lunar correctional facility Station 12,

24 degrees 45' 11.5 South

95 degrees 14' 12.6 East

Event: Inmate Kodor was unavailable for Guidance call today. No answer to several attempts. Third time this week.

Surveillance: screen images show Kodor busy at tasks assigned, but beginning to invent still more of own tasks, like building decorative junk items and displaying them on stands. Source of junk is unknown.

Recommendation: continue to file complaints on any violations to keep Kodor under control. *Do not parole.*

**

Complaint Filed Record second quarter 41,645:

Inmate Lily Freel

Praetorian Lunar correctional facility Station 13,

23 degrees 36' 25.9 South

95 degrees 14' 15.6 East

Event: Inmate Freel was unavailable for Guidance call today. No answer to several attempts. Fourth time this week.

Surveillance: screen images show Freel performing assigned tasks, but also beginning to invent own tasks: reconstituting fish balls and covering them with chocolate, heating numerous ingredients in separate cooking containers that have the appearance of soup. Screen images poor, cutting in and out.

Recommendation: file complaints on any violations, to keep Freel under control. *Do not parole.*

**

Lily gets me to understand, a few card games later, that she has found the incoming surveillance camera line and the "eye" for the thing in her place, Station 13.

Meanwhile I'm busy concocting weapons disguised as metallic sculptures of creatures from the home planet — in case I ever need them to defend our stations. I didn't mind my work here on the Terran moon, and I like life just fine with Lily around, so the only thing that gets to me is the surveillance. Nobody's gonna be spying on me in my own house.

Lily lets me know by more drawing that the next thing is to find where the surveillance line was located, and before the point where it branches out, cut it. I thought the surveillance camera just transmitted electronically to another place, without any need for cables, but Lily insists. So we stop playing cards temporarily and start digging a tunnel that should travel directly westward under the surveillance cable, according to Lily. I don't know how she could know, but I'm happy to dig with her. I've brought the tools back to the tunnel from the quonset, and anything is OK with her around.

"Gentlemen, start your engines!" She beams at me and points at the wall of our tunnel. I pat her hand and when she digs her spade into the spot I join her.

I decide while we dig that she must know how to hack into some of the computer systems on this rock. Otherwise, how could she have memorized a map of the power lines? Her intel has helped us do things fast, so far.

We have to do the digging in bursts, though, then get back to our stations for duty times.

While I dig, and while I make weapons, I can't help imagining the huge underground complex called Central. Like a dark electronic machine underground, underneath the light side of the moon.

It's been so long since Central hired me that I can't even remember all the terms of the deal or even the full name of the organization. Central Power Services? Central Manufacturing Espionage? But the organization seems to be micromanaging its personnel too much lately. Or did I just start to notice?

Now it's the middle of the "night," that is, the off-work hours, and she and I are doing extra digging time. I'm thinking while we work again, wondering about the other 498 or more stations and their inhabitants. Maybe when we get the surveillance to go down, I'm thinking, we can find out something about them, get together with the smart ones on some ideas maybe.

She halts me with her hand and cocks an ear at the tunnel face we've been digging out. Then she turns me around, jumps up on my back and reaches to touch the ceiling. We pull down dirt with our hands that lands in our faces and hair, but she's as right as a hunting beast: there above us is the underside of some conduit.

Tomorrow night, we agree, we can come back with the tools to cut it.

That will be the end of surveillance.

**

A ring from my Guidance phone wakes me a few hours later. Sliding into the bathroom I shake some more moon-dust out of my hair and check my good-lookin' face in the mirror before I go to the shiny black box and switch on the sound. They must have surveillance where the phone is.

The call has disconnected. They will call back, madder than hell I'll bet.

Lily has been to my place before but 10 Km is a long way to hike so we always split the distance as I've said. Surprise, she appears now, coming up the ladder from my cellar, her hair gray and her face caked with moon-dust. I'm hauling her aside, into the bath to get her out of the way of the camera eye, wherever it is, and make her wash-wipe-shake off the telltale signs of last night. But she's fighting away from me. I just don't want her seen, don't want us caught.

But wait, I shook her off last night before we parted in the tunnel. She was clean then.

"Lily? What—"

The floor begins to shake. Then it quakes, rocking back and forth so hard it knocks us both over.

The Guidance phone rings again and I struggle up to answer it. "No way Jose'!" she screams. It stops ringing anyway.

The floor bucks and sways. My ceiling is cracking and pieces fall. I grab emergency air masks. We crawl under a table to protect ourselves. What's doing this?

Then it stops. Silence.

I wait for things to shake again. They don't. I wait for the phone to ring again. It doesn't.

Lily brushes back her dusty hair and whispers, "Banzai, Baby!" She holds up a finger to me, then belly-crawls over to a wall near my desk. Rising to sit with her back to the wall she pries up a tile above her left shoulder with her fingernails, drops it, and with one fast motion, like a predatory bird, plunges her fingertips in where the tile was, plucking out my surveillance eye and tearing it from its connection.

Well, if that doesn't invite a visit from the Guidance meddlers, nothing will. I think, we'd better get Lily out of here before someone comes and finds her.

But she's up now, at my monitor and pecking fast at the keys. She brings up a video on the screen. I didn't know you could do this: it's live cam footage of the light side of the Terran moon with a time-tag 10 units ago, zooming in slowly, looking at the craters and the huge sea-like dark parts in the light plateaus, and then KABLOWWWWW — the entire width of one of the big dark spots erupts toward us with gouts of flame that must tower hundreds of kilometers, and kilometer-sized pieces of moon-crust flying toward us, spinning and rolling as they pass, nearly touching the cam satellite that she has hacked us into.

"Grand Central Station!" she yells triumphantly in my face. "Next stop, PhilaDELphia!" Who knows what she's talking about? Her hair looks like it's going to catch fire. Her eyes are full of delight, and more focused than I've ever seen them.

I feel funny: like a switch has flipped and an electronic scrambler in my head is powering down. From nowhere, now I remember coming here long ago under guard in a maximum security container. Not recruited, not hired. I remember drugs, pain. Things are coming back.

Suddenly Lily hugs me, getting dust all over my front.

"Look, you!" she crows, pulling a piece of paper from her coverall pocket and flapping it at me. Then she shrugs apologetically and corrects herself. "Look, Eldn!"

She's talking like a normal person. And it's a map, one that looks like the territory to the east of us, with the stations as dots. She repeats my name deliberately, as if she's practicing how to talk. But her crazed hair is almost setting itself on fire, her eyes are so lit up.

"Eldn! Poured the soup into the power line to Central — and sent surprises with it!" She pounds my arm and laughs so loud my sculptured weapons vibrate.

Then she says just what I'm thinking: "Hey. Want to get suits on and go wake up the neighbors?"

Found

TO SERA IT SEEMED THAT SHE HAD BEEN WAITING ALONE a long time, but it was probably just an illusion caused by anticipation. She sat very upright on a velvet-upholstered chair drinking water from a clear container that might be worth a fortune on Io.

Around her, what she could see was traditional Brahmine to the core, like the photos in the GeoUniverse articles about this crowded little planet, and she loved it: earth-pink clay or stucco walls were held in place at ceiling and doorways by heavily carved, richly-stained timbers, matching oiled and polished wooden floors and window sills, and open casements everywhere that allowed encroachment from those yellow-flowered vining plants, called perinya. She had seen the thick yellow flowers climbing up almost every wall in the city as the driver brought her from the port.

Sera listened hungrily to the city noises beyond the gardens outside. They were a steady buzzing, like a huge beehive. She could smell the rich aromas of foods cooking somewhere, and from somewhere a wildly mournful song burst into the air.

The electronic letters she had exchanged with the Varindhi family were encouraging: they were pleased with her credentials and prepared to pay well for a second-language teacher to teach Linnish to their third child. They had sent her account the usual travel funds, with the usual first month's pay, and made the return-ticket deposit in case the arrangement did not succeed. They had surprised her by adding a generous additional amount "as advance payment for services." But the letter translation had failed at the end due to some meteorological problem, so she never learned the sex or age of the child or its brothers and sisters before departing.

This was the kind of home a large family would own: they would fill this house with people and noise, thank heaven.

But it was too quiet now. Where were they?

She sighed. Hoping not to be caught, she stood and leaned to see herself in a decorative mirror, to make sure she was presentable: smoothing the weaving of her thick red hair at the temples, turning sideways to see if it still fell down her back as it should, in gradually diminishing bundles, to just below her waist. She wasn't tall or imposing. Her eyes were the plain gray of mollusks. But her hair, colored like copper wire, turned heads even at home, where redheads were common.

She had made it through the long, solitary trip from Io with the help of a huge download from the Io Universal Electronic Library. The ship was large, and full, but it had contained only returning students and newlyweds absorbed in each other, business people exchanging scans, and hundreds of predatory-looking, overdressed singles of both sexes who closed the ship's bars down nightly.

Sera missed Jax every day of the journey. He would have loved watching those unfamiliar stars and planets pass by in the ship's observation windows, finding them on the charts, talking about the places he had seen: their peoples and creatures, wonders of nature and art, their markets and foods.

At the port she had disembarked from IoAir flight #236 into a terminal as far from lonely as it was possible to be. The place whirled with bright colors and lavish varieties of costume, it smelled of spices she knew she had never tasted, and the air was filled with public announcements gabbling in about a dozen languages that she had never heard before.

All of that gave her hope. She was tired of being alone.

As she had looked around eagerly she caught herself hoping that Jax might show up again, shouldering through the crowd with his uniform jacket slung over his shoulder, his big grin and warm eyes seeking her face.

She fought that down bitterly one more time. He wouldn't be back, she knew by now. His laughing eyes had been lost forever somewhere outside Io's solar system when a mission went awry seven years ago. There was nothing she could do to help him or to change the way things were.

There was a spate of birdsong outside the nearest window. She sagged into the seat of the straight-backed velvet chair, her fingers feeling absently for the turquoise bracelet on her wrist — his gift from some ancient planet.

Where was the child? She was eager and apprehensive, both.

A whisper of noise made her turn from gazing out the vine-draped windows to find that three people stood before her.

She took them in as she rose bravely and bowed slightly, according to local custom; and the man and woman, about her height, nodded their heads. The man touched the child's back, and the little boy? or was it a girl? bowed deeply from the waist to show customary respect for a teacher. All three had dark, sleek hair and dark eyes. The child wore a simple tunic with pants and sandals, but the parents were dressed as you would see on the streets of Ringstrasse, her home on Io — in the intergalactic fashion of business people.

"I apologize for arriving later than I hoped I would," Sera said. "My luggage was lost coming off the ship, and it took two hours for them to find it..."

They had told her that they spoke Linnish, but they didn't tell her how little and how haltingly. They nodded politely, but her short description of her trip, meant to make them comfortable, only brought puzzled faces. Well, more pupils for her! She didn't mind. She would learn Brahmine as she taught Linnish to all of them. However many there were.

As she talked a little, and they struggled to talk and listen while the sober child said nothing, she took them all in. Certain, now, that the quiet child was a boy, maybe seven years old, and that something was wrong. "And your other children?" she asked.

The housekeeper who had admitted her to the house reappeared suddenly. She spoke quickly in Brahmine to Sera's new employers. Her message had an edge of worry and haste. A pair of male servants entered from another hallway, drawing and carrying luggage—but it wasn't Sera's. Baffled, Sera stared at them all, one after another.

"We must go," the boy's mother said apologetically in Linnish. She struggled to say more. One hand fondled the hair on the boy's head and then drew away.

The servant nodded and said something in Brahmine to Sera, which sounded like a repeat announcement, with many convincing details she couldn't understand, that still amounted to this: "They must go."

"Why? What is this all about?" Sera opened her hands toward them in protest and confusion.

"I will help you," one of the male servants said, in clear Linnish. He held up a hand and bowed his turbaned head. "Wait."

Then she stared, aghast, as husband, wife and travel cases exited with the three servants. The entry door shut behind them.

The room was silent. She and the boy stood facing each other, alone.

Her mind raced: the Verindhi couple, their names and address, their solvency, their electronic signatures had all been checked by the agency, which advertised "secure job placements at low cost." These people would have little reason to cheat or trick her.

The boy's eyes were downcast now.

Poor kid. No one had even said goodbye to him.

"What's your name?" she asked, and when he didn't look up, she added, "My name is Sera. Sera." He could not know Linnish, but she was pointing to herself to begin the oldest ritual in all of language: exchanging names.

His eyes remained on the flowered whorls of the fine old rug beneath his sandals. He was more than shy. He looked ashamed.

She knelt in front of him so their eyes were at the same level and raised his chin gently with her palm. "I am Sera." She pointed at her heart, and his eyes roved gravely over her face.

The Second Language institute, which had trained her in the method, had certified her, with high marks, for teaching of Mainstream Linnish. It was her native tongue, she was a quick study, and the teaching was one-on-one. Easy once you picked the technique up.

"What is your name?" she asked, doing it by the book, pointing toward his heart.

A large tear swelled in each eye and both rolled down his cheeks. He brushed at them hastily.

There was something very wrong with the boy. And also weirdly right. The painful silence and loneliness horrified her. —So much so, that she had to swallow her own sudden, childish wish to cry or run.

Then a voice behind her broke the silence: "He is Sai. He does not speak yet."

"Why?" she rose and turned toward the turbaned servant. Behind him the housekeeper moved through the room, carrying linens. It seemed the farewell party had ended and the parents were gone.

"I can tell you more. Later."

It was for the little boy's sake that she didn't demand more information right away, despite her mounting anger and worry. This wasn't his fault.

She showed Sai some snail shells she had brought him from Io, led him to the table when the meal was ready, and had him demonstrate how to eat each dish. A tiny spark of pleasure grew in his eyes as he helped her manage the unfamiliar foods.

She shook his hand, a gesture that was not unusual here, and let them take him off to bed.

Then she insisted that the servant, who called himself Veher, sit with her immediately and answer her questions.

**

Here in the darkness of the room they had given her, she stood at the open window listening longingly to the beehive sounds of the vast city out there, and reaching with her eyes toward the millions of blurring lights beyond these darkened grounds. Her room was a spacious and well-furnished place full of blossom-smells, but it sat in a house that was nearly empty and heavy with quiet inside.

She wanted to go back to Io. Tomorrow she would begin the process.

She brushed out her hair and considered what she knew now:

Sai seemed to be deaf-mute from birth, yet Veher had observed that he did selectively hear things; he turned his head at sounds, sometimes, or flinched if something fell. Veher had originally been hired as a tutor for the child, but he had never managed to induce the boy to talk.

The first two Verindhi children had died at birth or just after. There were no others. The parents, who had met as professionals engaged in exporting goods, seemed to have responded to their third child's disability as many people do to ease a loss: by plunging themselves more deeply into their work.

Three failures to produce healthy children had also made them isolate themselves to avoid the stigma of an ancient cultural superstition: that they had brought this on themselves and their children by evil deeds. Caught between science and superstition, the Verindhis had hired a series of physicians, therapists, holy men and tutors to help their son. They shrank from harming him further by their presence, in case their presence was harmful.

Sera was their most recent hope.

It made her heart swell with anger. They had not been honest. It was as if the boy had an evil spell, Sera thought, that she, a language teacher, was supposed to break. Alone.

Far out across the city, she heard the thudding beat and wild vocal high notes of some festival or concert. She closed her eyes, longing to be there.

**

The morning sun woke her. Sometime in her sleep she had decided to stay a little while, maybe a week. To be kind to the boy, who might feel abandoned by her if she made a hasty exit. He must already feel rejected by his parents. And no wonder the poor thing was ashamed: he must feel like he was at fault, along with his parents, for her disappointment.

She sat opposite him at their breakfast table on a sunny patio. Parrots burbled and squawked above them in some fat trees. Sai looked at her with mild, uncomprehending eyes.

She pointed to herself again: "I am Sera."

And to him, with her other hand: "You are Sai."

The boy began to cry.

**

She spent the afternoon reading in her window-seat, listening to the daytime clash and roar of the city, feeling worse than useless.

The next day at language time Sai only looked downward again, sitting with knees up on the painted iron patio chair, staring at his feet. She tried for an hour or more, but he would not even look.

The following day she didn't try. At her request Veher went with them to a market in a public vehicle, where they could be in a crowd and she could choose some fruit. Sai gripped Veher's hand, wearing a boy's belted tunic and trousers that were small copies of the man's, and stared at the people near them on the vehicle with intense curiosity. At least he wasn't looking at his feet.

She felt rejuvenated by the crowd; it was hard to keep from looking around her with the same wide-eyed fascination.

Sai chose his own fruit and smiled as he ate it on the way back to the house.

That evening they swam in one of the pools beside the garden and patio. The boy swam well. After traveling underwater like an otter for the length of the pool his head bobbed into the twilight air with a look of pleasure on his face and intelligence bright in his eyes.

And as they toweled themselves off afterward, she saw him turn his head at a sudden bird call.

**

Sera sat opposite him at their breakfast table again, listening to the parrots. A peacock on the garden wall spread its fan, then closed it and floated to the ground.

"Let's try again to learn some words," she said gently. Sai turned mild, unfocused eyes to her face.

She pointed to herself again: "My name is Sera."

And to him, with her other hand: "Your name is Sai."

His eyes darkened, but they landed on her turquoise bracelet and when she moved her hand they followed it. He watched the bracelet only, and nothing else, for several more minutes of Sai and Sera name-practice. Then he looked at her questioningly, stirred in his seat, and when she asked he answered "Sai," as if he were repeating an odd fact that had little to do with him.

Startled, she stifled her excitement. "Yes," she nodded, and pointed again to herself. "And I am Sera."

Again Sai watched the bracelet move, back and forward, back and forward, another hundred times. "Sai," he repeated finally, thoughtfully.

Not a hallucination: he had said it, twice. To celebrate she announced it was time to play and pulled his ball from under a patio-chair where he and Veher had left it.

She had forgotten how much simple-minded fun it was to throw and catch a ball. Sai even half-smiled, once.

After several of his throws had flown over her head, and she squatted again to pull the red ball from the undergrowth beside the wall, she turned to find him right behind her, delicately touching her hair.

"Sera," he said.

**

"Even at this age he still naps," Veher murmured as Sai drifted sleepily off down a hallway with the housekeeper after the noon meal. Veher's turbaned head and beard made him seem older than he was, she guessed. His eyes were kind.

She nodded. It was too early to tell Veher about her progress. Not clear enough how it had happened. But this was her chance to ask: "What do you think is wrong with him?"

He seemed to intend to give her an answer that he had learned would be acceptable. Instead he hesitated and shrugged. "I am a religious man," he said. "Perhaps you would prefer not to have a religious answer?"

She breathed deeply, irritated at his judgment of her. "Truth is best," she said. "What you think, truly."

He looked at her for a few seconds, measuring her. Then he said, "He has been hurt. As a spirit. He has to recover. He will talk when he does, whether it is this lifetime, or the next, or..." he shrugged again.

Her time was her own at this time of day. In her travel cases she found a book to read and didn't read it. This house was still too quiet. While the boy napped, in memory she saw again and again the small spark in Sai's eyes this morning when he spoke.

Tomorrow it would be a week since she had arrived. It was time to announce that she would leave.

But now she had made a little progress. Things were different.

Maybe crowds of people were as good for the boy as they were for her. She decided on another pursuit for the afternoon. When she asked, Veher agreed to escort them to a large park in the city, where he said there were walkways and small boats to rent, local animals in pens, a marketplace with vendors, displays of food and goods, and crowds, always.

Veher knocked on her door later with Sai beside him, rosy from sleep, the boy's jacket and his own over his arm. They would eat at the market, he explained, with pantomime, to Sai.

Sitting with the other two in a crowded car on the public transport, train, she found that Jax was suddenly in her mind again. Again she was hearing the impossible news: that his ship had disappeared into a heavy electromagnetic force, the tail of an uncharted comet, and had not reappeared at all on the other side. Or anywhere. Tracking records showed huge distortions in the ship's signal at the time of the disappearance, and then violent "sounds" that showed up only on a supersonic level. A sort of scream that human ears couldn't hear.

The park swarmed with people walking, bicycling, eating meals on thickly matted, viny lawns that were sprinkled with tiny flowers.

Children called and ran everywhere, despite the heat, like bright birds.

Veher let the boy help row them across the lake and back. The public-vehicle ride alone brought light to the boy's face, but the boat ride lit it with joy. Trailing a hand in the water, Sera watched Sai's face with amazement. "You look so happy," Veher said quietly to her, and she blushed to realize that her face probably matched the boy's.

The noise and color of the crowds seemed to feed Sai as much as they fed her. By the time they had canvassed the cages of creatures, the boy was radiant. He seemed taller and more robust, a little man.

They would all pick out their dinners, she explained to Sai. Veher watched, doubtful, but she was sure Sai heard and understood her. As they strolled down an aisle between rows of food-vendors' stalls, Sai and Veher were arrested by something savory cooking on spits, hissing deliciously in the twilit air.

She chose the stall next door to it for her own supper. She was tasting and adding condiments to her bowl of spicy stuff when she looked up and saw Sai striding toward her carrying his spike of spitted fish, a huge grin on his face, his jacket slung over one shoulder.

She stopped, utterly. He looked so familiar. He looked like — Her mind stalled. He arrived in front of her and stopped.

Time stopped.

"My name is Sai," the boy recited merrily in Linnish, parroting her teacher voice. Saying the whole thing for the first time. "*You*... are Sera."

Then he breathed deeply. His eyes were full of laughter and warmth. He said, "You are Sera. Sera, I am Jax."

Silver Alert

I T WAS RAINING HARD when Neil Raymond pulled up to the diner. The water streamed in sheets down his windshield between slashes of the wiper blades. The place was closed and dark, but a streetlamp revealed what the darkened neon scribble in the window said: Andie's Restaurant.

How could it be? He felt a little crazy. A small sign beside the door glared back in his headlights: Open 9 a.m to 9 p.m. He put his head forward on the old Chrysler's steering wheel, and with fingers knotted by age and trembling with fatigue, carefully turned off the ignition just before he blacked out.

**

She was there with him in the kitchen and they were making applesauce, the sweet smell of cooked fruit filling the place. She watched patiently as he ran the hand crank on the fruit masher so it pressed fragrant apple pulp through a sieve into the old mixing bowl and plastered the grated bottom of the masher with apple skins. Classical music played in the background.

She was getting old. They both were, but he couldn't afford to. She needed him.

She poured the sugar in, just a little, out of loyalty to custom. The apples were already so sweet. She stirred and tasted. "Mmm, it's good," she said, and smiled — the same smile he'd seen when he first met her, years and years before. Warm and complete, that smile always filled him with a feeling of endless plenty: loamy fields of real grain, hot pies in ovens, broad prairie skies.

The plenty she created had often been a source of secret wonder to him. Sometimes he privately felt that he had done nothing in his life, only helped her to do what she did so well: she made something out of nothing with endless art.

He just knew that he needed to preserve her.

Later, while she napped, he walked.

Almost forever, humans have designed ritual walks that contain prayer or magic, for the discipline of contemplation: the Stations of the Cross, pilgrimages to Canterbury, a shrubbery maze. His walking, too, was a kind of prayer to him. Up the street, turn. Up the hill, turn around and come back down. Turn right, up the shadowy walking path behind the library, and then out again down a long sidewalk. It was a pattern and it kept him whole as she dreamed in their little house.

The pattern kept him almost whole after she had gone, although he was never really whole again.

**

They first danced at the USO dance. He was a skinny soldier, still growing and always hungry. Her hands were soft. She said she played Chopin and Beethoven on the piano. He told her that one of the two recordings he owned was Beethoven's 6th, its wonders contained in six incised platters that were as heavy as café plates.

**

A sound like ripping canvas and gunfire shocked him awake for a second. The car was lit with lightning. The rain pounded the car roof. He saw once more the dark sign that said "Andie's." Then he was gone again.

**

He was walking one day, after she died, when she said something to him that he almost heard. He didn't greet the neighbor who passed because he was so intent on hearing her. Still, he couldn't quite. Every day after that he walked, listening. Through the distraction of bird calls and car noises, he listened.

His neighbors and friends began to think he was a little peculiar. There were disease names that he overheard when they talked about him, which they used to mean he was so old he was out of touch. But it wasn't true. Really he was trying acutely to be in touch. In touch with her, though; that was the important thing. He was rudderless without her. He needed to know what to do next, and maybe she would have an idea.

With practice, sometimes he saw and heard her. He saw her laughing. He vividly saw her hands on the keys, her young hands seventy years ago, the music pouring from her fingers in a flood that was pure pleasure for him. Sometimes he saw her sewing small coats for the kids, or making warm and fragrant things to eat. He was stunned to recall the plenty that she had made out of nothing much.

In memory he saw himself, over the years, doubling and redoubling his efforts to paint and fix and build. No wonder, he thought, seeing it all now as it was: he had been working to make things that were fit companions for the things she made.

Other times when he was walking he just heard her voice, without being able to make out the words. He was grateful to hear her, most of all.

One day he drove the Chrysler to the grocery store and found, as he stood among the produce displays, that he didn't know what she had asked him to buy. He left in disgust. Then when he was too tired to remember the way home, his son had to come from 12 miles away to talk with the officer who pulled him over for "erratic driving." After that the kids took his car keys away.

They left the Chrysler parked there by the house, though, as if to remind him of what he couldn't do.

OK, they cared. Should he feel hurt? He had no time for such stuff. He would just walk every day, and listen for word from her.

One day at last he heard words clear enough to understand. Did she really say "Good night folks, wherever you are"? It was a sort of joke, or a slogan for a television show, wasn't it? What did that mean?

He wondered about it for days, as he walked his customary route, listening for more. He passed old friends and neighbors unheeding, intent on his search for her voice. Nothing came.

On a morning walk when he was seeking the meaning in what she had said, a neighbor stopped right in front of him and asked, "How are you, Neil?"

Startled, he answered with the only thought he had to share: "Goodnight folks, wherever you are… Can you tell me where she is?"

But after the neighbor disappeared, he began to remember something: the weekend when they drove a long way to get to someplace in the Carolinas called Sweets, and there was this little restaurant, something about sweet potato pies. Owned by someone famous — Ralph Rimes, the guy who said, "Good night folks" — was that it? Good hot food, shrimp and fresh-caught fish and other stuff. His mother watched the kids that weekend, and she and he ran off like truants to be alone together for the first time in years.

Was that the place she was talking about? His breath came faster. She was sending him a message.

At home, he looked up the town in the Carolinas. It was on one of the road maps his son had let him pull from the old car, that day when he locked its dark-green doors and pocketed the key.

He must go find her; she was going to meet him there.

He would steal his own car, that's all, and drive to the Carolinas again. To the place called Sweets maybe. No time to lose. He was hungry, but there was a restaurant, and he would eat when he got there. With her. Take her out to dinner, someplace nice.

He had known all along that he had one spare key to the car in a junk drawer. Why bother the kids with such details? The old key was so tarnished it disappeared among the screws and bits of machinery, but to him it was as visible, when he opened the drawer, as if it were painted red. What better place to hide it in case of emergencies?

This was more than an emergency.

He found the way to the freeway after a while, and drove steadily southward out of Virginia, sensing that he was going the right way because of the sun, thinking of his forebears traveling in search of freedom. And of a medieval knight leaving home on a quest for something pure or magical. And the idea of a journey for love. That's what he was doing. He was desperate with loneliness for her.

**

A sign above the highway about his car? it startled him so much he slowed and pulled over to look at it. A truck roared past, blasting its horn angrily.

He sat and looked patiently at the sign, in case he had mistaken it. It said "Silver Alert: green Chrysler," year and model, and his license number. He didn't know what, exactly, the sign meant, but no one else had the same license number as he did. A sign for everyone to see, about him? They must be after him.

It made him chuckle. He smiled craftily as he started the engine and ran the car down the shoulder of the highway to the next exit. He looked at the sun again and headed south on the business streets. They were more interesting anyway.

He was hungry. But it was good to be hungry for a nice dinner.

**

Rain made it hard to see, in the darkness that had fallen by the time he arrived in downtown Sweets. The streets were covered with wind-shaken skins of reflective water that confused his eyes. Through the small gap in his side window, the cool air smelled wet and maybe a little like coconut shrimp. The restaurant would be here, of course, right downtown, where you could always find a gas station and a bite to eat. And there, he saw it, set back from the road a little: the Sweets Seafood Restaurant. The one with the pie Ralph Rimes loved — the famous old-time star that the kids today didn't even know about.

He pulled up into a parking spot near the door. But wait. It was dark. And the sign said Andie's Restaurant? The name was wrong. That was when he blacked out.

**

Nevertheless, he woke at the right place: the Sweets Seafood Restaurant. The sign said so, and now they had turned it on too, so its color was a friendly blaze in the dark, like a hearth fire.

And true to her word, she was there beside him. His heart swelled with happiness. She came, just as she said she would. She looked like an 80-something person, but sort of timeless.

At the entry door they passed the famous Ralph Rimes, who was leaving as they went in. He tipped his fedora at them both. Neil ordered dinner; nothing fancy, not as fine as she deserved. But something good, anyway. He was so hungry.

He couldn't resist touching her hands, and she smiled shyly at the unaccustomed gesture.

They ate the good food, happy, and asked for a bag for some of it so they would have room for coffee and pie. He spent all that was in his wallet, every last penny.

"Want to go somewhere, sit, and make plans together for the future?" he asked.

She nodded and smiled. It made his heart race.

He drove them through downtown and out toward the ocean; they pulled up in a sandy parking lot facing a beach. He rolled his window down a little, for air, but the salt and sea-creature smell of the ocean, the whispering of the surf, the warm, moist night, entered too and made him feel strong.

He took her hand again. They talked long about little things: what they remembered, what they forgot, what they were sorry they had said. The future kept eluding them. What should they plan? He struggled to think.

Then she said she must go now. But she wanted him to do well; she had come to make sure of that.

He protested that he couldn't do anything without her; she made something out of nothing, something that he never could do.

That's silly, she said in her practical way. We both did that. I would have made *nothing* out of nothing without you.

A soon as she said it he knew she was right. His relief was huge, expanding outward like a song.

Pre-dawn light was beginning to gray the sky, and he heard the drumming of the surf. Gulls rose to wheel above the water and cry.

He said he would follow her wherever she went. She looked hesitant, like someone being asked on a forbidden date. Then she brightened and said of course he could; hadn't they found each other before?

He struggled to remember other times or places than this one right here. He didn't think he remembered any.

She seemed to become pale and faded, pale as old cotton cloth. He felt, rather than saw, a distance between them — and sprang into motion, turning the key in the starter. It didn't matter, he'd stay with her and they would do those things they had almost thought of, every one of them...

She began to drift toward the dawning gray, slowly out across the water.

No. His heart would break forever if she got away from him again. He started up the engine, driving toward her.

As she faded away from him, he drove faster across the empty, grass-invaded parking lot, toward that creamy beach sand, toward the water.

He saw a barrier ahead. He didn't care; he gunned the engine and the car leapt forward, gaining… "I'm with you, right behind you," he reassured her, reassuring himself.

He burst into starry space and she was with him, on the seat again, laughing with a delight he hadn't heard in years.

**

An early beachcomber found the car and called the two on-duty town police, who came sleepily and were jolted awake by what they found.

Sergeant Morris took notes: the old Chrysler had been driven into the surf as far as it could go before it got sand and seaweed up inside and failed. Ballasted by sand, it sloshed with water and ribbons of green seaweed. Its nose pointed upward toward the sunrise so it seemed to be driving onto a shimmering road of gold tiles made by sunlight on the waves.

There was an old man in the driver's seat, waist-deep in the water, leaning forward with his arms embracing the wheel. Each wave rocked him as it hit the car; he smiled slightly as he rocked but his skin was cold. The registration card in the glove compartment said Neil Raymond, 96, of Virginia.

Morris' partner Shar learned, when she pried off the submerged back plate, that the car was on their broadcast list of missing or stolen vehicles. Something that they added to their report: It was not certain how the driver had cleared the four-foot beach wall to get the car onto the sand and into the water.

Odder though, was finding a takeout bag from Sweets Seafood

Restaurant floating in there beside the old guy, with a few pieces of fried shrimp in its soggy interior. Sweets? The restaurant that had become Andie's years ago? Andie's would be opening for breakfast in an hour or so, back in town.

There was enough that was strange about all this that the two police officers suspected foul play. Investigators took passenger-side fingerprints from the dash and window, and found those to be from another person, not the old guy. Maybe a kidnapper. There was also a little white hair in a small comb under a seat, so they sent that out for DNA testing along with the prints.

Later that day some State of Virginia records were returned showing that the prints and hair belonged to one Helen Raymond, 8 years deceased. The guy's wife.

The waves drummed on the beach as they winched the old Chrysler out of the water. Morris said: "Well, didn't the old guy put that car to some good use, anyway? One last fling for him."

**

Warm late-afternoon sun bathed in the water and baked the sand. Advancing waves seemed to strum the beach softly, almost musically, and smooth it again as they drew back. The tang of salt and seaweed rose to the tops of the palm trees and joined the perfume of magnolia blossoms and the toasted-grain smell of the beach grasses on the dunes.

A few bright umbrellas decorated the sand below. Was it a weekend? Neil didn't know. It didn't seem to matter.

It was easier to think now. Still, nothing mattered but this: He had caught up to her. He thought he knew how to find her again.

The beach withdrew beneath him, turning like one brightly illustrated page of a favorite old book.

Goodnight, folks, wherever you are.

He would go and find her now.

Kokopelli

K OKO LOOKED AROUND HIM IN THE DARKNESS. A rising moon lit the sandy ground and caused the cactuses and mesquite bushes to cast long shadows across its rises and falls. It lit the tips of grassy tufts, spires of yucca, and the tops of the other sparse vegetation. The air was cold and sweet — much colder than he wanted right now — but still it carried the smell of pungent kancha trees and the burning herbs for insects, and bitter ground-herbs whose local names he couldn't ever remember although he had bought and sold them many times. The smells piqued his hunger. Too bad his dinner had just left.

He chuckled dryly. Good joke on him. He had just returned to the secret launch location with his heavy sack of booty, only to find that they had left without him.

He was well-known among all the Peliua (pronounced Pelli by the locals) — the traders who came together from Io, of the planet some called Jupiter, to buy and sell among the people here in this part of Earth. He was also the one who was most often the butt of the traders' jokes because he was slow and often late.

He never minded being laughed at. He loved a good story or a joke, and traded in both as readily as he traded in goods, so it seemed impossible to most of the other Io traders that he would ever earn any profit at all. But because he was friendly too, sometimes he got the best trades. His profit was something he never discussed because the other traders might turn to thieves against him.

Now he swore, colorful delicious Io words that no one could mind, since no one from Io was here. Because the Io words sounded so excellently, he added more of them, enjoying for a few moments the timbre of his own voice in the clear night air.

But words would not help at this moment. No words would, and no stories or jokes. Because it was the cold season, he needed to get to warmth or his handsome Io body, the source of some vanity for him, would suffer quickly from exposure to the cold and dryness here.

How long till his trading group would return? Hard to say, but it would not be soon. It would be whenever they wanted, actually — and who knew when that would be? He swore again.

On Io, his wife would be disgusted and insist that his trade association schedule the earliest possible return trip. She would miss his caress, he knew. His children would be cross when he didn't return with the usual gifts. He would have a lot of storytelling to do when he got back there!

He couldn't help chuckling, anyway.

There should at least be some food stored down below.

It always made him happy to stow his valuable goods at the end of a trading run. This broad, flat rock at his feet marked the traders' secret meeting spot, but it also opened, its top layer hinging upward with the right pressure and words, to become the entrance to the Peliua rock-chamber.

With no one to stand watch, he would have to be quick; he leaped down the ladder, entering the cave-like hollow beneath the ground. Koko quickly checked the shelves, easily done because the traders had cleaned them out on departure. But the pigs had cleared out the food as well!

By the illumination of the thin light-strip overhead he stuffed his sack between two of his shelves in the storage space; he pulled from one a heavy cloak and the one other thing he might need, a wooden flute, tucking it in his broad deerskin belt.

He turned to look at the empty hangar, which normally would be occupied by their craft. With a sigh he leapt back up the ladder and pressed the hidden place to lower the lid on the cache. Closed, it looked like a flat, half-buried rock again, and nothing more.

He hesitated, thinking of living in the traders' cache till the Peliua returned. But there would be no food in there until he hunted or traded for it. It would be dim, dry and never warm. Hard for one person to defend, easy to be surrounded and trapped inside. And above all, lonely.

Standing in the bitter air, Koko could feel his skin beginning to crack, and with that the seriousness of it all set in. He needed warmth, fast. And hot food.

He was glad he had traded for some new moccasins this trip; his feet, at least, were warm. As he set out at a quick walk he sang quietly to himself — a local song, to the rhythm of his steps. This way, if anyone saw him, he would be understood to be friendly.

Singing helped him reverse the cold a little, but still he was very chilled by the time he saw the light of a small hogan far away. His skin was already frozen on the surface, his hands peeling and cracking, by the time he neared it.

He knocked politely on the wooden posts of the hogan door. An aging woman opened it and her eyes widened with surprise. "Koko Pelli?"

He recognized her too, without much delight, but warm air poured through the doorway and eased the pain in his skin. She urged him inward, her eyes riveted on the top of his head. He knew his crest must be conspicuous: blue and crackling dry now, the fingers of flesh rose above his head in a single row from forehead to nape like the jaunty, bobbing red crest on a male prairie bird.

He brushed one hand back over his head dismissively and distracted her with a showy wave of his other fingers: "I have come to play to you, Sisika, in trade for some warmth and food," he said. He flourished his reed flute and chuckled merrily, although it took some effort to be merry because he was so cold.

She broke into a broad, gratified smile, her teeth shining in some reflected firelight.

"Are they at home?" he asked. "Am I awakening you?"

"If you want to," she giggled salaciously. "But yes, they are here, all asleep." She stood aside and gestured at her family, bedded closely together on the ground around a small fire of glowing coals: her husband, several older boys, two little girls, a young couple. Thick blankets hung from wooden pins where the roof met the walls, and their earthen yellow, orange, and brown glowed in the swelling and receding waves of firelight. It was warm in here. For the warmth he thanked the Io gods and all local ones.

He couldn't be quite as thankful about finding himself at Sisika's hogan, though. She was a tough and devious bargainer.

He stuck the flute back into his belt, rubbing his rasping hands together, rubbing his face and head too, and easing toward the fire. Dead skin curled away from his hands and face, floating downward like feathers as he rubbed. She looked again at the top of his head, then turned away.

These people seemed to know he was different: who among them had this ragged crest that rose from the top of his head, like a blue ceremonial headdress? But, living as they did in a world lit and shadowed by magic they were willing to imagine that this was just some foreign species-emblem of the traders who came from afar, like the striped tail of one animal or the spotted hide of another.

She squatted and slowly poured some thick stew from a jar next to the fire into a large bowl. She reached to put the warm, savory-smelling bowl into his hands. She watched him some more while she did each thing. "You were leaving soon to trade somewhere else," she said.

"Yes. I told you that last trading-day, I know. But now I have some things to do here, before I go." He sat cross-legged and scooped some of the meat and greens, tubers and liquid with his joined fingertips to boost the hot food upward into his mouth.

The first mouthful hit his grateful guts and he sighed with relief. Food and warmth, right here. On this planet, pretty as it was, the cold was toxic. This hogan would be a good place to stay, until the warm season returned; that was the earliest he could expect the trading ship to come back anyway.

He was clever, and a trader, after all, so he spoke quickly. "But while I am delayed here, are there things I could do for you? For the honor of staying with you while I remain in this area?"

She sat and gazed at him for a long while, watching him with satisfaction as he ate. "Nothing we need," she said finally.

"Nothing?" He knew the look of someone wanting to bargain, and it was on her face. He sucked the leftover stew from his fingers.

"Nothing that we need. And food may be too short to share this winter."

"Well, tell me about some of the things you don't need, while I play to you a little," he said, with the merry look that had won him so many trades. Without her permission, he set down the empty bowl, wiped his hands, drew out his reed flute with the many holes drilled in all the right places, and began to play softly.

He had bought the flute from a tribe on the other side of the mountain, on a trading trip years ago, and they had taught him to play during a long snowbound month: the favorite local melodies, some breathy dancing songs, many humorous songs, and sweet tunes about animals or trees. Now that his lips were no longer dry, he could play for her and the sleepers: the soft warbling songs about beauty and new life.

He had never taken the flute home to Io. No one there would understand.

But this woman did: Her eyes closed with pleasure as she listened. Occasionally as he played a sleeper stirred, but always with pleasure showing on his face or her limbs, and always to return to sleep.

He paused. Her eyes opened. "Do you want me to labor for your family?" he asked.

She shook her head placidly. "We have many hands to labor. But not so much food."

"Do you need more hunters to get food?" He was no hunter, but he asked anyway.

"Yes, but you are no hunter I think," she teased knowingly. "Maybe a lover, but who needs those? Easy to find, costly to feed." She smiled smugly at him. "But tell me," she said at last, "How many children do you have at home?"

"Eleven," he said frankly.

Her eyebrows rose. She looked him over as if his buckskin trousers and tunic were not there. "Play again," she said, shutting her eyes, half-smiling.

He played for a long time, until sleep began to interrupt the notes and he was drowsing through the songs.

He had stopped and he was about to lie down when she opened her eyes abruptly. "There *is* something."

He strained his heavy eyes to focus on her, wishing only to sleep. But this was an important bargaining moment, he knew. He wiped his flute with the palm of one hand and waited.

"My daughter," she said, and it sounded like a decision. "Without child for three years after marrying. Herbs, magic, songs, none of them have helped. If you help she will bear many children—all the hunters our family needs."

"But—"

"I have told you my price, Koko Pelli. In the morning you will answer. *You are welcome to sleep here until then,*" she concluded the trading talk firmly.

**

When he woke, with the problem still on his mind, everyone had eaten and left. He knew Sisika would not mind, so he scooped himself some more cold stew and filled a small bowl with hot herb tea, the bracing morning kind that was a favorite in this region. While he sat in the warm, dim silence of the hogan and ate, he thought.

On Io, invading another family's bed was a capital crime. And it wasn't something he'd ever felt the necessity to do, either, he thought proudly. He wasn't inclined to start now, even with dire necessity staring at him. Also, he'd be back at home soon, and Rima would know it the instant she looked him full in the face. She was a hot-headed one, and she missed nothing. He didn't want to have to tell that tale while he was under fire from her.

Maybe it wouldn't even work to pair an Io body with an Earth one.

There must be another way.

**

At her mother's orders he went with Sisika's sad-eyed daughter, Sihu, on a walk into some hilly woods to help her gather pinon nuts. His skin didn't mind the warm afternoon sun. Later while she squatted and sorted her sack of nuts on a bed of pinon needles under a fir tree, he played to her and told her a story about a clever wolf-wife who used magic on her husband to make him do her bidding. By the end of the story, she sat with rapt eyes, right beside him with their backs to the trunk of the tree.

In the hogan, after dark fell and the evening meal had become nothing but empty crockery, Koko told a funny story about the night creatures fooling the daylight. Sad-eyed Sihu smiled a little and her eyes sparkled as she listened to him. Sisika rubbed her hands with great contentment, working to keep the gloating out of her eyes. Her daughter's husband must not suspect.

The next morning after Koko had greased his hands and face against the dry cold, wrapped his head in strips of leftover fur to camouflage his blue crest, and walked to the nearest settlement to trade, Sisika called her daughter to help her put the dried herbs into deerskin bags for the winter. Out on the sunny side of the hogan, where there was little wind, they sat on some sand to strip the dried leaves from the stems. The sand reflected the bright winter sun, warming their clothes.

While they worked Sisika checked with her daughter, delicately.

**

"What? How is it that you spent hours with her and did nothing?" she hissed at him, outside in the darkness later. Her scowl was ferocious, exaggerated by the starlight. Koko recognized this scowl from his earlier trades with Sisika. It meant that she wanted him to deliver twice-over to make her a happy customer. "You did NOT do your job!" she stormed.

As a trader he knew that to explain would be far less effective than to offer temptingly enormous future benefits. He described a greater plan, of which the last few days were only a small part, he said. He called for a gathering, outside the hogan of Sisika and her family, to which all the nearby residents would come; all would bring food and gifts for the host family and dress in festival clothes; all would dance and eat. These things, he reminded her, provided the very ingredients of successful reproduction.

His idea, which she could not resist, permitted him to trade throughout the area for the next pair of weeks while he invited all her neighbors, even the distant ones. He ate and slept in hogans great and small, and returned to Sisika's modest home between trips.

As Koko's clever trades increased his booty, he kept it in a large pile in her hogan where all the family could touch and admire his things and even borrow them for use: beads and leatherwork, decorated pots and jars, knives and farming tools. They were rich collateral for his bargain with Sisika.

They were collateral only, though: when he asked if she would like to accept his trade goods as rent for the winter, she only sniffed and said she liked the bargain she already had.

On the day of the dance, the families from the neighboring hogans began to arrive at noontime, pulling or carrying their food and gifts, and their best clothes. They would set up their family camping spots, wash and rest. Men and women would help set up the fire-pit, hunt for additional birds and small game to roast, and prepare foods, while the children ran in small herds wildly down to the creek-bed and back, having wars, playing at hunting with sticks and at cooking with stones and mud. Finally they would all dress for the evening, as the food aromas became unbearably tempting.

**

Near the fire, with his hands and face greased and his head wrapped, Koko began to tell stories: first the ones for the little children who were just waking from their afternoon sleeps, about coyotes and small desert quail and mighty hawks. Then the magical stories of their ancestors for the young girls and boys; then the shy local stories of love and heroism, always the favorites of those who were nearly adults.

Quiet settled only for a short while—while they all ate—and then Koko began playing and the young son of their nearest neighbor, Jow, struck beats on a drum while the young men danced, then while the young women danced, then finally while everyone danced, without formality, wildly and with joy, around the crackling fire. Koko danced himself, and laughed, as he played and sang.

Many hours later, when everyone was happy and fat and sleepy, the last reluctant children were sent or carted to their sleeping-places and the adults lay down beside the fire to talk softly and sing themselves to sleep.

Koko himself had put in a large day; he found a spot close to the fire, curled up among them and slept deeply.

**

A hard foot nudged his side twice. When he opened one eye the sun shone brightly into it, and he shut it again. The ground beneath him was rigid and cold but his blanket was still warm. Ahhh, what a pleasant night! Now a mouth at his ear, one that breathed out last night's spices, hissed: "You should be ashamed for forgetting, and getting me to forget, what your job was!" It was true: he really had forgotten it.

He sat up, hastily rearranging his thoughts for bargaining. He would need a good plan, so he invented one on the spot. A quick glance showed him young Sihu curled inside the blanket and the arms of her young husband. The look of contentment on both their faces seemed to bode well.

"Sisika, I need to speak with you privately," he began, because she seemed to like secrets.

Her scowl dissolved in a rich smile. "You had better have good news and good ideas," she warned, coquettishly.

"Oh, yes," he promised. They eased away from the sleeping circle that surrounded the ash-dusted coals of the fire, away behind some mesquite bushes. He drew her near him. She purred.

He feigned cowardice. "I don't want to have to fight her angry husband…"

"Did you think of that when you promised?" she scoffed.

"But here is my plan," he continued. His mind raced. The more devious the plan was, the better she'd like it. "Did you see how Tama and Honon from around the hill have such burdens to carry back home, with so many little children? And she is ready for another one."

Sisika sniffed irritably. "That is her fortune, or misfortune, whichever it is."

"Well, you know the old medicine: that it is easier to conceive near another who is with child?"

Curiosity and irritation fought in her face. "And?"

"She and I could walk with them on the long walk to their hogan, help carry their little ones and their things; and while we rest there, who knows? — Of course Sihu's husband would normally be invited to go with her on this errand of help, rather than myself..."

Her eyes lit with wicked delight. "But he must go immediately with my husband and son, on the Wolf Moon Hunt, or we will not have game for the freezing days to come!"

"Yes, that seems to be true." He winked.

She chuckled and squeezed his forearms possessively.

**

A month of winter had passed, and another two of bitter cold remained to threaten Koko Pelli's tender Io skin, when the hogan of Sisika was filled with happiness by the news that Sihu was expecting a child. Koko's relief was large, of course.

But the domestic celebration was shortened by a neighbor's calculation that the child had been conceived, after 36 moons of no luck, coincidentally during the visit of their flute-playing guest Koko Pelli. How likely was that?

Because someone without enough to do had introduced that thought, afterward his welcome grew thinner daily. Until finally one day, while he was helping Sisika peel tubers by telling her a story as she worked, she stopped, looked at him and said,

"I am sorry, Koko, but you must go. He has told me directly that he suspects you."

Koko wanted to tell her the truth: that if Sihu's husband wasn't the daddy, he didn't know who it could be. It certainly wasn't Koko. All he had done to advance the cause further was to play her some really inspirational flute music — the kind that makes you want to find a partner, quick — that night at the hogan on the other side of the hill. And on the way home the next day, whenever she gave him a melting glance — women always fall in love with the nearest musician — he reminded her of how her husband looked at her and how he must miss her. And he told her tales of what his wife Rima did to make things just right for him whenever he returned home from trading.

Home, he thought now: It would take a cycle of Earth's moon to get there, once he left. And how long before could leave?

As the final touch he had told Sihu about all eleven kids. By the time she got to the home hogan she was afire with purpose.

And that's all Koko did, if nothing but the truth were to be recorded forever. But he wasn't sure it was the thing to tell Sisika. Maybe she'd claim he hadn't delivered what he promised. Bad for business.

"So I have to go?" Koko complained. There went his promised winter security. This was serious.

"Wait," she listened for noises outside the hogan, in case the others were returning. She leaned toward him conspiratorially and whispered, "I have arranged another place for you, across the canyon, another hogan. I have spoken to the woman." A woman, she explained, whose daughter and husband seemed unable to conceive, after 5 years.

Koko would have laughed at this joke normally: so funny that Sisika had set him up with his next career opportunity, and no choice about it. He might develop a reputation. It was really very funny.

**

The midwinter snow whipped at his eyes. To get to the next hogan it was a long walk in the bitter, dry cold: steeply down a narrow trail, across the frozen stream, and up the winding trail on the opposite side of the canyon. The wind whistled against his hands and face as he spotted the hogan's dim light nestled among the trees.

The skin of his face was cold and cracking. He could already imagine the warmth by that fire...and as his moccasins reached the cleared snow of the entry path, the smells of hot stew and tubers sent him a welcome from inside.

To keep his Io-born flesh from dying of exposure, he would have to coax another baby from the air, like magic. And do it in such a way that he had nothing to hide when he returned to Io. And somehow avoid being slaughtered, or thrown out again, for succeeding. What a rich joke! What a challenge for his wits this would be!

Clever as he knew he was, Koko Pelli sighed. The frigid dry air made his chest ache. He withdrew the flute from his belt, conjured up a merry smile, and knocked on one post of the hogan door.

Author's note: Kokopelli is a legendary character who has been revered at least since the time of the ancient Puebloan people in the Americas. The first known images of him appear on pottery that may have originated between 750 and 850 AD. But there are some indications that he lived far earlier.

Legend describes Kokopelli as a traveling trader, a carrier of information and trinkets who was popular enough to be given a warm welcome by ancient communities; he is also known as a storyteller with a gift for languages and body-language, dance and flute-playing. And a reputation for bestowing or influencing fertility has followed him through the centuries.

Slaves

I WOKE TASTING METAL, with my head aching. That scared me. Long strands of my hair suck to the sweat on my face. Worse: I was staring at a strange orange light playing on an unfamiliar rippled wall. My heart began to pound. I slid my hand down into my boot where the stiletto was holstered and felt the handle hidden there with a little relief.

It was a hanging lamp, arcing lazily back and forth, that made the light slide across some thick tapestries. The rugs were old, done in rich colors, and pinned in place by polished wood rods, making a small boxlike chamber that smelled of spices, leather and cloth. And also of fear-sweat. Was it mine?

Somewhere outside these walls was the roaring of a primitive engine; it must be related to the motion I felt. I had never seen such a place.

I pushed myself upward with my elbows. When I tried to rise my head spun. A drug; that was the metallic taste. I licked the blood from my lips, salty and cracked.

With the thirst my last moments awake began to emerge from the fog in my mind: a local named Royen and I drinking hot jah at a classy spaceport cafe, talking about a weekend on the nearest asteroid. One fitted up as a spa. I had been working like a maniac. I wished the

Company knew how hard I had been researching.

When we met he invited me to join him in the cafe for a friendly cup. I deserved a little time off, he persuaded while we sipped. He offered a no-strings getaway, an old-style chance to get to know each other, and I was just about to agree. But I got sleepy, then.

Stupid of me to believe his sweetness, in a place where no one could be sweet. Stupider to drink jah that he poured for me. On Suyem, this cesspool, I'll bet no one was stupid enough to let a stranger pour these days.

Damn Royen. What I thought was a romance was a kidnapping. That was a bitter dose but it woke me fully, right through the remains of the drug.

The engine roared louder, then subsided again.

I felt around me hastily as the patch of orange light swung above, failing to illuminate much. The sleeve of my tunic caught on something soft; the floor of the box was strewn with greasy cushions, on which I must have slept. Disgusting. I rummaged faster among them and stacked them to one side. Then I went over the whole floor hand by hand — a flat carpeted area maybe ten hands by ten that rocked a little as I changed positions, as if this box were hung from somewhere above it.

The floor was empty. My pouch was gone. And with it the emergency kit filled with traditional remedies from the Kyaar homeland: herbs to neutralize drugs and stop bleeding, poultice for a wound... And local printed money in case of trouble in the spaceport.

I groaned. And my link, with all my contacts. How would I let the Company know about this? They couldn't send help to an unknown location. They might even fire me for disappearing.

They wouldn't be dripping with sympathy for me anyway, an underpaid biologist who got involved too easily in side issues, assigned to bottom-rung duty on planets like this one. I needed the job. Bad time to lose it, when I still owed money on my glider.

At least my captors had left me my tunic, belt and leggings — and the boots.

I rose to my feet, getting my balance with my legs spread as if I were standing in a little swaying boat, and edged my way to one corner of the tapestry box to run my fingers down the angle made by the polished wooden bar that went from ceiling to floor. The box rocked downward at my end, up on the opposite side. But my heart was thudding less now. I was beginning to be able to think.

Mine was a bookish sort of profession in most parts of the galaxy, and I was as bookish as the best of us, but it was rougher out in the field than the desk creatures at the Company knew. Your degree wouldn't help you when odd circumstances occurred, but you could sometimes work your way out of sticky places by looking around at what was there.

I kept looking. From upper corner to lower, there was no opening to the box on this side.

In spite of my balancing act, it tipped down wherever I stepped. Someone on the other side of the carpet wall might notice, and I'd rather not announce myself to my captors yet.

So, stepping carefully to avoid making the box move too much, I tried another of the right angles. No opening. And the next was the same; behind each wooden bar, each angle was formed by unbroken tapestry.

Not likely that the ceiling and floor were any different, but I tested the four softly gleaming bars that pinned tapestry into place to form the square roof, and then the four that formed the floor.

No openings. This seemed to be nothing more or less than a clever little cage. They must get people in and out by collapsing this structure somehow, like you do with a Guumi puzzle, to insert or extract their captives from between the folds.

And this might be some kind of slave caravan. It was a pretty reasonable conclusion, but my heart began thumping again.

I knew there were slavers on Suyem — revolting planetary cash business. But why go after me? Rumor was that they mostly trafficked in locals for sale to locals as laborers. I was healthy, but I was clearly not the sturdy wood-chopping, water-carrying type. Who would buy me as a slave?

A morbid chill came over me.

I pulled my stiletto, honed from razor-sharp Kyaar metal — so sharp it could slice plant samples to a transparent thinness for scanning — and inserted just the tip, no more, at one upper corner of the carpet cube. Slicing downward just half a hand, I spread the tapestry a little with two fingers and looked.

The bright light was blinding, but as my eyes adjusted, the scene was a surprise. My carpet cube was one of several suspended somehow above the deck of an ancient barge that was moving forward on a sort of canal. The canal cut a wavering path through a flat valley, among large hills that sat like conecakes on a green plain.

With the barge so low in the water, I could smell the tang of the canal and the bitter scents of plants and decay not far below me. I started, and almost lost my balance, when the engine that powered the barge stalled, coughed and roared again beneath me.

Ahead on the barge deck were tall stacks of cartons made of metal and straw. Among them were some made of the greenish native wood that told me right away I was still on Suyem; that wood didn't travel well, so it was only used for local transport. Seeing it was some relief. Suyem was a slum, but at least I had been here a couple of times so I knew it a little.

Then the moving part of the scenery came into focus for me: enormous beasts of burden, a train of them, shambled forward beside the canal in single file, chained together. And suddenly, directly beside me was the huge bewildered eye of a creature that plodded alongside, passing my carpet cage.

I let the slit collapse quickly, mentally putting together the rest of what I'd seen: the line of creatures laden with cartons and packages, treading a path beside the canal, were members of a species that the locals on this planet called yosima, meaning "big slave."

InterFoods, the Company, had sent me here to do the usual: gather information about local fauna, with the idea that there might be money in some of them, in uses that ranged from food to pets. They had told me to leave the yosima alone, though. Too controversial. That also meant I didn't know much about these creatures.

I had at least learned that they were used for all kinds of labor, hauling and carrying; although now, hundreds of local years after settlers had crowded onto this planet, naturalists had begun to argue that the beasts were sapient. Their arguments that these beasts could think were the subject of many local jokes.

Still, considering the arguments, I was surprised to see so many being worked here. When I called this a slave caravan, I wasn't thinking of such slaves.

I braced the slit open again. The beast had moved ahead faster than my tapestry box and now I was facing its thick, leathery neck, encircled with wrinkles that made the blue-black flesh look like a bunch of fat leather necklaces. It wore a colorful tapestry under its load, which was laced onto its huge back and around a bulging belly with crisscrossing ropes. Judging by the symbols I could make out, someone had strung an identifying chain of numbered beads around the base of that long neck. The creature sighed as it lumbered on, and its long tail arced up over its back to slap at an insect on one shoulder.

I needed to get out of this cage. Out there, the caravan drivers would be armed; not safe. But waiting politely in this little rug-box to find out what they had in mind for me — that wasn't going to keep me safe either.

I saw no other way. I tied my hair into a knot at my shoulder. I pulled the knife again and slit the tapestry with a whisper, almost down to the floor. Saying a prayer of thanks I sheathed the Kyaar blade — thanks for its lightness and the metal that didn't register on most detectors.

I reached through the slit. And missed. My rug box swung back a little.

I waited for a reaction from anyone below, but in the drowsy heat, with the barge engine making so much noise, I heard no sound from the animal drivers or any boat crew.

The cargo-loaded part of the beast was almost past me. When my carpet box hit the end of its swing and reversed to move back toward the yosima I leaned out, caught a section of the load ropes in each hand, and swung over to the creature's midsection with my legs dangling down its side.

The beast snorted.

Between the drug and the thirst I wasn't at my strongest, but fear is a great spur. Hastily I hauled myself upward on the ropes, like someone climbing a ladder hand over hand, to the top of the giant's load so drivers walking somewhere down below wouldn't be able to see me. I lay down, getting my breath, on the painfully sharp corners of some big containers.

The animal had stopped. It knew I was on its back. An angry voice called out below. It was local language, something I didn't know.

"Please don't give me away," I whispered.

There was the whistle of a stick against the beast's hide, maybe his leg, way down below. The giant sighed deeply and began to lumber forward slowly again.

It stank; but then, I probably did too by now. Thank heaven the creature had decided to move.

I liked living things, with emphasis on "living," and I found that animals were usually easier to understand than humans. I had earned Expert Qualifications in classification and prediction of fauna, meaning that I was able to predict their behavior by observation, grasp patterns of genetic similarity from planet to planet, and determine which animal species in a new environment might be most useful to human or human-like inhabitants. InterFood hired me to do studies on planets that interested the Company's expansion planners.

I felt around in the load on the yosima's back. I found that there were some big sacks of stuff, softer than the carton that was digging into my stomach right now, and I edged sideward over to them, finding a hollow between two that would help hide me.

It was time to make the rest of an escape plan. I could probably slide down off this giant at a rest stop, take off across country, get some help... To get a better look at the countryside I put my palms down on either side of me and pushed my head and shoulders up a little.

My left hand slid off a sack and down between two bundles, deeper into the load, and my palm pressed flat against warm leather. The back of the beast quivered, and an odd contentment came over me. I relaxed for just a moment.

**

When I woke the dark was complete. It reeked of urine, vomit and intense fear sweat. I choked down panic by feeling around the spot where I lay. There was soggy tapestry under me. And a smooth rod along the floor at arm's length made it clear: I was back in a carpeted box, this one with no light.

The sweat absolutely didn't smell like mine. My knife — it was gone. So were my boots. I groaned. All they had left behind, besides my clothes, were the small gold hoops in my ears, a Kyaar coming-of-age gift that they probably had been unable to remove.

Stupid of me to fall asleep on the back of that beast. I must have been wiped out from the drug.

Maybe the creature had turned me in to its keepers as unwanted extra weight.

For a moment despair pinned me right here and now. I was like one of those pathetic insect specimens at the Biological Training Institute, where they had ancient collections of winged or shell-armored dead things stuck on pins for observation. The things on pins were supposed to be for study, but to me they were really no more than trophies, like the preserved heads of beasts hunted to extinction by someone. I spat to remove a puff of smelly pillow-stuffing from my lip.

Every planet seemed to have the same kind of stuff: someone began by admiring a creature so much that its beauty or strength became something to capture and own. Someone wished to possess the attributes of ocelot or monarch butterfly or Kyaar dragon, and all they could think of to do was to kill it and preserve the remains.

I shuddered. Captivity and death were too close and too personal to me at this moment. To shake off the fear I began to inspect this carpet cube to see if it were constructed differently from the previous one. Floor, sides, corners.

And while I felt my way around the box I couldn't help considering the yosima, because it's my training to weigh these things. Some animals seemed to be happy to carry passengers or haul for people. It was something to do. Some, like the dogs of Earth and Kyaar, were happy to associate with people as friends. But other creatures were unwilling to enter into such agreements in any form, at any price. Those would kill first, or die.

I made it a part of my job to let the Company know these things, although they didn't always listen. The bloody massacre five years ago at Colony One on Guumi had resulted from their ignoring my report that the Guumi lizards were not suitable as beasts of burden.

I ran my fingers over the fourth corner of the tapestry box.

So I was good at figuring out animals, and clearly not good at figuring out people. But I could have told anyone that before. Look how willingly I trusted Royen. And what about Aben, and Carter, and the Ares Guild before him? Those stories might be funny over dinner with colleagues, but not so funny now.

Finally I had to conclude that this box, like the other, had no opening that I could find, and no seam. I tried to still my heartbeat and breathe, keep my mind going. Not the time for panic.

It was clear that without a blade I would have to figure out the trick to opening the tapestry puzzle in order to get out of this box.

**

By the time the box stopped swaying, my fingernails were worn down and broken from hours of prying at the tapestry. I realized that our caravan had ceased to move. My stomach went heavy as I realized we might be at our destination. My destination.

I was desperately thirsty. I thought of the long string of shambling yosima, wondering again whether they were willing beasts of burden. Doubting it, somehow. What if they really hated hauling bags of grain?

There was no sound from them. Were they still beside us? In memory I felt the warm, wrinkled leather on that one's back, and sighed. A question formed without my intending it, and it came out as a whisper: "Are you still here?"

Something slapped against one side of my box, setting it swinging. I scrambled to my feet and reached one arm to press a hand cautiously against the convex carpet. Something hard there, curved and hard. A big head? I let my palm rest on the curve for a couple of seconds, just because it felt warm and a little comforting.

Could the creature have understood my question?

I considered for a minute, and decided to ask another. It was part of every survey interview I did on members of a species that seemed intelligent. I said softly: "Are you able to think?"

Knowing that one thinks is one of the primary evidences of sapience, according to the Galactic Statutes.

A wave of warmth washed over me, but there was no concept in it that I could get. So I asked another question: "Do you like to carry loads on your back?"

The creature screeched loudly, blasting me backward onto the floor of the box. Similar voices bellowed and screeched nearby, and further off, then further away. The noise continued until there were human shouts, and weapons fired into the air, and the sound of quirts whipping at the soft blue-black leather of the legs nearby.

I sat very still, wincing while the whipping went on. Now I heard the sighing of the nearby beasts, a sorrowful sound that went on for a while before it dwindled into silence.

The silence became a long one.

In it I thought of the next question:

"Can you help me get out of this box? Without harm to yourself?"

I felt the head slap against the tapestry, a sound like wind hitting a tent suddenly. But there was no concept with that, either. The creature seemed to be listening, at least.

I tried again: "I think I may be able to help you. But I have to get out first."

The head pushed closer, denting that side of the cube a little more. I heard a deep sigh. But still no answer.

Well, it's a big universe. Maybe there are creatures who listen better than they talk. I visualized the box I was in, and what I knew about how it was made, as if I were drawing a diagram in my mind. I said very quietly:

"If we give every side of this box a number, the top side is one. The bottom one is six. The one you are touching is two, the next one to its right is three, then four, and five...Tapestries do not have infinite length. I cannot see where these end, but they must end somewhere, maybe outside where you can see..."

I waited a long time. The poor beast might be confused by the numbers. Maybe it didn't even comprehend what I'd said. But it had seemed to understand something. So I hoped, faintly, standing very still.

The beast sighed loudly. It really was a sorrowful sound, like the sigh of someone lost and lonely.

I wondered abruptly: what if it has been talking and I haven't heard it?

The head slapped the side of the box again. *There are creatures who talk better than they listen!* I heard it as a sudden gusty sigh, huge and diffuse, and as nearly silent as a warm wind. Kind of a quiet roar.

The beast had scolded me. I was more excited than chastened. "So tell me again, louder, can you? I'm listening hard! Trying."

I closed my eyes. I was very silent. I made everything as quiet as I could; I slowed my breathing, and even my heart slowed, I think. Then the noise you hear in your ears when there is no other noise began to seem different to me, becoming something imponderably slow and low, speaking in a cavernous space, and it came in waves: *Get up. At the top. And stay there! I will push.*

Why she seemed female I couldn't say. Maybe because the orders were like my mother's, back on Kyaar. Possibly I'd just made this all up. But I was ready to try anything. And glad for my bare feet, which helped me to brace against a couple of corner poles and hang by hands and feet with my back pushing upward against the roof of the box.

I would not have believed it, but when the creature's head pushed upward on the floor of the box, the cube cracked inward and turned to triangles of carpet along predesigned seams that had been impossible for me to feel. Her nose was where the floor of the cube had been. The barge deck below me was faintly visible beside her head.

I didn't need to be told; I dropped as delicately as I could onto her nose and clung to the warm leather while she ducked downward out of the box. The seams closed above me. The stink around her was enormous, but I patted her leathery, whisker-studded face gratefully anyway. I was out of jail — and almost as good, I had conversed with a yosima. Contentment poured over me.

Around us the sky was dark and the air sharp. I caught sight of a swathe of stars and a thin sickle of moon as I lay down on the top of her head and tried to be invisible for the moment. Her huge head swung away from the vessel and its dangling boxes to a position above the path. From that angle I could see the unmoving barge, sitting still in the water among reflections from the small bright campfires far ahead; and the sleeping barge crew; and nearer, the staked mounts and the rolled sleeping blankets of the yosima drivers. Silhouettes of a few night guards squatted beside fires, some with their faces lit, gaming. Their laughter and arguments came quietly across the still air.

Abruptly I had the impulse to run and speak to the guards, inform them that I was an international scientific guest on this planet and that meddling with me was breaking the law, and request sanctuary according to Galactic Statutes. They would have to grant me that.

But then it occurred to me that our captors were people who didn't give a high priority to the Galactic Statutes. By all galactic guidelines these giant creatures were sapient: they had reasoning and speech, the ability to act deliberately, and from the outcry earlier it was clear that they were aware of themselves as individuals — as individuals with rights, too. They should never have been enslaved.

Furthermore, on this planet even obvious humans were bought and sold by humans. These slavers were not the people on whose mercy you'd want to fling yourself. Here, already at their mercy, were these gigantic slaves. And here I was, also at their mercy, not free or safe either.

But what safety could there be with the yosima? If they could escape, wouldn't they have done so already? How smart would it be to trust them, let alone help them? This one had helped me. But maybe the rest hated humans.

It was certain now that these creatures didn't choose to be named yosima, "big slaves."

"What do you call yourselves?" I whispered.

There was a long pause. She shifted and sighed.

I realized that I might not be listening well enough again, so I tried harder.

QuoLen, the wind seemed to say.

"Quo Len?" I said quietly, and felt a flood of warmth.

QuoLen, the creature repeated. *Moonfarmers.*

I couldn't help smiling. It seemed to be an unlikely name for such creatures. Such people, I reworded the thought.

Listen now! the moonfarmer roared almost silently, and this time I could make the voice out better. *We must go. Tonight. Before you are caught again. Then there is no more hope.*

Right. But I had seen their huge shackles. How could they remove them? And how fast could these enormous guys move? And what happened when the guns of the guards started going? I'm a biologist, not a martial arts expert or a warrior...

The head tossed me straight up into the air a little and caught me delicately again, like someone flipping an ofrid egg expertly. She seemed to be telling me to pay attention.

**

The barge was dark but now and then a flashlight started up out of the night, like a star, and the grasping arm and hand of its beam raked across the canal water, touching the deck and rigging and the grassland or the beasts.

I was doing as I was asked. Was I stupid to go into league with these QuoLen? Because the one who undid my box-prison had heard a thought, I guessed that one or another of them was hearing this thought as well. But too bad: I had a history of being entirely too willing to trust, and I didn't want to be caught being stupid again.

So far there were good signs: the moonfarmers had a startling memory for the positions of things, and they had remembered whose back carried the stoneworker's toolbox. They passed me from nose to nose till I arrived on the back of the second one in their train, who coached me to find the case of tools in the huge wallowing load, and lowered me to the ground to begin with chisel and hammer on the primitive cuff of the lead QuoLen. The cuff was large enough to hold four of me together around the waist.

The leader lowered his long neck as if grooming his foot, to hide me from view. The other heads craned out to the left and right from their bodies, all watching me carefully and taking turns making noises to mask each strike of the hammer with a snore or a groan or a cough. I had been nervous about the noise, but it only took eight or nine hard strikes before the crude latch on the cuff split.

As the lead QuoLen shifted his loosened foot and sighed, I scrambled up onto his head so he could deposit me beside the cuff of the one behind him. A few coughs, a few more groans, and off went that cuff; another giant head presented itself for me to scramble up on; and turning slowly to reach behind him, the owner rolled its neck to let me off feet-first at a spot beside the next chained leg.

Many hundreds of hands of chain seemed to be strung as usual beside the canal, the attached cuffs as usual seeming to bind the ankles of the QuoLen, at the time when I broke a welded joint to open one huge link of the chain itself. That was right behind the first six uncuffed QuoLen.

To a distant observer the long train of QuoLen would be standing asleep as usual, doing a very-slow-motion dance that seemed to involve using their heads to scratch numerous itches on their own or each other's hides. At the end of this dance, I knew, they would have chewed through strategic ropes that attached their loads to their backs. That much of the plan I understood.

I was sweating in spite of the chill, now, working as fast as I could make my hands go, chipping at the cuff of on QuoLen Number 7 of twenty-seven with a spare chisel and hammer strung through my belt. I would get five more uncuffed, then break the welding on a chain link after Number 12. And so on.

A flashlight went on far ahead, and I ducked to make sure I was in shadow behind the protective lowered head of Number 7.

The long beam of light skimmed across the canal and the deck of the boat, wove in and out of the legs of the QuoLen, and swept out across the grassland. Then back across the canal, deck, legs and grassland again, and back, as if the idiot guard had nothing else to do to entertain himself.

The unpredictable light show must have thrown the QuoLen off, because one had just failed to make a noise to cover the clank of my chisel on the metal. A human voice far ahead shouted warning or alarm.

The covering noises began again, and I began chiseling again, and there were restless motions from the huge bodies and legs that I guessed were supposed to be the sounds of beasts disturbed in sleep by the human noises.

But the humans actually seemed to be waking, going into motion up ahead. I could hear the movement and the murmur of voices, see sudden stabs of shadow thrown by someone moving before the fire.

An order I didn't hear must have been issued among the moonfarmers.

The six freed QuoLen ahead of me went into synchronized slow motion, like dancers. They softly swept their cuffs, and the hundreds of hands of chain attached, simultaneously into the canal, then went forward at a surprisingly light-footed four-legged jog, left-right-left-right, fanning out as they went: straight at the shouting and confused clumps of men ahead.

Number 7's head nudged me roughly to climb aboard, and then I was lifted into the air by it, so I saw from there what happened next: Numbers 1 through 6 were stamping on the fires, blacking them out. Without hesitating they dumped their heavy loads — sacks, bales and crates — onto the nearest group of men, the yosima drivers and traders. Lying, sitting or standing, the men were all pinned by the heavy loads.

I couldn't help grinning at the sight, until a few struggled to free themselves, some reaching to grab or recover weapons.

I almost flew off my observation perch when it went into rapid motion. We were taking off. I slid down the fat, warm neck to my mount's shoulders, holding on to this giant's ID necklace: Number 7 and the rest jogged toward the chaos in single file, still chained together, and like dancers they encircled the entire camp of men just as a few shots fired.

There was a roar of pain and anger as one shot connected with a circling beast. I ducked and lay flat against Number 7's neck.

With Number 7 leading, our circle of QuoLen became a noose tightening toward the center of the camp, pounding feet shaking the ground, stampeding the humans, who screamed with horror as they ran in every direction, turned and ran again. I clung to Number 7's necklace with all my strength.

Below me Number 7's gargantuan legs pounded rhythms into the earth, and to my left and right the moonfarmers thundered and leaned, neatly pouring their loads — probably more than 75 tons of cargo — to cover the swarming humans in the noose.

At that, all twenty-seven QuoLen went into a lumbering jog, off at a right angle to the canal and path, with the six unfettered ones taking the lead.

Looking back I saw no figures moving and no lights going on in the camp as we loped onward through the grassland toward the nearest hillside.

**

The morning sun was warm on us. We rested in the grasses beside a small stream, and drank. They knelt or lay or crouched much as giant dogs or horses would, sighing a lot, but contentedly, grazing and sometimes rolling in the thick bluish-green grass. The wounded one was being healed in some fashion by one of the others, who chewed herbs and licked them onto the wound now and then.

Awed by their huge bulk towering above me, I sat beside one after another of them, chiseling off the remaining cuffs one by one with blistered and raw fingers. I didn't mind at all. I was beyond hungry, and I would have to find a way to get food, but the air smelled fresh and good up here on the hillside. Here we could look out over the valley below and feel safe for the moment.

I had been, for a little while, a slave like them. I had tasted the rot of slavery. Now I was free. We were all free.

One by one, as the chains came off the QuoLen, they took turns wallowing in the stream, damming and rerouting the water with their huge bodies, blowing water through their nostrils, joyfully slapping mud on their hides and rolling in the grass to scrub it off. I was happy to think of doing the same soon: washing off the stink of captivity.

We were captured and enslaved. Because we trusted them, one spoke in answer to my question. I was getting better at hearing the large slow sound of their speech, more air than sound. Why the language was so understandable, once you could hear it, I couldn't guess.

While I chiseled at the last of the cuffs, leaning against a leathery leg, I realized that this moonfarmer had not managed to drop the load of cargo from its back. I asked if I could help remove the things for him. Or her. The beast — that is, this huge intelligent person — crouched low, chewing apart the knots and allowing me to help part some of the ropes with my chisel.

"You are nomads? But also farmers?" I asked while we worked.

At each new moon we plant, wherever we are. A new forest garden, for us or anyone, the vast QuoLen explained with a practical air, its voice sounding like the slow roar of a waterfall: *The gardens grow fruits, and vegetables and herbs, that feed animals. One garden per moon.*

When it rose to shake off its ropes at last, and the load slid off onto the grass, I advanced to pick through the huge heap in case there were useful things in it. I was surprised to find myself looking at bales and boxes, tins and bags, of human food. The giant person answered my amazement: *We eat plants, roots, fish. All easy for us to get — when we are not fettered. Knew you might need these.*

I opened a container of fruit, tasted one slice, offered one to the QuoLen. This moonfarmer liked the flavor and stayed to eat a little more.

When we reached the bottom of the can, and this final QuoLen had headed off for bath and spa treatment, I dug around in a sack of containers for the next course.

With no link, no ID, no money, and no map, as soon as we neared civilization I'd have to beg use of a public link to call the Company. The Company would blame me, regardless of my plight, but in a pinch my gold earrings — still there, the tips of my fingers told me — might buy me passage off this place.

The story about the yosima was going to rock the galaxy. I knew it. The Company would probably fire me for releasing the information, but it was the least I could do for these moonfarmers. I could find another job before my glider was repossessed.

On the other hand, the Company might want to keep me on the payroll, just to own the right to put its name at the top of my report.

Fun City, Callis

S HE WAS LATE.

Fenn came to a quiet intersection in one corner of the city din, eased into a black alleyway with no one looking, and faded out, made invisible by the disruptor.

She stepped back onto the walkway beside the street and began to run, lightfooted in tekryl half-boots on the dirty pavement. She wove in and out among the shabby, drooping pedestrians unseen. Deep drafts of steamy, dirty Horenopolis air filled her lungs. Lights blared around her, creating pools of darkness deep and rich. One of those was waiting for her.

She might be reprimanded for arriving late, though.

Nearing the fountain encircled by the roadway, where three roads intersected to make a six-pointed asterisk, she ran among hovercars to the fountain pool and sat on the low wall that rimmed it, putting her fingers into it for the coolness. At a quiet pause in the movement of traffic, she squeezed her left wrist, depressing the disruptor button on the wristlet, and the disruptor faded her back in. Anyone observing her closely under the lights would have seen her pale eyes, her tightly woven red hair, and her multipocketed travel tunic, crisscrossed with backpack straps. She would look like a tourist from Io. Or Ares, or anywhere.

It had been this way every time they came to get her. Excited in spite of herself, she watched and waited.

But she was supposed to leave, already? She'd only been here on Callis for two years.

An hour passed, in which no extraordinary pools of darkness had appeared and no visible persons had come near. She faded out, rose and went on the move again.

The notification had come when she was on one of the galaxy's biggest Ferris wheels, looking downward dizzily on the blazing plain strewn with clots of jeweled lights. The lights, like gems carelessly thrown, were interrupted by the spotlighted rises of dagger-like towers.

She arrived for the rendezvous a little late. So what? You get off a Ferris wheel when they let you off; she couldn't have interrupted the ride.

—Yes, she could have, she had to admit. She just didn't want to. She was sitting at the time with Bern, a humorous fella who kept her laughing as gusty winds rocked the central tower back and forth. He was irresistable, a true Callis citizen of the classic type: all fun and games.

It was her own fault that she was late.

Now the only remedy was to keep moving, fading in and out of visibility, until she connected with the correct dark pool.

She would miss Bern. Compared to him and his friends, the city types here in Horenopolis were corpses. Worse news: compared to him, so were her Sol Corporation associates.

**

It was her duty, according to the Sol Corporation Investigations Manual, Callis Edition, to keep moving and searching until she was retrieved. But two weeks later, when no retrieving signal had emitted from any pool of dark, she gave it up, sick of eating the Horenopolis street food and sleeping in trees or under bridges. She had to keep at it for a while to make up for missing the first call. It made her nervous to skip out on a direct order, but they could send another notification if they really wanted her.

With her handprint at the lock, she entered her little flat in the park district (she had called in favors for a good view when she was assigned here) and dumped her pack beside the door. She looked around, sighing with relief at being home. She was happy to stay here a little longer.

She had softened the synthetic opalescent floors, standard in this building, with patches of thick fiber: rugs she had traded for, when she was on leave, with the local primitives up in the hill country. Shelves and cupboards stuffed with books lined the walls except for the alcove where food was stored and cooked. Her sleeping loft hung cantilevered above the kitchen, beckoning to her now after so many nights on the move.

But she had things to do first. She slumped into the seat at her desk, which floated on a raft of rug in the center of the apartment, and began to upload two weeks of observation notes and statistics from the files on her holophone to her desk unit. It was her first duty, always, on arrival — because who knew what could happen next? From the secured desk unit she would dump them uphill to Central.

While the files processed she looked through the window wall overlooking the park below. The trees were heavy with those unpronounceable blue fruits, the kind that visitors shouldn't eat. They looked unbearably refreshing down there when they were ripe, like now, in the hot season.

Fenn looked around her at the familiar comforts of home: At her right a couple of utility tables strewn with maps and charts occupied one side of the large space. At her left a low eating table sat on one of the softer rugs, holding up a longsuffering plant. It was wilted.

Whenever it was that she actually left Callis — and that could be soon, or it could be years from now — her books and maps would be reconstituted at her new location.

But the park view and the rugs would not be. And Bern would not be.

She hated desk work so she had learned to keep it short. As she traveled around the province she keyed or spoke her observation data, and entered holo recordings, onto her link phone in files that echoed the categories required by her reports. Then when she was uploading into the report forms, as she was now, she could just grab a section of data and pitch it wholesale into the correct category: Flora, or Fauna, or Native Shelters, or Native Peoples, Industry, Agriculture... nothing political, which was fine with her. She had actually been awarded for her excellent reporting, when really, it was just that she was lazy.

While she awaited the next screen she looked longingly at the book lying at her feet. The novel showing on the screen had been awaiting her since she had dropped the book to answer the door two weeks ago, and opened it to let Bern's impossible grin in.

She had dumped all the data to Central by the time the orange sun dropped low enough to get into her drooping eyes. She climbed the loft ladder and closed them, asleep before she was even prone.

**

Now the city lights blazed festively in the night outside the window wall. While Fenn spooned pickled fish and vegetables into her mouth, she stared at the unit screen, reached and touched, stared, swiped and touched.

"Project News" headed the confidential employee news screen from Sol Investigations Central. She read again from the top, slowly. No, she hadn't misunderstood: the entire notification group from two weeks ago, in which she had been included for pickup, had died on arrival at Phobos. Some local electronics storm had caused ship controls to malfunction and order detonation just before landing.

She stared. A storm? Not likely. That was Central Investigations code for "We're not telling." Probably the truth was that competitor pirate vessels had attacked the transport ship, and it was being hushed up to keep the employees from worrying.

As if it would.

And she had managed to miss that pickup because of a freak Ferris Wheel date.

Fenn stared out the window a while, considering the people whose names she didn't even know who had just died. They might have gone to school with her and she would never know their names. Sometimes Investigations was way too cloak-and-dagger. The secret arrivals and departures of the staff, for instance: who cared about their being here, or anywhere? But that was done "to avoid corporate espionage and keep Sol Corporation's unbeatable advantage in this part of the galaxy."

She shuddered and thought of Bern, who had kept her laughing too long on the Ferris wheel. Or had kept her laughing just long enough to miss detonation at the Phobos port. Thanks, she sent off to him mentally, wherever you are.

Her phone signalled.

Bern.

As she admitted the call, but just before his voice came in, a new notification signal from Corporate sounded on her link.

**

The Ferris wheel was a fad on Callis these days, one import from Io's solar system that was wildly popular here. Callinese had their own amusements, which they thought far superior to most of the sedentary pastimes of Io: things like very fast undersea scooters that permitted cavorting in company with the enormous fishlike population of the planet. And things like catching rides by dropping unannounced onto certain pterodactyl-like flying lizards who travelled in migratory herds as the seasons changed.

And those were only the favorites of city-dwellers. Out in the wilds the amusements included more deadly sports, like catapult battles between opposing teams or racing over some spectacularly beautiful waterfalls in flimsy vessels.

"Bern?" she said again in Callinese. Learning the language hadn't been hard. It was a simple one, with lots of verbs.

He crackled into hearing. "Time to soar, dip, sail, my love," he crowed. "I knew you would not be gone long!"

Well then, he knew more than she did. She thought she was about to be gone forever. For years, at least.

It was hard not getting involved with the local citizens of these places, and hard to tell the ones you were involved with that you could disappear at any time — sorry, it was just part of your job. She had actually told Bern, a few times. But he ignored all of that.

Now she laughed at his cheerfulness. It was an antidote to contemplating her own almost-death.

"I'm arriving now!" he replied. "With saddles. Let's gallop!" He disconnected.

Who knew what he had in mind? Delighted, she swallowed the last of the pickled stuff, popular local fast food, and was already pulling on some tough, sporty leggings when she realized how hard she was blocking out the notification that had just rung in.

She had been notified. She was leaving. It was a sea-change, something that happened once in many years, usually. Her duty was to respond by going mobile and locating where to be picked up.

She didn't want to.

This was an unprecedented quandary. She rummaged hastily on her screen, as if the shifting electronics there might offer some information to solve the quandary — before Bernd could arrive, before she decided to do her duty, and said goodbye, and left.

Her Central managers had called her an "exemplary hire." She loved her job — at least the travel part: learning about the races and cultures of the planets that supported human-like life. She performed as reliably as a Mars automaton for them, and they seemed to eat it up. She had never had a disagreement with Central, although there were some who did, and there was some grumbling here and there about Central's involvement in politics. She doubted it. They never bothered her with such stuff.

She ran her scan aimlessly over the mapped planets of this system on her screen, looking without focus, dreading Bern's knock at any instant.

Recent Central news items rose to the screen as she scanned the map: trade deal signed, spaceline route opened, transport accident, new team assignment, diplomatic relations with new planet, transport accident, another transport accident...a holo of a shattered hull rose toward her as she scanned back to the accident story: a ship leaving Cypria with a team of Sol Central investigators, half of them from Callis, taken out by an unpredicted meteor shower. She slid her scan to the previous transport accident: ship leaving Thaaro, enroute from Callis with a team of Sol Central investigators, mysteriously lost before arrival at the corporate home port on Io.

She had learned from ten years of investigations: if more than two of something occurred, there was something to find out. She scanned back: a previous accident, 12 local days earlier? There: ship leaving Vulcan with a team of Callis investigators on leave — breathable air accident caused by a disgruntled crew member who disobeyed orders and also died in the airlock breach.

Fenn sat barefoot in the riding leggings, staring out the window-wall at Fun City Horenopolis, seeing nothing but the images in her imagination: unwary corporate investigators like her, maybe 10-year alums of Io University like her, evaporated somewhere between here and the company homebase at SolPort, Io.

There was a small sound outside her door.

She hit the security screen view of the hallway outside; no one there, but it looked like a package had arrived… There was another small sound, near the floor. Her heart had begun thumping. Quietly she lifted her handgun from the rack at the door, wiped off the thick coat of dust, and hefted it. Recalling her training, she slid back the setting to Stun, and slid open the lock.

Bernd fell inward softly.

His body curled around his limbs like one of those Callis tree-bugs. She felt choked. She shot stun-waves before and above the doorway behind her, as she had been trained, then in all four remaining directions, in case someone was hidden by an image disruptor. Each crackle of the gun was followed by silence, so she hastily pulled him and his shoulder-pack inward and locked the door.

His back had a deep sear, sickening, that penetrated into the skin. How deep? His cheery face, relaxed as a sleeping child's, rested on her rug. Hastily she pushed away the shoulder pack and tore the back of his shirt.

She wiped bluish blood and fluid from his shimmering dolphin-like skin with a wet cleaning cloth. But the skin slid apart shockingly and lifted away. Her supper rose in her throat. He had a sort of carapace of hard stuff beneath it. An implant?

Astonished, she tapped at the skin and the carapace: she was looking at a protective manufactured body-shell, with an artfully created imitation skin, fluids and all, on the outside. At his abdomen, after she opened his shirt, she found tiny closure tabs and released. It all came off then, leaving his own healthy skin — always fascinating to her — beneath.

On Callis, evolution had engineered sun protection into the skin of the land-dwelling bipeds. The skin that must have been shimmery white at his birth was now tanned where the sun had reached, like hers. And pale where it hadn't.

He blinked awake, grinning to see her. "Clobbered!" he said in Callinese. "Bashed! Shoot them?"

She tried not to chuckle. It wasn't funny. What if he had died, here on her floor? Worse: what if he was actually some kind of criminal, and Central was trying to save her from him?

Trying to save her. What about the three or four shiploads of her fellow Investigators, dead or missing? "No, I missed," she answered.

He grabbed her sticky hands, despite their coating of blood and ooze, and pulled her down onto him, kissing her hungrily. She had taught him to kiss, and he had a very athletic fondness for it as a way of greeting her.

She knew him better than to try to contradict him right then.

But when he took a breath, she said, "Time for you to tell me things." She sat and tugged him upward. Pointed at the unbuckled carapace. "What is this, Mister?"

"It protects." His liquid blue-and-black eyes were still.

"I know. Why?"

"Come. I show. —I demonstrate," he added in Universal Language, with dignity. He led to the map table, which he had rummaged curiously on a visit a month ago. He found a large chart of Horenopolis, the harbor, the shoreline and rivers that ran into the sea. "Sol Corporation Central Intelligence. Underwater fortresses here. Here." He thumped the table with his palm at each spot. "Here. And here." His hands left oozy prints on her maps.

She shook her head, openmouthed. None of the corporate briefings had included any hint of such data. What would a food and commodities company be doing with secret fortresses?

He leaned toward her. "You want to know why does Sol Corporation do this? To break Callis governments and demand to take our planet. Run it for profit, turn it to sad dirt like this city — Horenopolis, Fun City Callis —" His arm swept toward the window wall. His grin was nowhere around now.

She felt his eyes searching deep into hers. She knew he saw her disbelief. "But Sol Central isn't...Sol is not political," she stammered in Callinese.

"Wants you to think it is not." He tossed his head back. It was a gesture he usually reserved for the pleasure of challenge, as in a game. Now it was a different challenge.

Over there next to her unit screen, another notification signal sounded on her link.

She had a great job. An enviable career. They liked her.

Liked her. The last few notification groups from this system were all ex-career investigators now. Maybe all of them were liked too.

She struggled to think. "Do you know who shot at you?"

"I know which ones. One of those shot, high power! I have excellent shield. Good friend to help me too." He looked at her, with the faintest trace of a smile in his eyes.

"You told me you were an engineer. What do you really do?"

Lying on the floor over there, his bloody carapace tugged at her eyes. She hated politics, skullduggery, border wars, any kind of wars...

"I am stunning engineer! Power engineer! Engineer Corps hired me to understand, report, 'figure out' (he used the Universal word with great dignity again) what is in the fortresses reported to us by the ancestral family undersea."

Their ancestral family? The dolphins maybe? "And?"

The Callinese word she used called for more verbs, so he gave them. "Found, discovered, uncovered weapons. Discovered directions of force. Dismantled, refocused, redirected circuits. Repurposed fortresses for use of the real owners of this place." Once again he tossed his head back and forward, then looked at her levelly.

The things she thought she was certain of were going liquid in her mind and being replaced by...what he said. Hard to believe what he said, though.

"Show me."

"Put on boots, I'll put on my shell, let's fly!" he said puckishly.

Impossible person; impossible to dislike. But her job was to investigate. That thought gave her some kind of stability in her confusion. She should investigate. She slid into her boots, pocketing her link instead of opening the connection when the third notification rang in.

**

He didn't explain how he knew that the utility ladder and trap at the end of her hallway led to the roof. Or how they only had to stand near the roof's edge and one of those cattle-sized leather birds arrived immediately to balance, teetering and grasping the roof edge with his leathery claws as they mounted, then sprang up to soar across the dizzying canyon of air toward the Ferris wheel and the waterfront. He held her in front of him, protected by his shell. Her one look back and up at him showed the delight in his face as they dove downward toward the water at 200 km per hour.

**

The air inside the "fortress," which looked like a mobile biological research station, was better than the steamy, thin, almost-air in the descent tube that sank through the sea for hundreds of feet to get to it. The station interior was tidy and bristling with levers, screens, dials, keypads, buttons.

"How did you know enough to get us in?" she demanded. After their plunge into the warm offshore waters, they had entered, feet first, an air/water lock and slid wetly through the damp tube.

"Powerful reverse-engineering," he grinned.

As they shook off on a dryer mat, he pointed to the title stamped on a log book on the nearest workstation desk: Sol Corporation Biological Research Unit #2. She shook her head in wonder at the title. He pulled her close to it with her boots still damp and ruffled the pages. No log entries since installation ten years ago. No one had come to maintain it in ten years?

From an inconspicuous slot below one desk he pulled a flat metal case with the same stamping that held schematic drawings and ten full years of entries in Universal Language — describing inspections and maintenance on the complex patterns of keys and displays covering the consoles around them. The diagrams and instructions explained functions for preparing, positioning, aiming and firing weapon after weapon — hundreds of them.

She wasn't battle-trained, but she could imagine what these could do to the city and beyond. Sol Corporation, maker of "Goods and foods for the galaxy," had also made this?

She said, "You knew this when you met me."

He nodded.

Suspicion dawned. Her fondness for him sank.

"Did you meet me deliberately, for some purpose?"

He nodded again. "Fun, flying, Ferris," he grinned. At her look, he sobered. "Also to save you. And me."

Fenn couldn't deny that he had saved her. Only an ingrate would quibble about that.

He offered one hand. She stared at it.

It looked like she had forfeited her job with Sol. It seemed certain that keeping that job would kill her, anyway. Not keeping it might kill her too, if Sol Corporation was determined to snuff out all the investigators on Callis. Maybe, like her, the Investigators all had learned too much?

"Time to fly now! Let's run, rise, return!" Bern clamored. "We have much to do!"

She'd lost a job, but it looked like she was being recruited for a new one.

He reached the hand toward her again.

She took it.

Dark Chocolate

THERE'S SOMETHING ODD about the face of the guy behind the scuffed-up counter at Hodges as I hand over the chocolate bar and some cash. Hodges is this little family store on my block here in the City, run by Mrs. Hodge, a motherly person with a red-haired son and (sometimes) a hot temper.

It's the kind of place that's jam-packed with shelves of food, hardware and household stuff, with aisles so narrow you can't pass someone without getting very close. There's only one place to pay and that's this little counter beside the door, whose front is plastered with notices, testimonial letters, and product logos, and the person behind the counter at the cash register is framed, above and on both sides, by an array of cigarette boxes and lotto tickets.

The guy behind the counter seems to be new. I've never seen him before. He looks at me for several seconds with a kind of polite curiosity, as if I have just revealed that I am an important celebrity instead of an impoverished painter. Then he rings the sale up briskly and hands the bar back to me. "Thank you, dear."

The little bell on the door jingles as another customer enters. But the guy behind the counter doesn't let it distract him. Again he looks at me funny: now he has added a benevolent smile, as if he's presenting me with something special. Not just a free-trade Dark

Cacao chocolate bar. Something priceless.

I tell him to have a good day, and break out a half-smile myself. I've been painting for days to get a commission finished in time to pay rent, and trips like this out into the real world have been few. I'm a little out of practice on the social graces.

It's still raining as I step outside into the noise of traffic and water; even under my umbrella the wetness is suspended in the air. My sneakers are getting soaked by streamlets and puddles in the uneven, tree-tilted sidewalk that leads to the building where I live. I tiptoe around the puddles, musing. The clerk seemed like a leftover Flower Child: love and light and peace to all. I'm not complaining. Kind of nice, really.

I must be in an odd state of mind, to be so struck by that guy. For sure I'm in an odd state of something, anyway: stuck with an unfinished painting that I can't figure out how to finish, with back rent to catch up so I don't get evicted at month end, five dollars left and no groceries in the house except a stale baguette. And now some chocolate. Maybe I'm starving and I don't know it. How do you know your mind is getting weird? Mine seems to be.

I walk up the four flights to my place, a studio in which I also eat and sleep. Opening the door I almost always feel happy because it's my place, and it's comfortable to me. It's home, all the home I've got. But this time, as I unlock and open the door my attention goes right past the coat rack and the little corner kitchen at my left, the bed and the wardrobe at my right, to the easel near the rain-streaked windows and the unfinished painting on it. Suddenly I can see what's wrong with the painting.

Still staring at the canvas across the room, seeing it all so clearly— what to do to make it terrific—I shut the door behind me, drop the soggy umbrella and my coat into the fresh puddle at my feet. I'm unwilling to take my eyes off it for fear of losing what I see right now.

I walk over and pick up the brush.

Later I realize that the sun has gone down and the light is getting poor. I haven't eaten in 12 hours. But the painting: it's as finished as it will ever be, and it's beautiful.

**

I stand by my easel, waiting for him to speak. The noonday sun is moving fitfully in and out of clouds, and the traffic is noisy down below, outside my windows. The windows are speckled with dusted raindrop-marks. Jake has come during his lunch hour to witness my creation, which is still drying from yesterday's paint frenzy, and to pay me before the actual delivery so I can take care of the landlady and get groceries. I showered before he got here and brushed my hair into a ponytail, then braided it down to my waist. It's a good thing "bohemian" is the right look for this occasion, because jeans and a hoodie are all I have that are clean enough to wear right now.

"You're going to love this one," is what I told him on the phone earlier. Jake doesn't pay me gallery prices, that's for sure, but he pays right away and right now he's agreed to pay before he takes possession, even, to help me out. He uses my work to furnish his law offices and his house, and he could easily buy good reproductions but he wants the real thing. And he always likes what I do.

"I don't know what happened, Cara," Jake says, eyes wide, shaking his head slowly. "I really hate it."

**

After a while I rouse myself and lift my head off my folded arms to sit up here at the kitchen table. Jake has gone. I'm not sure what I said to him but it must have been something like "I'll fix it." I'm still stunned.

And I'm a little scared. That's the trouble with having only one patron: if he's not pleased, you don't eat.

And I'm hungry now, for the first time in 24 hours. I get up and find some old half-and-half in the fridge and pour all that's left over a hunk of stale baguette so the bread turns to mushy cereal. I sit at the table and eat that, staring at the painting at the other end of the room. I don't see one thing I should change.

Not much of a meal. I remember the chocolate and decide that I can pretend this is a French garret, in which I eat baguettes and chocolate for breakfast.

I find the bar in my coat pocket, the wrapper rippled from sitting in the damp fabric overnight. It makes a whispering noise as I open it.

Some people excuse eating chocolate by saying it has copper or tryptophan — or is it endorphins? — something like that, in it. I just like it, though. Especially dark chocolate.

But listen: When I snap off the end section of chocolate at the place where it's grooved so it breaks into squares, there's handwriting underneath on the wrapper.

The wrapper was sealed. How could someone write in it?

I think: oh no, what if some maniac opened this to make me his next serial poison victim?

Bad timing, fella. I want to eat this chocolate really badly.

The broken-off piece is starting to melt on my fingertips. I get a plate and drop the gooey thing onto it, planning to return the bar for a good one. I dump the rest of the bar out onto the plate too, so I can read what the maniac had to say. Then I remember to slit the glue and open the wrapper with a clean knife and fork so I don't disturb the fingerprints—as if they aren't disturbed already by now. I picture the police thanking me for helping them solve this serial-killer crime. Maybe there's a reward.

I break the glue seals at both ends and spread the wrapper all the way open on the table. The message says:

Come to Hodge's Natural Market 3 p.m. March 31. Bring the painting.

It's printed in ballpoint-pen ink in what looks like everyday writing. Nothing special; it could be a shopping list or the kind of note you write to yourself when you're on the bus with no paper and you realize that you have to get green onions for the salad you're making for the Art Students' Co-op Potluck. Something that ordinary. But this note is inside a factory-sealed chocolate wrapper?

March 31 is the day after tomorrow. And the person who wrote it knows I paint?

Bring *which* painting, anyway?

**

Normally I would think this through more, but this time I don't. I'm too hungry. I throw on my jacket and grab the heavy thrift-store plate full of chocolate and wrapper to go return the bar.

While I'm locking my door, my neighbor Bron opens his and sticks his dark shaggy head out. "Hey, want some leftover lasagna?"

I must be gaping—because that sounds so good—so he explains: "I overdid it again. I'm going vegan for the week." He dives back inside his apartment, a studio like mine, and I hear the refrigerator door thump. He's in front of me again, holding out a foil packet as big as two bricks. "Glad you can use it," he grins into my eyes, "Come over later. Got a painting to show you." And he disappears inside. His door clunks shut.

Well, I am stopped right there by this brick of lasagna. I unlock again, walk right in, slice off a hunk and eat it cold, standing up in my jacket. After that I add some hot tea for a civilizing effect.

Now that I'm not so starving, I consider the message again while I drink the tea. All artists are hopeful, let's face it. Or most of us are. Most of us are dreamers. Maybe a secret admirer of my work wrote that note? I don't even try to think about how the person got the message inside a chocolate wrapper; that's just impossible.

My thinking goes like this:

Suppose I *did* go to Hodge's at 3 p.m. on March 31st. And took a painting. It couldn't hurt.

I couldn't take Jake's commission, because I have to finish that for him or get evicted. And I still don't know how to finish it. But I need to figure it out, fast. All I have besides Jake's commission are a couple of failed paintings and no more stretched canvases. No more canvas to stretch, either.

Thinking is over. I decide that I really do have to take the broken chocolate and wrapper to Hodge's and maybe find out something about all this. At very least I can get another bar. Maybe by getting out for a walk I'll dream up another solution to Jake's painting.

I take the plate, shut myself out of the place, and go down the stairs, all the way down to the first floor.

In the entryway of the building, below the mailboxes just before the door, something new has arrived: there's a pile of junk leaning against the wall and resting on the chipped, soot-accented marble tile floor. It wasn't there yesterday. Not really junk, though: wood and cloth, with a scrawled sign that says ARTISTS, and it's actually a roll of canvas and an assortment of stretchers, good wood ones.

My mouth drops open. The small print on the sign says, "Have to move, my loss is your gain. All yours—" with a signature that's impossible to read. There are usually at least half a dozen painters living in this building. One less now, I think. It makes me sad. And worried.

And that reminds me of the landlady's threat: catch up the rent or leave. My stomach gets queasy.

What weird luck, bad and good. I stagger back up the stairs with the plate of chocolate in my left hand and the heavy roll of canvas under that arm, and eight rectangular stretchers of various sizes strung like huge floppy bracelets on my right arm, clattering against each other and banging on my side. I think of sharing them with the other artists in the building, and I just might. But right now I might be the one who needs them most.

I'm thinking that right now I'm having a little lucky streak, as I turn my doorknob with one elbow. But when I put down the stretchers and the canvas, I notice that something's changed.

Then I realize what it is. Jake's painting is missing from the easel.

I sit down for a minute, still wearing those giant wooden stretcher bracelets, and let the plate down on the kitchen table. Missing? I'm stunned, for the second time today.

Then thinking takes over: can't be missing. How could it? I stack the stretchers and canvas near my easel and begin to methodically search the room, as if my painting, which has been sitting right there on the easel all day, has just taken a very reasonable walk to another part of the room or gotten mixed up with some books due to a wind coming in under the door. Or by some poltergeist it has ended up in my bed between the sheets. When it doesn't show up anywhere, I look out my windows at the street five stories below and check the window locks. They are unmistakably locked. The locks are even covered with the usual layer of dust. And there's nobody outside on a scaffold or anything.

Did I remember to lock the door? The hinges squeal faintly as I open it and stare at the scarred wood. No one has ever stolen one of my paintings before, not even when I went away for a week one time and forgot to lock up. I go next door and knock to ask Bron if he happened to see anything odd. No answer. Where could he have gone so fast?

Back in my studio I pinch myself, just in case this is one of those painting nightmares I get sometimes. Unfortunately, it's not.

End of scientific investigation. We are in the realm of mystery.

I feel sad that my best painting, ever, is missing. Maybe I should be flattered that someone stole it, right?

OK: I'll play along, I decide. —Maybe I've been breathing too much of my own paint fumes, but that's what I decide to do: play along. Something is going on, and I don't have time to fight with it. Rent is due and I need a finished painting for Jake.

I always think better when I'm not trying to think. So from the roll I found in the downstairs entryway I cut eight canvas pieces to the right sizes for the new stretchers. And staple them on with the staple-gun, first the center of one side, then stretch and staple at the center of the opposite side, then the center of the perpendicular side, and the center of its opposite, then the rest of the sides and corners, tight as I can: doing a high-quality job because it looks better and the paint goes on better. I always feel better charging for a painting with a top-quality stretch job, so I don't do quick-and-dirty ones.

This process is soothing. Next I stir up the fat jar of gesso, creamy-white and aromatic, and put a first coat on each stretched canvas with my big gesso brush (really just a wall-paint brush from the hardware store a block down). The gesso fills the pores of the canvas and makes it shrink so each canvas on its frame is tight like a drumhead. When I've primed the last one there are eight of them, various sizes, leaning against the wall, the window sills, and the legs of the easel, drying so they can take a second coat of gesso later.

All the while, I've been looking in my imagination at things I could paint, trying them out and weighing them. The spring sun is heading downward; I can see it glinting in some of the windows of the buildings across the street. The afternoon sun has warmed the dust on the sills and floor here by my easel, so the air smells like toasted dust and gesso. And here's what I've decided: that I should go where the luck leads me, and maybe it will turn into more luck.

I know I can get the second coat on that night. The next day is the 30th and I know what I'll do, even if it's absurd.

**

I'm up early the next day, and it's more lasagna for breakfast. While I chew it up with some mint tea I calculate and figure I have enough left of the slab of pasta and cheese to last me for today and tomorrow.

I prep my palette, put the first canvas up on the easel, and start painting.

**

By the time the daylight fails I have all eight canvases started, believe it or not, and two of them finished: both still-lifes. The still-lifes are done from an arrangement of wax fruit and other odd and ends, and another arrangement that includes a vase of silk flowers with a book — pretty usual stuff but with a little zing added, the way I like to do it: loose, with more color, more motion. Jake has a couple like them in the entryway of his office. These new paintings aren't as good as the one that's missing, but then that one was my best ever. I wonder again why he didn't like it. He never said.

The other paintings are on their way, kind of like a race: the ones that are finished first will win. A sailboat in a harbor. My street in an evening rain, summertime. A re-take of the one that's missing: Jake's father's house and barn in the country. This one isn't set in afternoon light, like the photo he gave me; it's done with imaginary morning light, as if the sun has washed the colors toward pastel and melted the edges of everything—the way things look when you're little and morning sun is all it takes to make your day. Maybe Jake won't like it that I've changed his idea, so it's good that there are lots of alternatives sitting here.

I have a sort of plan: to use the rest of the canvases for different angles on Jake's commission. To make enough paintings of the house and barn that Jake can hardly help buying one of them. I can throw in a freebie (it's a bad practice, but I'm desperate) to make sure he does.

After lasagna for supper, heated up and with lots of black pepper for variety, I take up the chocolate plate again and leave for Hodge's. This time I make sure I lock the door to my apartment.

**

Wet wind is whipping around the corners, biting cold, as I make it into the protected doorway at Hodge's. I stop to catch my breath, then push through the heavy green door and stop, letting the entry bell jingle. The owner herself is at the checkout counter straightening up some displayed items, a copper-and-silver curl falling out of a headband into her face.

"Hi, Mrs. Hodge," I say.

"Cara. Haven't seen you for a while."

I'm glad it's Mrs. H. She would know. I display Exhibit A, the dark chocolate wrapper, and tell the story. She looks as mystified as I am.

"Maybe the cashier from that morning would know something about it?" I suggest.

She thinks a few seconds. "That would be me. Or Luke, noon till closing."

Luke? Her tall, redheaded son? "No, the other guy, the new one."

She shakes her head blankly. "We don't have another clerk. Luke and I have been managing it ourselves for the last month."

Now I feel sure my mind is in trouble. I describe the guy: short, well-padded, round face, nice eyes — brown, maybe. Hair... maybe. Maybe I'm losing my marbles. She keeps wagging her head, looking at me in that embarrassing way that parents do when they notice their children's lapses. The way my dad would look at me if I told him I was broke again.

"You been doing drugs, Cara?"

"No, Mrs. H." I say it gravely.

She brightens. "Maybe it was an angel!" she says. My turn to look at her funny. But I get it: I'm a regular customer, so she's trying to help me out.

"Well, thanks, Mrs. H."

"Here. You can still have a replacement bar, honey. I'm sure you got that one from us, so we owe you one anyway."

**

I wake from a deep sleep, in which I had some kind of very satisfying dream. I wonder: Am I going into a pasta-induced state in which a full stomach blends with the morning sunshine and all is well? I laugh for a while, very amused at myself, until I sit up and see that the clock says almost noon.

I was painting till 3 a.m. All the canvases but one are done, and I think that one could pass for done if a buyer liked it that way. There are more finished and unsold paintings here than I've ever had piled up all at once. Actual inventory.

Then I realize it's the 31st.

I drink some tea to clear the pasta out of my voice, and call Jake. He doesn't answer. Great. What if he's away today? I need rent money. I leave a message that he should come by to get a painting—"after your workday is fine," I add so I don't sound desperate.

Because I really can't eat any more lasagna right now, I decide to invest in a can of spinach. Once I've showered and dressed again in my almost-clean jeans and hoodie and I'm about to leave for Hodge's to get the spinach, I remember the message in the wrapper.

I sit down and stare at the mostly-dry canvases for a minute.

I'm playing along, right? So here's what I do: I gather up the dry paintings, four of them, in both hands, spacing them with my fingers so they don't touch each other just in case. I leave for Hodge's and just shut my door by flipping it toward me hard with my foot. *Really, who cares if it's locked?* I'm thinking.

And I carry them to Hodge's. Along the way a couple with a dog asks me if they are for sale. I say yes, just follow me, humorously. They follow me into Hodge's and I set the paintings down, leaning back against the counter. Mrs. Hodge cranes her neck to look over the gum display on the counter, trying to see.

Maybe I should make this short or you'll think it's a Shirley Temple script: This couple reins in the dog long enough to buy the pair of still-lifes. They give me her card — she's an interior designer of some sort — and ask me to call. Two customers walk in off the street, ask prices, and buy the others. And that's before I even have time to ask for a can of spinach. All these people pick out a sack of Mrs. Hodges' groceries each, while I'm paying for my can and some more half and half with my remaining five dollars. It doesn't occur to me to buy more food with the new bills folded in my other jeans pocket.

"Mind if I go get the others?" I say to Mrs. H. Who knows what this is all about, but I'm still playing along.

At home I open the spinach and practically inhale it. Spinach must be the complementary opposite of lasagna, just like the color yellow is to violet. When I open my door to go carry the rest of the paintings to Hodge's, there's Mrs. Arnis, the landlady. "You're not moving out." she accuses. An unframed painting hangs from her left hand.

It's Jake's painting, the one he hated. My landlady is the thief. Remind me to lock the door, always.

"You were gone," she says, seeing me stare at it, "when I came to collect. I wanted this. I'll take it for the rent, OK?"

I nod, thinking that's a good deal for her, but OK. Happy landlady, happy life.

At Hodge's I set up the final four paintings against the counter, one with a sticky-note above it saying "WET! Don't touch."

Just as I back away, Bron walks in grinning. "Happy birthday, girl!" And then a bunch of my friends slip out of the first display aisle and yell, "Surprise!"

My birthday! I totally forgot. They've brought a dark chocolate cake. Mrs. H cuts it for us and we share with her, too. No one remembered candles, but they sing happy birthday and we all eat the cake till it's gone, laughing at what pigs we're being.

Here it is, the 31st, and I have brought my painting as the note ordered. *Paintings*, that is. All of them. While we are telling funny stories and ingesting cake, the rest of the paintings sell to random people who come in off the street. No kidding; I am not making this up. I stuff the bills deep into my jeans and hoodie pockets. We're having so much fun I almost don't care. Besides, I've made rent already.

I ask, but none of my friends knows anyone who looks like the guy who sold me the chocolate bar. Or at least they won't admit it. And none of them own up to the message in the wrapper, either.

At the end of the day, I have still not heard a word from Jake.

I decide: On his next painting the price goes up.

Shale

GARETH LAY ON A FLAT ROCK overlooking the next village, holding the reins of the beast in her hands. Her only companion: an enormous barcla. She shaded her eyes from the brilliant orange rays that lanced at her beneath thick clouds. The wind, which smelled of calcium, was cold enough to sting as she rubbed her chapped hands together; it inflated her robe so the heavy woven fiber swelled into dust-colored bubbles of air around her.

The thin snow that iced the rooftops and outlined the roadway below told the story of this place. There should be more snow than this.

One of these days she'd see Shale again, riding her own lumbering barcla toward her, a dot at the horizon blooming, as it neared, into the friend she had learned to count on. Maybe that speck she could see now out there at the horizon, that small dark place, was Shale.

But she was already hungry and thirsty; she would only get colder as well by waiting. No choice. She rose to go.

They would recognize her as soon as she entered the village: her plodding, shaggy, big-footed beast and the telltale leather packs it carried. The welcome would depend on how desperate they were.

"Move, Yang," she insisted. The barcla snorted, disliking the footing. Her bootsoles and his hooves slid as gravel rolled beneath them on the hard earth. There were few plants on this hillside, and that winding stream below seemed to be barely enough to sustain the thirsty farm-shares, probably planted with tubers and grains, that crowded alongside it.

She had begun this work in the tenderhearted belief that she did good for the poor people of this planet. Now that she was familiar with the layers of deceit and cheating here, it was impossible to tell from day to day who was helped, who was harmed. Maybe Shale was right to quit. If that's what Shale had done. One day, she was just gone.

Gareth refused to think of any of the other things that might have happened to her.

Gareth wasn't cowardly or weak. But she hated being alone. Still, no choice.

She loosened the robe, and beneath it straightened her tunic and leggings as she walked. She pushed strands of dark curls back into her headscarf. She touched the hoops of the earrings that proclaimed her an admirer of the local culture, although her gray-green eyes and the freckles on her sun-browned face would announce without a doubt that she was a foreigner.

A voice trumpeted from down below. She stopped and watched as a distant figure ran toward the foot of the hill, coming nearer and seemingly calling to her. As she passed a canted slab of rock enfolded in bushy shrubs, she saw some kind of smoking missile moving toward her through the clear air. She pulled Yang down into a heap and dove at his side with the reek of the animal's sweat close to her nose as the object flew above their heads and hit the jutting rock. Yang shrieked and leaped to his feet, tore the reins from her grasp, and galloped downhill away from the concussion.

When she saw that the figure below continued to run in their direction, she leapt after Yang, running and sliding downhill toward him. As a townsperson, that stranger might provide them a safer location than the naked hillside: who would shoot at their own people?

But as she neared, she saw that the stranger was dressed in the colorful rags of a busker — what busker could make a living in this impoverished district? — and that he carried a large empty basket. He was no townsperson.

For one frantic moment she thought that he must be the target of the explosions — that she and Yang were running toward the bullseye. But silence had fallen and he smiled as she stopped, panting, in front of him.

"My lady," he chirped in the national language, ignoring her dusty clothes and worn boots. "You seem to be in a hurry." He blew on his fingers.

She hadn't met anyone with a sense of humor since Shale disappeared. This person's hair was dark and straight, like a local, but it was cut short and ragged and his eyes were pale gray in pale pearly skin.

"And you too, sir." She tossed the words back to him as if they had begun a game of Pock.

He grinned. She smiled politely, waiting.

"This town, my lady, is not in a friendly mood. You will not find much welcome here for your water-magics."

"How do you know?"

"I'm being chased away empty-handed" — he displayed the air-filled basket — when at least my tricks and jokes bring them some fun. Your remedies will just make them poorer."

She glared at his bad manners, but he didn't seem to notice. He said affably,

"Would you like to see a trick?" and unbidden he found a small ollis egg behind her ear. He cracked it delicately against the bleached-wood handle of his basket, deftly peeled and ate the boiled creamy interior. She watched hungrily in spite of herself.

He smiled a knowing smile at her, pulled a second ollis egg from behind her other ear, and handed it to her with a courtly bow of the head.

While she ate he lifted the trap at the bottom to show how his empty basket could carry a concealed cargo: most visibly a few more eggs, a bunch of greens tied with a stalk of grass, and a local favorite: lumps of grain and cheese wrapped and roasted in carn leaves. The smells made her hungrier. But her eyes snagged on the little tattoo on the inside of his wrist.

"Do we stand eating eggs in the face of a hungry village? No wonder they were shooting!" she warned him as he reached in for another egg.

He shrugged and went down to a squat, with his back turned to Yang and the village, and cracked another shell.

He was crazy, or else he was protected by the local gods.

Ignoring the hunger she began to set up her things.

**

The clouds were heavy and lowering. They often were, all the long winter, in this part of the country. But in this decade the tantalizing clouds didn't loose their moisture as often as they once had.

She had taken up the usual place, before the village gate. Beside her the roadway turned toward the gate and entered, if the gate were opened, into a shadowy street that meandered and disappeared among thickly clumped earthen buildings. A low wall, then higher walls, separated the nearest dwellings from outsiders. A fenced corral, a little distance from the roadway, embraced the usual chattel and some horses protectively.

A headman had come to stand and watch her. His hair was pulled back and braided, shiny with oil as befitted his rank. His robes were faded but he stood with dignity, here at the bottom of this barren bowl of hills.

She polished and stood the final urn on its silvery stand, then polished away some dust that the wind had strewn newly onto one tray and one platter. Presentation was important, she had been taught by the Guild masters.

And those who seemed to have driven the Guild-masters from this planet? In her mind she saw again the tattoo on his wrist — this busker, or whatever he really was.

She saw the skepticism in the headman's eyes, the curiosity and amusement in the busker's. Turning she saw more curious eyes straining above the walls behind her, peering from windows in the nearby buildings.

Each new village was an unbelieving audience. When she left, they were usually changed. It was the one thing about all this that made the weariness and hunger and the stink of the barcla's sweaty hide tolerable.

There were a thousand back-country dialects on this continent. She and the headman had already determined that she didn't speak his, but she suspected that he knew the national language even when he would not reply to it. Although he was not willing to converse, she had learned that it was best for her to speak to make her intentions plain and her actions unsuspicious. So she named each thing she was doing.

She lit the small wick below one urn and poured a little handful of snow into its shining metal throat. She encouraged him to watch and inspect each thing as she did it: the way the snow melted to water, just a small amount of water though, with no waste. The way she quickly poured bluish grains from a small vial into the water and extended the wick so the water began to boil and steam. Then the lid she placed on the slender urn, and the curling clear tekryl tubes through which the steam wound, and the segmented pipe that went together to extend at least 15 hands into the air...

"Busker — Charlis? — Charlis, please hold this pipe firmly." Getting her audience to assist was also recommended. Not much of an audience, but to the headman Gareth said, "Please look at these grains of incendiary powder: they are familiar, right?" Must be; someone in the village had used them to shoot explosives over her head. "They will throw the blue solution" — she waved at the steam traveling through the coils — "into the clouds." To illustrate she flung her arm skyward.

Now she opened a pitcock just below the vertical tube and injected the powder into the line. She closed the pitcock neatly just before the hissing began and a blue jet of steam shot upward from the pipe Charlis held.

It climbed higher every second. The headman's eyebrows rose. Around them villagers had appeared. They were crowding, without his permission, to get a better look.

Charlis gripped the shuddering pipe with both hands now, staring upward.

When Gareth saw the first signs of success, she knew they were also the first hint of breakfast for her: where the column of blue steam intersected with the belly of the cloud, a barely-visible darkness had begun to collect in the thick wooly layer there. She pointed, and the usual murmur stirred through the little crowd around her as they saw it too: her magic was making the cloud above look ripe with moisture.

Charlis turned to her and grinned in a way that clearly said, "You've fooled them now; good trick." Aloud he joked, "Now might be the time to suggest some food or pay, my lady."

She shook her head. She pointed upward again. Her audience, a respectable size now, inhaled in unison: snow was falling, a column of it about 20 hands or more in diameter, expanding and rippling as it dropped downward toward them and began to sprinkle her stands and urns and bottles of chemicals.

Arms lifted; fingers spread and reached to catch the flakes. Crystals melted on swarthy faces, and teeth showed in the somber features around her.

It was the Guild method, and it always impressed them.

**

They fed her, after that first display. Her customers almost always did. Sitting cross-legged on the ground before her equipment — she didn't dare leave it — she had tucked a stray curl into her headscarf, and moved her hands and head in the local prayer of blessing over her breakfast: the eggs and greens and some kind of cattle cheese. No water had been offered to wash her hands, and this ritual at least gave a symbolic attempt at purification. With water scarce, both this food and the hands that had prepared the food might not have been washed.

The villagers who watched her nodded with approval; probably approval for her good sense as well as for her piety. Local customs were there because they worked, the Guild manual said. Her heart warmed to see them there.

But why does the busker remain here? He and his odd smile were supposed to be on their way out of town, weren't they?

Before she ate she accepted and drank the precious little flask of water with relief. As she ate she smiled and licked her blue-stained fingers, nodding her appreciation to those who fed her. In front of her the ground sloped downhill to the ragged farm-shares and the small stream bed — which was mostly a sandy bottom cradling a thin ribbon of water.

She longed for more water to drink but none was offered. When she had finished eating she swept a small pile of clean sand from beside a rock and scrubbed the oils from her hands with it, and only then did she take up a small handful of snow to finish cleaning them

— to show respect for the precious water of her hosts.

Now it was time for the next step. Clearly they had never seen the Guild demonstration before, because her performance had impressed them enough to earn her breakfast. Even Charlis, who sat nearby, watched her with steady appraisal, looking less like a busker now. Looking more like something else that she couldn't quite find in her memory...

The next step was the Guild "water magic," *manea curisan*. The name was what people in this region often called what they were about to witness.

But first it was necessary to strike a bargain. It was something that Shale always excelled at. Gareth disliked it.

She rose and stood before them with as much height and dignity as she could assume, despite the wind whipping the ends of her hair into her eyes. Her over-robe billowed. "The price must be settled at the beginning," she said in the government language. She must show confidence that they would pay. "I will need food," she began, "and water for my ongoing journey. I will need more of the blue powder for the next village. What can you pay me?"

She saw that the national tongue was understood. Some of the villagers nodded to others: of course there must be payment. Many faces grew longer and their eyes dropped.

"We can give you food, after the next crop grows," the headman said finally, grudgingly using the national tongue.

She nodded. It was true that her result was not a certain thing yet. She was often paid in future food, which she would collect when she travelled that way again. If she ever did. But she had to get something she could take with her to trade, too. She waited.

"This I have to see! I will give two government pieces if you can produce an hour of rain."

Gareth stared at Charlis. This ragged clown had coins? More

mystery. She held out a palm and he displayed his own, cupping a pair of blue-white metal coins that caught the light. Thieves and fake coins abounded in this country. She took one and scraped it with a fingernail, turned it and inspected the stamping, checked the edges for nicks.

She looked at the headman, who scowled first at her and then at the "busker."

There was something here that she didn't understand. She returned the coin to Charlis, looking into his light eyes. A veil fell across them, deep inside. Whoever he was, he was hiding things. Maybe the headman had noticed too. To the headman she said, "Does this village have other valuables?"

After some moments a woman stepped forward, drawing a youthful furry bull-chattel with her, a small version of the chattel penned in the common stockyard just over there beside the village gates. Clearly the little bull was a prized possession. Gareth had seen no other young; this may have been a poor year for new births. Her stomach hurt with empathy.

"This," the woman said. The headman's eyebrows raised, but he nodded. Something like resignation drew down his face, and the woman's.

"One-tenth of your first crop, and that." Gareth nodded her assent to the bargain. "For rain for two hours or more today — and more tomorrow if your prayers are answered," she said to them all.

"If there are not two hours or more of rain today, no bargain," the headman said. He closed his eyes with finality.

She wished Shale were here to say confidently, as she always did, "We hope all your prayers are answered."

She turned toward her equipment. Charlis' eyes were on her, steady as the eyes of an Inspector.

**

For good measure, an unusully large scoop of the blue stuff went into the tall flask. With the little syringe she ejected incendiary powder into the pitcock quickly. And snapped the little door shut with haste. Charlis gripped the tall pipe as blue steam flew skyward, buried itself in the cloud above, and spread through it like a bruise.

The villagers — all sixty or seventy of them now, of all ages — gasped and sighed, breathing with the magic, willing the impregnated cloud to burst into life for them. Willing it to bring water and give them life too.

The darkening bruise above swelled until it seemed to fill the entire sky. Soon all sunlight was blocked, and the noon twilight made a few babies wail. Chattel in the corrals lowed and screeched nervously.

As always, she was captivated for few moments by what she had done. It was easy to feel like a magician at this time.

But now she began to disassemble her equipment, for safety in case there was chaos next. She had only a little time; she had learned that bad or good chaos, either one, damaged equipment. She wiped and stacked, wrapped and stuffed her things into the heavy packs, looking around for her beast just as the first drops fell. Cries of pain, joy and release burst from the villagers, mixing with the pattering drops and the puffs of dust.

"Good fella," she said when Yang arrived. She began to load.

**

Yang's flank steamed with his body heat, for which she was grateful. She and the barcla squatted under an overhanging roof, watching rain pound the hard ground and carve the beginnings of gullies in the parched earth there at the entrance to the village.

After filling all their pots and dishes, drinking-skins and pails, the villagers had joyfully dug ditches to carry the water to their fields so the precious stuff didn't just disappear into the swelling stream.

Gareth sighed with contentment, watching.

"Greedy, aren't they?"

She found Charlis beside her, drenched. Where had he gone? To her, their hunger to capture and keep it all was understandable. Scarce things are treasured.

She thought again of Shale.

Down below, sopping young men and women hoed and spaded the soil in the fenced growing fields, mixing dust-dry soil with wet lovingly — as Gareth remembered, on the home planet, someone mixing dry into wet for a cake.

The rain was still falling when the headman and others had run out of ways to use or conserve the pelting rainwater. But they had been quick to invent the ways: a small pond in the cattle enclosure, where the cattle were crowded now, drinking all they could; a crude cistern within the village to catch wash-water; a bathing pond in a little hollow above the creek, hastily buttressed by stones. Down there the mothers of infants knelt on mats in the downpour and washed their babies, cold as it was; then, made shy by the tremendous luxury of it, stripped to wash themselves. Their families joined them.

Charlis had been silent but now he made a sound. When she turned, Gareth's eyes widened with shock: he held a laser weapon at her. "My lady, I hereby arrest you," he said, as lightly as if it were a game of Pock, and added: "On behalf of the Farayyun National Government."

What bad joke was this?

She demanded, "What is the charge?"

"Poaching rainwater from the National Government Stores. Many counts, probably." He slid back the release on the gun.

Her mind whirled upward like the jetting blue smoke, and struck something, and the truth rained onto her: his tattoo. The seal of the Inspectors; he was one of them? When did the job of Inspector become this? And the National Government, known for its dubious integrity, now owned all water? Since this government had been seated 10 years ago, water shortages had run farm people like these down into slavery and begging. And crime.

She saw the headman nearing, drawn by the sight of Charlis fastening a shining metal chain and cuff to her ankle. The weapon in Charlis' other hand now pointed at her face. She saw the older man scowl fiercely, quietly speaking imperious gutterals in his own dialect to those nearby.

An arm appeared at the corner of the building, whipping around the mud wall, and something it threw struck Charlis' head from behind. His weapon flashed out, just as a hand pulled Gareth's leg out from under her; someone shrieked, and mud from the village wall flew in every direction. Her skull landed hard against the huge bony head of her beast.

**

When she woke she was cold. She lay in a dim room that smelled of clay and cooking, and seeing her eyes open, the householders went to fetch the headman. Her head hurt where there was a painful lump on one side. Was it safe in here? She should leave… Gareth tested her limbs. No blood, nothing seemed to be broken.

Shale would have said something funny now.

Where is Shale? Moving her limbs awakened a few places that hurt, but she raised herself to sit upright.

She had never once been inside a village dwelling; the manual recommended against it. She was surprised to see that these clay interior walls had been stained an ochre color, and edged near the top with skillful vinelike patterns that bore flowers and symbols. She saw, in memory, the colorful wall-striping everywhere on the home planet and the silvered metal decorations that her family favored.

The woman returned to Gareth to wash her face with gentle

hands, help her comb and re-bind her hair, and prepare her to be visited. Liking for each other connected the two women. Gareth smiled at her gratefully, feeling less alone.

The headman entered. He seated himself on the floor opposite her. Her assailant had been tied up and placed under guard, he said. He had been suspicious of "Charlis the busker," but the tattoo had made them afraid to antagonize him, he explained, so they had merely given the fellow food and tried to drive him away.

So the village had supplied the food for Charlis' trick basket. They had not refused him. If he would lie without cause about such a small thing, he would lie about bigger things.

The headman said, and she knew it was true: every year someone came to collect the tax for "government protection of the water." She knew it was a bitter joke in the villages that since the tax had begun, there was less and less water to protect.

The headman recounted legends from travelers that the capital city and the large farms around it were green everywhere, and water was cheap there.

She had been there. He was right. How odd that the rain only fell in the vast green capital district, and was so unwilling to fall on poor villagers.

Had the Guild left this planet because its help to the villagers ran counter to the plans of the Farayyun National Government?

A small boy rushed into the room, handed her a piece of home-woven paper, and dodging the grasp of the headman, ran away.

She stared. Symbols crowded the paper, written in the practiced hand of a scribe or hired official. Which of these people could write? But the writing was in the national tongue. She could read it. Her eyes took in the message hastily: "Wiser not to trust him. He is less your friend than I am, although you may not believe it. A test: find out how much of the water tax he takes—"

The headman snatched the paper from her and glanced at it quickly. "He is a lying scoundrel."

Not a long enough look to read what it said. Besides, what village headman could read? And how did he know who wrote it?

The message had to be from the busker. But how odd that the headman knew so much about this fake busker: recognized his writing, expected his lies?

The headman was looking long at her, sharply, considering.

"What does he say?" she tested.

He drew himself up proudly, nodded at the paper, and informed her, "He threatens you and me." He began to rise.

Hastily she begged for a little tea for her parched throat. To force him to stay and honor the laws of hospitality while the bowls were brought. He sat again. She had bought some time.

A new wave of rain was falling outside now; a small ventilation slot high in one wall transmitted the sound and sight of falling water. The prayers of the villagers had indeed been answered. But if this man's prayers had been answered, the answer didn't light up his face. He stared broodingly at the slot as she drank, only sipping a little now and then himself.

"You spoke of the tax. I have heard about that tax," she began, nodding knowingly.

His eyes met hers, pulled from other thoughts.

"It seems very wrong to take from a hungry village in that way," she said. "But I have heard, and maybe you have too, of clever headmen who take a percentage of the tax in return for collecting it for the national government. Maybe you could also —"

He waved her to silence, imperiously. "Of course," he said. "I have thought of that. Half goes to me — as befits my rank."

She nodded silently. Half goes to him, and not to his village?

"Good to hear that half of the tax comes back again to your people," she said, deliberately misunderstanding.

His eyes veiled.

So his people never saw the money again.

But what did it prove that he was a paid tax-collector for the national government? Just that he was no better than Charlis the Busker. He was no less a pretender in some greedy game.

She missed Shale again.

In memory she saw the notice they had received months ago that the Guild was moving its headquarters from this planet. Work would continue here, the letter said. She and Shale and other volunteers were thanked for her persistence in the cause. If they should ever need help, the letter assured them, they could just contact any of a very short list of people.

Soon her tea would be finished and the headman would rise to go do what he had in mind. He would probably make sure that Charlis the Busker couldn't do anything further about anything. Possibly this fellow had the same sort of plan for her.

"Sir," she bowed her head with an extra measure of courtesy, stalling for time to think. *Gods, Shale. Where are you now?* The roads she and Shale had traveled for the last three years were long and their work had made them subject to threats often enough that she and Shale played a game as they rode on their shambling barclas in the heat and cold: What Would You Do If. As a result she was pretty good, even alone, at thinking of ideas. Shale was best at it, and Gareth's were not always brilliant — just numerous.

"I have an idea about the 'busker,'" she announced, and she lowered her lashes to give her speech the right veils of secrecy and confidentiality. "—an idea that may bring some wealth to your village. Can you take a moment to hear it?"

He grunted limited assent.

**

The twin moons rose. She had learned that they spun at reckless angles to each other, astronomically — but now, lit as they were, they seemed to be exquisitely in harmony, like matched crescent pendants hung from a pair of chains too fine to be seen.

She slipped out of the house with the flowered ochre walls — now silvered with moonlight coming through a window — and out of the house to the village street. She made her way to the corral where the barcla was loaded and tied, according to their plan.

After a quick check of her packs and equipment, she swung her personal satchel up ahead of her, and the well-schooled beast offered an extended knee for her to mount from.

She would have only a quarter of a quarter of a quarter to be away, before he followed.

**

The moons hung further from the horizon now, above the dry treetops. She and Yang, who was muzzled, were sheltered behind some rocks when she heard the shuffle of footsteps along the roadway. She craned her neck to see him passing, looking right and left for signs of her: Charlis, the busker/Inspector/liar.

She had already located his hidden transportation, a small laser-propelled kite with mothlike vertically folded wings, dun-colored for camouflage, hidden in a small cleft among the rocks on the opposite slope of the ravine. She had guessed a vehicle might be there: of course this clever fellow was not really travelling on foot from village to village.

Now he sat down on a rock by the roadside, and the moonlight cast his shadow long on the pebble-studded, gravelly ground beside him. She was horrified at the treachery that she knew was intended against her. The desire to survive it made her pant, but she throttled her breathing.

The beast tensed and struggled to rise. She stroked Yang till he was still again. His sensitive ears had heard what she only now began to feel, through the ground: the footfalls of people and horses, coming.

"Better hurry," she whispered to Yang. He rose gratefully when she tugged, and they walked downhill the short distance to the road.

"Charlis," she called softly. He stood. His face was handsome, and his smile was charming, as if he might have something funny to say.

But his gun gleamed in his waistband, struck by the moonlight, and he kept his hand near it. The headman had returned his weapon to him; if she had any doubt before, she knew now how things stood.

"Quick," she said, moving without delay to stand beside him. "We must hide." She must move faster than his treachery. She took his arm and drew him away from the road among some dry brush, where a protruding elbow of layered rock would protect them from view. "I have news," she concocted. "They are coming to kill you, intending to make it an accident blamed on me. Your vehicle—" She saw his surprise when she tossed her head toward its hiding place, uphill from him. "—To fly is our only chance."

She took his hand and drew him uphill without pausing. Impulsive people like this one were easily surprised and redirected, the Guild had taught. She dragged Yang, poor reluctant creature, behind her with her right arm as she urged Charlis with her left.

The kite sat in the shadow between two upright slabs of rock. They panted steeply upward to it. "Prepare to take off! Quickly!" she begged, in a voice heavy with dread, turning to tie Yang to the rock-hard exposed root of a dead tree.

Charlis the Liar hastened to move the kite out of its slot in the rocks, lower its wings and engage power. He held out a hand to draw her in through her door to a seat next to him. She reached. He engaged power, the kite began to move, and at that moment she pulled away to turn to her beast. "Yang!" she pretended to scold, loud enough for the sound to echo noisily in the ravine.

The kite had begun to move downhill. She turned and ran to its side again, saw his frightened face, made a fake attempt to reach his hand, then sagged weakly, giving up. "Go! Save yourself!" she urged.

It took no more than that: he was airborne, spitting gravel and dust behind him at her, banking sharply to avoid the opposite wall of the ravine, just as shouts rang out from below. The Liar's weapon crackled twice in answer. Horses and men screamed. Shots hissed from below as well. She heard the bellow of the headman, rallying his little troop.

She panted uphill to Yang again and tugged him into a squat in some snow-dusted brush. More shots and screams echoed from below. She huddled next to the beast, trying to envision what she heard: hissing weapons, a rattling impact, a harder one, more screaming horses, and an explosion. And a crash, far down in the ravine.

Then silence.

She waited for a little while. When she stood, dust was still rising in clouds from below. She couldn't see much else.

She would not wait any longer. She tugged Yang up and walked uphill quickly with him past the hiding place of the kite and onward to the top of the ravine.

There she looked down through the clearing air on the small moonlit pile of dead things far below, at the bottom of the ravine. Pieces of broken kite lay over everything.

She breathed and looked for a long time. She had tricked her enemies into doing away with each other. She wished Shale were here to make it funny.

It didn't seem funny to her. It was the saddest thing she had ever known. The village that was already teetering on the edge of extinction had just lost a headman and several fathers.

She should be glad she had saved herself. She had never been like this, so grief-stricken she couldn't cry.

She led Yang away from the ravine's edge. When she touched the back of the barcla's near knee, he raised it for her to mount from. She settled on his back, turned him with the heavy reins, and rode slowly away.

It seemed that Shale was riding silently beside her, and in a moment she would begin crowing about their success with the village rain, their victory over those criminals, the Liar and the Tax Thief. She could just hear it.

But Gareth had killed all those people down there. Without Shale to share the responsibility. No one here but her.

It was self-defense! She had never killed anyone. She was here to help these poor people. She couldn't help what had happened...

Where is Shale?

A few seconds ago she had glimpsed something — and now she saw it for certain: at the far rim of this barren country, out at the horizon, a speck that seemed to be Shale riding toward her.

Gareth rode a little faster, staring ahead into the bleak landscape at the speck. After a kilometer or two it didn't grow or change.

Shale was not coming.

Alive or dead she was not coming back. Even if she had the ability, it would be unsafe for her to try.

Because of the loneliness, the silence unbroken by Shale's victorious voice, Gareth also began to see what she had not seen before.

She had decided to live instead of die. She had pitted her two enemies against each other and yes, that killed them. But then, wasn't it true that they had done their part of the killing too?

She had come here to fight against the drought that hurt these people so badly. And once she began the work, her life had seemed inevitable. Now all this was tantalizing her with something new: the suspicion of a choice.

And choices beyond that. More than she had imagined before.

She saw the smoking chimneys of a village ahead, to one side across the rolling arid terrain — another village with dry and desolate fields, badly in need of rain, its poor villagers slowly starving.

Gareth assessed herself more coolly than she ever had. She was weak from thirst and hunger. She had been forced to leave her small bull-chattel behind — the one she could have traded with the next village for supplies and food. Who would a half-starved water magician convince to feed her next? And when the national government heard about the last village and sent someone to find her, would they understand that she had only done what she had to do? There was no Guild here anymore to defend her.

She had never considered leaving with the work undone. But this was a fight she was losing. She could die alone like a martyr or get out and fight another day, some other way.

It was forty kilometers to the nearest city, barely possible with a thirsty beast and rider, where her Guild certificates would help her get Guild protection wired in and a flight to the planet where its headquarters lay. Such a decision was out of the question before. Now the choice was hers and no one else's.

Laboriously she considered, as the barcla plodded aimlessly on.

And then she chose: to ride onward to the city.

Her choice. Knowing now that she would choose again, and again, and all of them would be her choices.

Sometime in the future, she might be proud of her choices or regret them. But this much was certain: she chose not to quit.

Sister of a Crocodile

THE VICE PRESIDENT OF CONNECTIVITY simpered at her. She was amused at this attempt to connect but Serith threw a baleful look at him when he turned his eyes away to glance at the water. Bloated parasite.

The tall reeds surrounded them both. This steamy little tributary to the Nile was very private. While he sat on the single bench-like seat and sweated, she poled the little skiff fetchingly, allowing her long braids to swing back and forth past her waist, letting her bangled bracelets rattle like the clacking sound of the reedflies, ignoring his blandishments.

Around this curve the crocodile awaited, probably yawning in the tawny sun and anticipating the promised snack. "Either way a snack," she had promised him early this morning, her finger resting with hypnotic pressure on the tip of his nose. His eyes had drooped in acquiescence.

"About your offer," she said to the VPC. "It's not acceptable."

"More sweets?" he enticed.

"More lapis," she said firmly. "More gold."

They rounded the curve.

"But that is impossible!" he croaked.

She waved to the croc, who slid forward and snapped, one smooth motion that removed the VPC from the barge. He was so surprised he didn't even splash much. She regretted that his Sensor had to go with him. But the device would draw humorous attention to the crocodile's snack.

She poled on, humming a small song to herself, considering. One down, nine left. How to eliminate the next Vice President?

They were usurpers who had landed in airships one night a decade ago, and taking the shape of humans, they were stealing positions of power to make a slave farm of Egypt, of Mesopotamia, of Phoenicia and Greece. They were mostly not as stupid as this softheaded Vice President of Connectivity. Taking out the next one would be harder.

But this morning her life seemed like a clever game of Senet. A delightful pretense, in which charisma protected her.

**

At the wharf she tossed the tether to one of the wharf-boys and stepped out, her gilt sandals caressing the wooden planking.

She carried only a thick fistful of reeds and lilies with her. On the packed-earth street, she bowed her head to left and right as the townspeople dipped or curtsied and moved aside for her. When she stopped at a cedar door on a quiet avenue, the one with the awning of painted cloth above it, she knocked — then entered without waiting.

She shut the cool, heavy wood against the heat and market-noises outside, smelling its cedar fragrance near her face.

He stepped from the shadows before her eyes adjusted. "Serith," his voice smiled, and a large hand wrapped around her handful of stems.

Rakhen kissed her, then tabled the flowers and scooped her up as neatly as the croc had taken his treat.

It was acceptable: she had commandeered him the night before with just as much insistence. They understood each other.

**

When she woke, Rakhen was gone. Rebellion business, probably. She hummed as she put the fragrant lilies, slightly wilted, into a vase that she filled with water ladled from a sweating kitchen urn.

Only when she set them on the table again did she see the pool on the polished earthen floor: in one place only, lit brilliant as rubies by afternoon sun that entered beneath a window shade. Her heart stopped and the floor fell away inside her.

She slid her knife from an ankle sheath and searched the little house, her heart pounding now.

She exited through the garden door into an earthen-walled space smaller than the house. Its innocent flower perfumes shocked her now, and the quiet hum of bees, the soft splash of fountains.

With shaking hands she pulled her cowled robe from its hook in the mud garden-hut and hid her sandals there beneath some pottery on the shelf. Barefoot, she left the garden by the back gate.

She entered the back street as a bowed figure whose face was in shadow, whose dusty bare feet shuffled as she walked.

**

At a market stall Serith fingered a small garden tool and asked the vendor, "What news today? I have been up to my wrists in mud."

"No news." The gaunt, white-bearded seller moved around her as if to see under her cowl.

She turned away. "Gods bless you today."

Of a seller of sweet grains, she asked again: "What news? Your cakes smell heavenly."

The plump vendor neared her, watchful for theft, and said, "No news. Good to have no news these days."

"Yes. Gods give you blessings."

Serith worked her way through the market until she saw a vendor with a receiver in one hand: the electronics end of the market was always better-informed. "What news?" she asked, inspecting a shadowy hanging display of devices, probably smuggled. The vendor, a muscular tattooed woman wearing outlandish boots and an almost-sheer tunic, edged nearer to protect the merchandise.

"The news?" she murmured. "There was a murder among the Lords this morning." Again Serith felt the ground drop away from beneath her.

"Who?" she choked out, and coughed to cover the quake in her voice.

"One Lord Rakhen, arrogant son of a crocodile." The woman's scent, body odors mixed with heavy perfumed oils, made Serith choke again.

"Killed, or killer?" She clung to a final hope.

"Killed. Lord Khamis, Vice President of Conduct, claims this victory."

She sagged. "The more blessings to you, my dear." And she left, affecting the wandering gait of a person too old to think well.

She was in fact staggered by the news. While she had slept — and in her presence — they had taken his life.

And with it, she realized, they had taken her protection. Wasn't the pool of his blood on the floor message enough of that? She was no longer safe. She had been located. And she was powerless to defend herself now.

Above her head a hawk circled above the back streets, looking for prey. She staggered to the small hut, on the rim of the city, that she rented as Garrut the gardener, a poor widow. She locked the flimsy door behind her and sat in the one chair at the single crude table, put her head on her forearms, and fainted.

**

Serith woke to the pale leak of evening light through a window, and with it came some clarity to replace her wretched dreams.

143

The Rebels had suffered a heavy blow today — the death of Rakhen, their leader. They also had scored a victory, which would only be discovered when the remains of the missing Vice President of Connectivity were found. As one of the 10 Vice Presidents who administered the current tyranny, he left behind nine more armed and still in power.

She thirsted to get the rest. But the final piece of clarity arrived: because she herself was too vulnerable, she needed to find a new place of safety or be no good to anyone, not to the Rebellion and not even to herself.

Rakhen, my love. Why had the killer not killed her along with him? The answer must be that she was too much liked, and no crime had been allowed to stick to her. She was too thorough.

**

On her way to the waterfront she let herself through the back gate into the garden again, thankful for the thin new moon just setting. It would be a dark night. The dark cloak she had worn since morning covered Garrut the gardener from its hood down to her dusty bare feet. She held the coarse cloth together tighter now.

It wasn't just that the sandals were a gift from Rakhen. The sandals would be part of her costume at the first port; an aging gardener couldn't hire a long passage without suspicion but a prosperous female trader could.

Inside, on the garden hut shelf, she felt under the stack of pottery for her little gilded sandals. In the darkness her fingers closed on them.

A rough hand clasped her wrist.

Her breath stopped. She feinted, pretending a quick struggle to pull away. With her other hand she grabbed at her ankle and brought the knife upward, curving as it slashed, into the heavy, grunting neck of her captor. Blood gurgled and the sick wetness soaked the front of her robe, covered the sandals in her hand. His grip slowly went lax and he sagged to the floor, pulling two shelves of pots and tools loudly down over them both.

In this part of the city, so near the wharves, domestic noises could be expected at times. After the silence that followed had continued for a while, Serith let the last pots slip from her shoulder quietly down on top of her assailant and slid out, doubled over in the deep furrow of a garden path, to strip in the shadow by the larger fountain and wash the blood from the sandals and her clothes.

She hung them all on a small fruit tree near the earthen wall. The warm desert air would dry them, while she slipped into the darkness of the fountain pool and bathed with the knife on the rim beside her.

Revulsion at the grunting killer's blood on her, horror at Rakhen's blood on the polished floor... she drove them from her mind for now by scrubbing herself hard.

The Vice Presidents had demonstrated that they would be perfectly content to kill her, but only on the sly. Not so the deed could be publicly known.

Time was short. She dressed, now, and strapped the knife back onto her calf, hung the bloody hooded robe in the shed again above the body, and slipped out through the garden gate, carrying a potted flowering plant that gave her the look of a local resident on an evening errand of friendship.

Sewed into the hem of her linen tunic were gems and coins — and lapis for small purchases — from the little cask she had buried in the house of Garrut. In the pocket of her linen trousers was a Sensor that she would jettison if she were ever caught.

The Sensors had been brought by the Vice Presidents, and some of them stolen by spies of the Rebellion. They gave certain powers that she was just learning. The Rebels would not use them until it was necessary, because use would expose the users.

When she appeared at the wharf with her potted flowers, the wharf-boys grinned at each other. "An errand of love?" her favorite teased, untying and drawing her skiff forward. She smiled wickedly back at him as she stepped in. She pressed a small uncut lapis into his palm. "For your help," she whispered sweetly.

And she poled away without looking back — upriver toward the next small city.

Where she would sink the raft and hire passage on a boat at dawn, downriver again toward the delta.

Toward Greece.

**

The boat rose and fell as they sliced through the waves. Salt and coolness edged the air she breathed. The little pots and jars she had bought in several steamy delta market-stalls served as part of her disguise: with them in a colorful woven bag she shouldered, she was an ordinary vendor of cosmetics who also could be hired as a cosmetician by any ladies on board with enough money and enough time on their hands to have their looks freshened on the way to Gythium.

The sailors added and trimmed sail. The unceasing creak and slap of boards and sails, and the hiss of the water, were in her ears day and night. Some days seabirds cried, and in today's bright sun the salt and spray flung themselves over the deck passengers, wetting her braids. She was seasick and alone, but she was alive — and many leagues away from anyone who might wish to find her.

One fellow passenger interested her: a comely young man with a modest face, who treated her with great respect. They talked politely. Without noticing, she spoke to him as she would talk with a trusted servant or one of the more educated townspeople. The accent of his speech seemed familiar, but he was from the delta region, traveling to take work as clerk and scribe for a trading company in Attica. The familiar sound in his voice seemed to be the sound of friendliness.

She heard the same friendliness now: "How are you faring today, my lady?" he asked. "Still unable to eat?" His hand reached down to her where she sat on a deck cushion, offering her a string of fat dried dates that some date-seller had temptingly tied like beads on a chain of braided reeds.

"Yes, I—" Something caught her eyes as she raised them toward his face. Then what she saw disappeared, leaving his own eyes bland and humble.

She had seen the betrayal in his eyes.

How did he know her?

When had the "my lady" speeches started? Who was he really?

"Later maybe," she nodded. "Thank you for your kindness."

She pulled the stopper from her goatskin, sipping the very-diluted wine that all passengers were issued, and watched him walk away down the deck toward the prow.

They were nearing the coast of Greece; by tomorrow, dawn, they should be in port. She considered.

While the afternoon sun shone she napped among the women who huddled for warmth on the windy deck, nursed their children and gossiped. She kept to the center of this little herd of ewes, and although she was aware of his returning several times, each time she pretended to sleep as long as the others formed a barrier that kept him away.

But with sunset, the women scattered to share food with their men and children. Serith's solicitous fellow traveler came and sat beside her, at a polite distance. "You are the only woman traveling alone on this boat," he said. Once again he held out the dates, which in spite of her hunger she waved away.

"I offer my protection for tonight," he said. "You may need it. It is on the last night that thieves usually make their moves. Even those gamblers on the forward deck will be doing their best to lighten the pockets of all the passengers before we arrive in port."

Serith thanked him warmly for his offer. *So the last night is the night to make victims of other passengers?* She held out her hand for his dates when he offered again, promising to eat them when she could.

She shifted her woven bag to settle it behind her as a pillow against a coil of rope. As she did, she slipped her knife from its ankle sheath into the hand that was least visible to him. Like him, she sat with her goatskin on the deck beside her and drank a little. She had rested well; she wasn't tired.

**

A half-moon rose from the water, lying on its back like a hammock. At an arm's length from her he stirred and sat up, opening his eyes. "I slept!" His surprised eyes slid around the deck between the two of them, searching. "The dates?"

She nodded. "The dates were very tender: what excellent quality you purchased!"

He smiled with satisfaction, unstoppered his goatskin, and drank deeply. The two dates that she had minced fine while he slept and shaken into his wine would be unnoticeable on the way down. The others of the bunch were overboard, feeding the fish perhaps. —If the fish were as stupid as this one, who was just beginning to retch and choke a little on his own poison.

Now she saw the lights of port appear through some mist, far out in the graying darkness. She rose and shouldered her bag to take a morning walk around the deck.

She would be the first one in line at the gangway when they had tied up at the quay at Gythium.

**

The clamor of the market at Gythium was far louder than the

sounds of the boat at sea. Here the shouts of the boat crews putting in at the wharf barked above the buzz of bargaining voices. The clangor of a bell announced a religious procession that wound along the wharf, utterly disregarded by a busker who played an Egyptian flute while his partner sang and writhed sinuously in the path of the priest.

The glare of the sun flashed from sweating bodies of every color, and from bright cloth and shining metal that hung upon hundreds of wooden racks and awnings. The smell of roasting meats and baking grains mingled with the stink of the unwashed and the unloading cargoes of fish and mollusks.

Slipping between the sunlit stalls at the wharfside to the tiers of shaded stalls beyond, she quickly made the trades she needed: trading her cosmetics for food and a long, coarse cotton dress with a pair of sturdy walking sandals. Her Greek seemed to be decent enough that it didn't draw suspicion.

She had donned her new costume, that of an ordinary foot-traveler, between two of the ragged saplings that clumped behind the breadseller's stall, wrapping her gilt sandals in the linen tunic and trousers, stuffing her cloth bag with them all.

To speed her travel away from the port she ate her bread as she walked. Half an hour's progress inland, at a more expensive market, she passed a place where in other times she would have checked into a service room, and as a tired traveler who wished to look well on arrival, she would pay for a massage, bath and makeup, have her hair skillfully braided again, and close the blinds to nap awhile in air that was fragrant with flower oils.

Today, she would not.

**

She strode in the brilliant sun, under blue sky flocked with clouds, toward Corinth. Her companions on the roadway probably knew nothing of the Sensor wars, had never heard of the treacherous Vice

Presidents of Trade, Taxation, Conduct, Disease and the rest who masqueraded as princes of Egypt, or of the Rebellion that sought to retake the fertile Nile valley from them. But here in Greece, at Corinth, she had heard one could find friends of the Rebellion. She had never heard their names from Rakhen, but somehow she would learn them.

Rakhen: the pool of his blood returned to her mind again and the image almost strangled her. She shook away the horror that followed and walked faster. A shadow crossed the roadway, brushed her toes, and flickered across the tops of the small trees beside her. A great raptor, circling far above, hung motionless for a second in the air and then plummeted after its prey.

It was a five-day walk to Corinth, a fig merchant at the northern edge of Gythium had told her. She had bought a little grass basket of his figs and olives, but she couldn't bring herself to buy his dates.

She had not needed his warning about traveling alone. She was already alert for other travelers going the same way who might make safe companions.

**

It had not occurred to her that beauty was a reason for the treatment she received. In the world of her upbringing, all the women near her were beautiful: makeup and the right braiding, the glow of gold at ears and neck were all it took. Even the matrons, swelled like gourds from being mothers of many, were beautiful.

The women she knew were treated like queens by stable-hands, boat-boys and stall merchants. And by maids and makeup women and hair stylists. But the market women were not. The gardeners and farm-women were not.

And now, with her braiding gathered roughly up and tied to hide its disarray, and without baths and oils, without daily makeup and gold or crisp linen to set off her skin, she was not beautiful either.

Like goods at the market, those that were not beautiful must become useful.

"Bring me that pot." The stocky woman called, pointing to the wide-mouthed brown jar beside her. Serith was startled until she saw herself as the woman saw her. Woodenly she stooped and hefted the heavy cooking pot toward the charred rubble of the fire site.

"Now fetch water while I build the fire." The woman's plump forearms held a large two-handled pitcher toward her. There was no cruelty to it; Serith saw it all. She walked to the streamlet nearby — not once but several times — to return with the full pitcher on her shoulder or her head. She poured every drop into the pot. Earning her protection and her place by a fire at night.

Later, the stars were vivid above the hillside where they slept among the hummocks of sweet grass, the woman's family nestled together for warmth: her husband, a daughter with a husband and two children, a cousin and an old uncle. Nearer to the embers of the fire, but sleeping solo, Serith was cold. At the next village she must find a way to get a cloak. She shivered, slept and woke and dreamed fitfully.

Around them were fragrant trees with sharp, needle-like leaves. The fattening moon shone into her eyes now and added another cause for restless sleep.

She sat up. No rest tonight. Carrying pots for cooking tomorrow…Yesterday was humbling, but not something she needed to repeat. Serith rose quietly and retied her braids, shouldered her bag and walked on toward Corinth alone. She would take her chances on the moonlit road.

**

At least she wasn't cold as she walked. In fact, the rising path and the bracing air brought life back into her, a sense of free motion again, and determination. In Corinth she would find a place to bathe and dress, have her hair rebraided, and while she did she would ask clever questions…

Rakhen had been proud of her cleverness. They had been playing a sort of Senet game. The risks were exciting when he was playing too.

Now the westering moonlight was almost directly in front of her as she topped a rise. She stood among the weathered cliffs and piles of rocks under some of those hill trees, breathing the scent of their sharp, needle-like leaves.

A calloused hand gripped her mouth, hard. She felt the point of a knife at her back. "You are in the wrong place," an imperious male voice announced in Greek.

She twisted downward, gasping as her motion dragged his knife through the skin between her shoulder blades, and grasping at her calf for her own weapon. She knew the alternative could be death, or worse.

The hand at her mouth flew downward cleverly to capture one wrist, then the other, and turn her around so any movement hurt.

She inhaled, ready to shriek, but now his knife rested at the front of her throat. "You will be quiet, because it would be very easy for me to just—" he jabbed lightly at her neck with his knuckles, illustrating.

He had dark curls and swarthy skin, a well-made face in spite of his rough voice. He wore the heavy sandals, woven tunic and simple winter trousers that most of the locals wore.

He turned her to face the moonlight, inspecting her and giving his report aloud: "Eqyptian, traveling alone. Quick to go for the knife..." his sandal toed her left calf, raising her dress just enough to expose her expensive blade. "High-born, probably." He considered for a few seconds.

This scum-fed thief was estimating her worth.

He backed her up against a stack of weathered rocks and said, "You are a lady. If you act like one I'll let you go sooner than if you squall like a pig."

She could feel the trickle of blood descending and wetting the back of her dress. Worse than pain was the degradation; her perfectly unblemished skin had just been scarred by his filthy knife. For a second she wanted to die, right now. But she saw where her chances lay and nodded.

He clamped the knife quickly between his front teeth — which forced him to bare them at her like a captive tiger from India — and pulled a cord from his pocket. Her eyes widened. But he wrapped and tied her hands.

"You would tie a lady?" she scoffed. "Then you are no gentleman." Such a taunt would throw some men off-balance, but it brought no success with this one. Still flashing his knife and moonlit teeth at her, he made her sit while he pulled another cord and tied her ankles.

This game that she had entered months ago with Rakhen: it had ceased to be an easy amusement. She could lose, painfully. Why was she still playing?

To find a place of safety, she answered herself. There was no safety for her in Egypt...

Now he sheathed his knife and jabbed hers inside his woven belt. He took up the cloth bag from the ground beside her. She watched furiously as he pulled from it her tunic, making a show of using his fingertips to locate the little lumps in the hem where the coins and gems were sewn in. He pulled out her gilt sandals and raised his eyebrows at her. "No ordinary traveler."

As he turned to her bag again, the rest of her answer fell out of the silence: why was she playing this game? To get beyond intrigues to a life with more skill and beauty, less brute force. But all of that would require freedom.

Why had she not suffered her road-companions long enough to get to Corinth?

When he withdrew her trousers from the bag and reached into one pocket, she remembered — and her heart began to race.

But by the time he had plunged a hand into the second pocket she was ready with a story clever enough to fool an ignorant high-country thief, and an offer of bribe that could free her of him...

He lifted the Sensor, a palm-sized metal square engraved with symbols. Unlit, with its little windows dark.

She raised her chin proudly toward him, smiling with her teeth. "You have never seen one of those, right?" she began. "It's a religious artifact I bought in another country. Holy, but not at all—"

"Clever lie, sister of a crocodile. I *know* what it is." He held the Sensor in one palm as if he were balancing it between the two of them, while he looked for several long seconds into her eyes.

He said, "I think you will find I am a friend to your enterprise. If you will trust me, my fastest horse will take us to Corinth to meet the others."

She stared. The others? This was not the kind of ally she expected. What if he were a liar, planning to sell her and the Sensor to enemies of the Rebellion?

"I will even untie you" — he grinned — "if you can promise not to attack me or my horse on the way."

She saw again where her chances lay. And now, again, she saw a game that could be played. On with it, then.

She smiled again, teeth only. "I promise. And *if you keep your word*, son of a raptor, you'll see me keep my promise."

Escape Route

AT FIRST BEN DIDN'T SLOW HIS STRIDE; his bare feet whispered onward in the silt of the trail and he only squinted ahead to concentrate his vision. Tall eucalyptus trees all around him threw patchy late-afternoon shade on most of this part of the valley, allowing shreds of hot sunlight to lie across the path and the undergrowth. Something about thirty feet away caught the light funny, then: a twisted reflection under a cluster of thick, dusty leaves. Seeing that, he stopped, wary; and the eucalyptus scent that was heavy in the air, now that it was unstirred by his motion, settled into his nostrils and lungs so densely he could taste it.

The sunlight that dappled the ground at his feet also lit a bit of reddish cloth over there in the leaves. Something flashed, like metal or glass. A hiding human? His hand glided down to the knife at his belt and he drew it out. When there was no sound and no motion he squatted low to look, craning his neck to the side.

The heap of red and flashing stuff was small and still. Years since he'd seen a person, and what if this was one that was dead? The hope and the fear together made his heart begin to thud as he circled off the trail and around the heap, watching from every angle.

When he had made a full circle, he hesitated, then kneeled quickly and pushed back the fat leaves, leaning close.

**

The Way In

The cream-colored yurt was lit like a lantern by sunrise. Ben woke from a dream about Dana, who, when he left five years ago on this mission, had been his fiance. He doubted that she was his fiance now, although he could still smell her hair in the dream. Of all the things about her to hold onto, why the smell of her hair?

He had assumed that the mission would last no longer than his two-year National Militia military service requirement, but that seemed to have been his mistake. Also it seemed to have been his mistake that he obeyed the rules and never let anyone, not even Dana, know what he was going to be doing or where he was embarking from.

Around him the octagonal yurt looked bleached and faded by all the light pouring through the walls. It was tidy, just because he liked things that way: a thick foam mattress with white sheets on the rug-layered floor, low white bookshelves full of books, audio and pulp, and music, with a player that would play any of the audio stuff. A white refrigeration unit held some food and water, and there was a pantry with neatly labeled enameled-white steel shelves custom-designed to contain the food they dropped. As if he cared what the labels said. It was all trash.

**

It was hard for him to remember when he became crazy, but after a while he knew he'd done it. Stationed here in this dry, treeless place, with no one he could talk to and nothing living visible to befriend, he had begun to look for ways out. It was a strange notion, to be looking for an escape from a voluntary job, but now he realized that it was what he had been seeking for at least two years.

Despite the food that they air-dropped in, the books for "intellectual stimulation," the music recordings and a remote-controlled glider for amusement, there was no one to talk to and no transportation. And no live electronic connection with the rest of humanity was available: no audio, no visio, no holo, no mike; not even mail or messages of any kind.

When he signed up for this as his required military service, thinking he would avoid participating in the latest jungle war by volunteering for a "study mission to further the reach of space travel," he had not known that he was what was being studied. It wasn't other races, unique species, or off-planet locales; it was him. And apparently the name of the study was "How long can Ben Argin last before he cracks up?"

That had seemed obvious to him after about two years.

**

Electric Fence

He first thought of escaping his voluntary mission duty on the third anniversary of the day he signed up. They had kept him so busy for the first two years that he had no thought but to do the assigned tests and send back the observation reports on time: Weather tests. Wind measurements. Soil tests. How blindly and faithfully he had kept his word, expecting the same in return.

After the first two years were over, and the time had arrived when his mandatory military service would normally end, he spent the next year expecting to be picked up and pulled out any day. —Still delivering his experimental data faithfully, day after day, going the extra mile like a colossal sucker.

After his third mission anniversary, he stopped shaving or cutting his hair. He began exploring further and further from his yurt, seeking signs of civilization. Looking for places to go. What he found: no visible human settlements out there anywhere — what desert was this, anyway? — and instead an electric fence or magnetic barrier of some sort, about a mile outward in every direction from his yurt, that resisted him. It kept him bottled on this desert floor like a bug some kid had left imprisoned in a sandbox beneath a glass jar.

He had tried every day, for two more years, to discover a break in the fence. He had found none. Even the airdrops occurred at random times, often at night, through some kind of temporary hole in the electronics of the glass bug jar that imprisoned him.

**

The Door

Now he exited the "igloo" — his humorous name for this yurt-prison, his home — into the blazing morning sun. He wasn't even able to think things were funny anymore, he noticed dully. His flagpole and the drooping red flag (necessary so the airdrop could find him) wriggled in the heat waves rising from the earth. The summer season had begun, so he could not engage in the pastime of building a fire and cooking his first meal of the day; too hot for that. He just stirred the embers from last night's fire, idly. Instead, he would open assorted unappetizing airdropped containers to feed himself.

But he wasn't hungry, either. Not for that airdrop garbage. He tried to remember the taste of eggs and bacon...He longed to see what he had never once seen here: any living creature at all, even an ant or a lizard. He stared at the wriggling flagpole and went back inside.

He could read now, more of the Complete Works of Dickens. Or play more of the Complete Works of Verdi. Or pack up more of his used books for the robot-controlled airdrop to pick up, along with soiled laundry, at the next drop-off time, whenever that was. He had given up thinking of drop-off time as an event to look forward to. He had given up sending notes To Whom it May Concern in his "Return" bag. They were never answered.

He sat on a pillow seat on the floor and gazed at nothing.

Sometime later he looked down and realized that the pillow beneath him had changed from sand-colored to green. Resting plumply on one of the camel-colored carpets, it was a deep, rich, satisfying green, the color of grass in the shade of a leafy tree.

That was when he found the first door.

**

Passageways

Ben stood stooping under the low yurt ceiling and ate something right out of a container, ignoring the cream-colored dishware stacked neatly in the white cupboard. While he chewed the flavorless stuff, ignoring the parts that got into his beard, he looked with great interest at his emerald-green pillow. Its color was nourishing, and the plumpness of the thing was perfect for a floor-cushion.

He tossed the food container in the refuse bag, didn't bother to Reseal For Sanitation, and sat again on his pillow with a sigh.

He sat a long time looking at the sun-illuminated sides of the yurt that faced him. Gradually his gaze became unfixed from the sides of the yurt and became a look at everything and nothing.

After a long while, he again found that he was gazing at the inside walls of the yurt, but they had changed. They were made of sunlit water now: cool light sea-blue, thin and shimmering as silk stirred by a mild breeze. He looked hastily at the pillow beneath him: it remained deep blue-green, like spring shadows. As if he suspected trickery, he slid his eyes to the yurt walls again. To surprise them in the act of betrayal. But they were still there: walls like water formed of silk.

He rose and touched one wall, enjoying the feel of it, then went outside to the sanitary location among some rocks, a little distance from the yurt, to relieve himself. The waning sun made small rocks and hillocks throw long shadows across the stark sand. There was no breeze, but the sand radiated heat. As he returned to his yurt the outside walls were sunbleached white, as always.

As if nothing had changed.

Sudden anxiety clutched at him. He hastened to unfasten the yurt door, to look inside — and sighed a little with relief to see that the inside of his prison still looked like infinite ocean. Entering, he shut the door behind him carefully and locked it.

After he ate he read a while, with the dimming water that surrounded him now trembling in twilight balanced on the edge of darkness.

When it grew dark he slept. He dreamed that he had a pet lizard.

**

He woke as dawn broke above the waters of his tent-walls.

Terror broke over him with it.

An oblong shadow grew across the roof of his yurt, flapping like a flag. He smelled a cindery odor. Was it an animal smell?

He stared as more shadows massed and fluttered, altering the light that lit this lantern-like place all around him. Had he left something too near the embers of his last fire? Was this flapping from the wings of gigantic birds? How could such creatures have come through the invisible barrier out there?

He was sure he heard panting and heavily inhalations. Taking in his scent. The smell became nauseating.

He had no protection except a desert knife, probably rusty, in one of the tidy white cabinets. The catch on the yurt door was still locked but it wouldn't hold back anything serious.

The desire to live, even when life was miserable, was unrelenting. In fright and confusion he looked at the water-silk wall at the opposite side of the yurt.

It seemed to him, for no clear reason, that it was his only way out.

With numbed slowness that he tried to spur into speed, he opened a cupboard and quietly stuffed two containers of food in a day-pack. Along with a white cotton shirt and desert pants. And a belt, also for no clear reason. And an old hardbound copy of Oliver Twist.

The flapping things outside growled and hissed hungrily now.

He opened a cupboard door: no knife. He tried another: no. Two more he pulled softly, panting shallowly, openmouthed as if being quiet would keep him hidden.

There: the knife. He grasped the handle tightly, with relief, pulled it from the leather case and slashed downward through the sea view at the back of the yurt, between the food shelves and the refrigerator. He twisted his body through the slit.

One bare foot, and then the second, sank into cool sand at the edge of shimmering, silken water.

Palms leaned over the beach, left and right of him, making pools of shade. Thick beach grasses stirred in a moist breeze. A bird — or something living — called from above.

He looked behind hastily: the yurt was gone. The snarling creatures were gone.

The trees and grasses that had replaced the yurt shifted rhythmically with the wind, and a lizard ran carelessly past his feet. A creature. Live like him.

Dull with astonishment, still holding the knife, he waded into the cool water up to his waist and stood a long time. Minnows clumped and fled, swarmed and dashed around his ankles, like migrating blackbirds in spring skies somewhere, sometime long ago. Although the water was salty, he drank some from a cupped hand. It tasted good.

After a while he realized: he had found a passageway.

**

The beach curved back away from the water on both sides. A piece of survival lore came to him: he pulled free a thick armful of vine that extended from the shadows out onto the beach, and neatly wrapped the nearest beachside tree-trunk with it, round and round and then tied, to mark the place. In case it was just a little island — so he would know when he had walked completely around it and returned to the same stretch of beach.

He set off to his right, clockwise, counting his paces like a kid playing Robinson Crusoe until he lost interest in that. To his delight, a bright green parrot-like bird flashed above him, squawking a raucous greeting. His eyes followed it raptly.

Deeper in the thickets of trees that edged the sand, more birds began to call and chirp now, filling the quiet. As he plodded along, the beach lizards scuttled up and down the trunks of the nearest palm trees. He heard some insects swarming. The noise and motion were irresistible. Maybe they were even dangerous, but his senses fed on them.

The sun was high when he reached a shallow stream that cut across the beach, flowing into the sea; after he drank he changed his plan and turned inward, walking along it. Where there were streams there might be people.

He was almost frightened at the thought.

**

Discovery

A long day's walk had brought him from the wet air and close vegetation of the beach to this sandy valley where there was no longer any ocean in view. He had eaten one of his containers of food after walking a long while uphill. He had drunk from the stream to wash away the taste of the meal.

Now here he was kneeling, holding his breath, among the trees where the afternoon shadows were long. Something red lay in the shadows in front of him, under some large-leafed low plants.

The eucalyptus scent was heavy and cloying as he held apart the leafy stems and let his eyes adjust.

Wonder opened his eyes and mouth: it was a child under the leaves, all dusky skin and long-lashed eyes, curled on its side — wearing only a long earth-red tunic, a pounded-metal amulet that flashed at its neck, and a small smile. When he touched, the woolly head was warm and sweaty. The child stirred a little in its sleep and the sweet, unfamiliar smell of another human was so startling to Ben that tears stung his sunburned face.

**

In a rush he began to remember things: where he had come from. What he had done. Dana's eyes.

In a few minutes he rose and looked around in the dusk for other humans to whom the little kid might belong. Parents. A tribe or school or something.

The sun had set; twilight might be deep here under the trees. Were there animals that might hurt the kid?

He heard voices, faintly, cheering and shouting some distance away. He left his pack to mark this place and walked toward the sound — which grew louder as he neared it — passing dimming trees along the twilit sandy trail. He could eat the last of the disgusting yurt-food in his pack and sleep somewhere around here tonight, but first he should find the kid's people...

The people were nearer now, maybe cheering at a game or celebration. His heart pounded with excitement. More people, after so long.

He felt suddenly shy. What if there was danger?

But the draw was strong. They would need to know about the little kid. He walked on.

Ahead he saw a door, oddly placed near the trail ahead, among the trees. He couldn't make out the building, but as he neared it the door was clearly open, with light pouring through.

He stepped into the light.

Inside a large room, people rose and stood facing him. Tiers of people at computer monitors, in office clothes. They began to yell and clap in the glaring light of holocams. It smelled like ozone here. Ben blinked and squinted at them all.

Someone stepped forward wearing a military uniform decked with medals. Ben pawed at his scruffy beard, glanced down at his bare feet and pajama-like desert clothes.

The man reached to shake his hand; it confused Ben for a moment before he recalled the gesture. "Congratulations, Mr. Argin, on successful completion of the experiment. First ever."

Ben stared at him. Completion? In memory he saw Dana's face just before he turned away from her to board, how many years ago?

A dark-haired guy with a noteboard arrived, running, and pulled up alongside the officer: "We had begun to think the maze was too difficult, Ben. Mr. Argin. If you don't mind I'd like to interview you right away, while memory is fresh."

The eager eyes looked him up and down wonderingly. Ben gazed back at the neat hair and clean-shaven face.

"The little kid back there—" Ben pointed. His voice was scratchy from disuse.

"—Yes, but what I mean," the eager face explained, switching on the mike clipped to the noteboard and swiping to reset the screen, "is that we'd like to hear about how you found the doors."

One Basket

PALE ORANGE SUNSET ALREADY, and Llania was clearly far from the city. But she didn't know exactly where she was or what the dangers of nightfall could be. She blew out an exasperated breath: Useless space-kite! A lonely wind fluted over the Greccan landscape; she sat on her heels, here at the top of the rise, and looked out across the unbroken hills and valleys of naked sand.

The air, which she had faithfully tested for safety before depressurizing and exiting her little rented craft, felt thin as it filled her lungs; it smelled of heated lime and silica. The waning heat of the day radiated from the grainy sand through the soles of her sandals, making her sweat inside her heavy homespun desert robe and the face-protecting pesht.

Not a lot of time before nightfall. With her eyes still searching the landscape, she shifted impatiently and let her feet slide downhill from beneath her so she sat on the crest of the dune. She lowered the pesht and opened the robe for coolness, so the dry breeze could pull moisture from her.

No one in sight for miles. She might as well enjoy the air on her skin while she could; the knee-high woven sandals, short pantaloons and belted tunic of Zoana, her home, were not acceptable here, she had been told. She would have to keep them covered in the city.

As soon as she landed she had checked her vials, like a hen inspecting its nest: not one was broken in the crazy landing, and the colors were all still good. She sighed now with held-in relief.

The flimsy craft had spun when she hit the lower layers of atmosphere, as if an invisible wind was making whorls out of the air. She was no shabby pilot but it took all she knew to get it out of the blackened spiral that was driving it off course and drilling it down toward the earth. She did it, though, and now she smiled, remembering how she'd touched ground just in time to sled down that enormous dune into the deep bowl back there and slide to a stop halfway up the other side.

She stood. The solitude was suddenly oppressive, just as it was at home when she poled a boat through the marshes, watching the starlight stir in the surface of the water. Her people were quiet and solitary by nature, fluid and soft-tempered like the marshes and grasses. Never ill themselves, always nourishing others. And so complete they never needed anything; no wonder the traders never tried to sell them much.

She wasn't sure why she didn't feel complete herself, but she didn't.

All she had was a three-day Greccan trader's pass to sell her little vials in the market at Athos. After days of solitude that was supposed to contain contamination on the *Hillenken*, she had been delighted to get off the trading ship and ready to plunge into another crowded marketplace full of new faces.

But now that she had missed landing at the city, she would have to re-navigate there quickly, if she expected to earn enough from this market even to pay the vehicle rent. Let alone make some of the cash she wanted — to buy a caravan for a little traveling clinic on Brinh, the sickliest planet in the system. Where she would always be busy, never lonely...

She turned to look behind her and made another irritated noise, this one directed at the metallic glint on the slope below. Flimsy cheap kite. The nav panel wasn't too complicated on this model, designed for short-term rentals like hers — and for renters who were far stupider than she was. She was tired from battling the winds. But would she be safe resting here for the night before she took bearings and set a new course?

Probably not.

She stepped off the crest of the dune into midair, her dark curls and the robe flying around her, letting gravity draw her downhill in long sliding leaps to rejoin her kite.

**

The lightweight tekryl craft had passenger doors on each side, and behind the seats a small cabin where one could sleep and eat, and where personal items could be stowed. She climbed up and inside. It still smelled of some kind of cleaning fluid and a hint of disgusting perfume from some prior renter.

Shedding her cloak in the cabin, she was mesmerized again by her treasures; she lifted a few of her vials with long fingers, lovingly, from the woven circular carrier she had set on the table. Each one turned the overhead light into a beam of color that fell onto the floor.

The vials themselves were clear molded silica, no longer than her thumb, and because their manufacture was too rare and precious on Zoana, she had traded for them. That had been the beginning of her trading, actually: her first trip off the planet into the big noisy marketplaces of the solar system. And on that trip she had found the only places where she didn't feel alone.

She raised another vial to the light of one rearward window. It was deep blue-green, and perfectly clear. The liquid inside the vials, in colors that ranged from amber to emerald to rusty plum, was sealed in with resin, bound tightly with grass fibers. She replaced the ones she had checked among the dozens of others that were arranged in circles in the woven-grass carrier basket, made so each circle surrounded the last; there was a taut woven handle, attached in four places, to lift with.

She had made the basket herself, as any child could on her grassy planet. And she had filled each bottle and plugged and wound it herself. Her remedies, harvested from the marshes and beaches of her home (still called "The Planet of Healing" in this part of the galaxy) and mixed and distilled as her family had always done, were eagerly sought in other places to ease the usual injuries and indiscretions of life. To relieve many unusual ones, besides. In each new place she went, she found that the inhabitants had somehow found ways to be ill or to abuse themselves.

But she was letting her mind idle. She should hurry. Dark was falling. She slid into the pilot's seat and pulled navigation maps from a compartment, powering up the kite's nav screen.

When Locational Positioning on the computer gave her the coordinates, her map told her that she had spun out of the sky onto a giant desert, but in a location only an hour's flight from the city. Her heart beat faster in anticipation. Time to get this thing to take off again. Time for market!

She had just run her eyes over a map notation that described the desert as uninhabited, when the passenger-side door clicked open and a small person entered, followed by a file of similar people, all carrying wicked-looking sawlike spears and all robed in colors that looked like sand. Their eyes were the colors of lizard eyes, pale green. They arrayed themselves before her in a crowded semicircle. Sitting frozen, at eye-level with them, she berated herself for dawdling and lack of vigilance. She'd left the doors unlocked, on top of everything else?

Her only weapon, the laser-gun that still made her wince when she pulled the trigger, was somewhere in the back with her clothing.

She stood, on an impulse to make her long limbs seem more formidable. The small people raised their weapons instantly, eyes and weapons all pointing upward at her face.

She saw all the possibilities of this, pouring as quickly as a tide-rush through her mind. It could get bad. She was no fighter, with or without a weapon. What could she do?

The usual, she guessed.

"Can I help you with something?" she said in Universal Language, signing with her open hands as fluidly as she did when she displayed her remedies — to ease the ragged spirits of those who came to her in the markets for help, to let them know she would do them no harm.

In the silence, she felt her solitude again. As if no one was here, whether friend or foe; just no one. In the markets full of strangers, each one who came for some help broke the solitude. Their faces, when her remedies worked, eased her sense of loneliness for days, sometimes.

This was no market, though.

The leader of these people gestured, without taking his eyes from her, to the others, sending them into the small cabin behind her. Probably to search. They must be robbers.

Her vials! She had seen what happened when destructiveness was stirred in people, and their gentleness overcome by aggression. She had seen the child and the monster in all kinds of people.

"Please don't let them hurt my vials." It came out in her native language. Then, without thinking, she said in Universal Language, with signs, "Shall I show my vials to you all?" The child in everyone was curious, she thought hopefully.

Only a bodyguard remained with her and the leader. The leader said something curt, in an unfamiliar language, toward the ones in the cabin. Two arrived with the basket of little bottles, another one hastily trying to re-pack a stopper into an amber-colored vial as he followed behind them. She saw how the skin on his hands was leathery-looking, scaly and a little like the skin on a tortoise's neck. So were all their hands, and their faces.

The leader held out his fingers for the partly-opened bottle, held it up to the light, and raised it to his lips to taste.

"No!" Unthinking, she reached to stop him. A blade lashed out like the tongue of a snake and sliced into her forward hand. She clutched it, stared at the oozing blood, felt numbly in her tunic-pocket for a cloth. The spear-tips pushed closer to her but they withdrew when she pulled out the cloth instead of a weapon.

Lonely had been replaced by hostile and painful. Things could get worse. She bound the hand by wrapping it with the bit of work-rag, tucking in the ends; taking this moment, while their attention was fixed only on her blood, to consider what to do.

She sat slowly, to face them at eye-level again. Then, to the leader she said, with the gentle gestures reserved for the very ill, "That bottle. It will not be good for you." She pantomimed weakness or illness. Raising her forefinger in the universal sign for waiting or thought, she pointed at another of the vials, and then to the leader, and pantomimed strength. This deep blue-green liquid came from roots known to feed male energy and balance. The other, a stringent cure for a woman, was likely to bring weakness or pain to most men.

Soberly, he instructed the lackey who had opened the first bottle to unseal the blue-green one. And drink some of it. His face and gesture clearly said, "Let's see what it does to *you*."

The lackey looked trapped, but he opened boldly and sniffed. He seemed drawn magnetically to the stuff. He should be! It had taken months to make, from the finest poruan roots. Then he restrained himself and took a delicate sip.

That would be plenty for most people. She told the leader, in her most soothing way, that it might take a while to work. While they waited, would he like her to tell about some of the other vials?

He quizzed his crew, who had all returned now from searching through her things. She guessed they were reporting on the inventory in the cabin, and their gestures said there wasn't much. He shrugged at her and held his palm outward toward the grass basket; it meant "Go ahead." She was their only entertainment right now, and entertainment seemed to be her only value to them.

It was so in many of the marketplaces: she was interesting to watch for a while. As in the markets, for the first time she now looked at this small fierce man not as a threat but as someone who might want healing. His eyes seemed ill: too much white showing. Also, two of his followers had bad teeth and malnourished-looking skin. Using her marketplace gestures, she lifted out a vial and explained its virtues to them all. Then another, then another, in Universal Language with graceful hand-signs.

There seemed to be no women present but she explained that if children were not coming, here was one vial that often helped the woman, and another that could help the man. They grunted and nudged each other at that information.

There were a lot of bottles, and a long night ahead. She longed for sleep and some part of her neck ached from the landing. But this was better than being prodded with spears.

**

Halfway through the basket of vials, they moved rearward into the little cabin so the visitors could sit on the bare floor in a circle around Llania, with the leader in the chair at the table. She opened the kite's food storage cupboard and brought out all the food she had carried from the trading ship, spreading it on the table as any host would: some fruit and nuts, cheese and some of the little bitter berries that Greccans were known to prize as stimulants. It was good that they had their own skins of water, because she had little.

In moving around she realized that she wasn't wearing the robe, but when she snatched it and the pesht to put them on the leader waved them away, gesturing to say that he liked what she wore. So she used the robe to make a place on the floor for her ongoing demonstration.

When at last she had finished their tour of the vials, she asked if one of them would like help with something; but the leader held up his hand to stop her. He surprised her by saying clearly in Universal Language that he was going to arm-wrestle his lackey — the one who drank from the blue vial. All the men grunted and laughed: a good joke, a good test. Llania's part of the entertainment was over now.

Leader and lackey pushed up the sleeves of their robes. She saw some of the joke: The leader had strong-looking arms, with lots of muscle and thickness. The younger man was skinny and sinewy. Llania watched, as they stood on either side of the table and positioned themselves.

It wasn't the first test of her wares that she'd seen, but she was still relieved when the younger one took down his leader's arm in one smooth motion. And when that caused an uproar, he did it again. And from a different angle: he did it again.

She sat smiling through the noise and joking that followed, watching them all with the kind of impartial fondness she felt for each person whose sickness she could fix. This, now, was a whole group of them. She breathed the thin air deeply. It was very satisfying.

So much had the present scene changed for her that when the hands started grabbing for her vials, she stilled them all by ordering them to stop, saying in Universal, "Each bottle costs one Universal Ounce. Please pass the proper coin to me, tell me what you want and I'll give it to you."

By sunrise, her guests had joined together and bought the whole basketful for a bag of ounce-pieces, on the condition that they could send for more of their group to come and learn the proper use of the vials.

These did seem to be career bandits, so she decided wryly that she had better engage the child in all of them pretty fast. She explained to their leader that to teach their people she would require tents to shelter them all from the heat of the day, and water and food for everyone present, and protection while everyone rested, including his men. "For best results," she explained.

This project engaged them, without a doubt; and full of eager plans to win wagers by out-wrestling or out-fighting their unsuspecting fellow tribesmen, they began to plan and squabble happily.

She ushered them out through the two kite doors, locked the doors behind them, put the bag of ounce-pieces in her pantaloons, and slept.

**

When she woke, much later, the kite was hot from the day's sun. She was thirsty. She stared out the side windows of the rear cabin at the long shadows and the waning light, and knew she was dreaming.

It looked like a fair out there: dozens of dun-colored tents surrounding her silly craft, running down into the deep bowl between the dunes to a much larger tent that occupied the center of the bowl. There were pennants and skins hanging on the sides of that tent — camouflaged decorations, maybe —-and smoke rose from some fires on the rising slope of the opposite dune, on either side of the long skid-mark she had made in landing. On one side of the giant bowl she also saw, unmistakably, twenty or more traders' tents, displaying wares on their sides. Hundreds more of the small dun-robed people swarmed about carrying food and water. Even from here in the kite, she smelled food cooking.

She smiled. She shrugged on her own robe and the pesht, quickly hid the bag of ounces in the one compartment in the cabin with a lock, and locked herself out of the kite. Her gun was missing from the clothing compartment, she noticed; she would have to get it back from her hosts. She loped downhill, letting her robe fly out from her in the wind.

She was now missing the Athos market. But another market had just traveled to her. She thought it was too bad that she had no more vials to sell at this market; but then, she had never before sold a whole basket of them in three days, let alone one day.

A robed figure intercepted her and spoke with gestures that meant an appeal for help. Probably a woman, who seemed in need of the gray-green vial, the parmi fruit. Llania was led downhill toward a waiting cluster of others, where, the woman gestured, she would show her who was sick, who wanted to learn.

Smaller versions of these desert people — who must be children — seeped out of tents and joined Llania, pooled curiously at her ankles and clung to her robe as she made her way down the sliding sand. A very little one reached chubby arms upward to be carried.

With or without her gun she knew she was safe enough here. When she stopped a moment to boost the tiny warm bundle into her arms, she saw some early stars breaking through up there in the dusk and froze to look at them, as if they would tell her where she was now.

At home on Zoana right now, where her people loved her but would never need her, the lonely stars hung above the marshes.

Right now, the rest of her stock of vials waited for her in a cooler far above on the *Hillenken*, ready for the next market stop and the next.

It was quite clear by now that she would never get to this year's Athos market, even if it was only an hour away.

And actually, she didn't even know how to start a kite uphill on a dune.

Right now she didn't care. What mattered was that she wasn't alone.

175

The Knife-Thrower's Assistant

JOEL SET THE PAINTBRUSH DOWN CAREFULLY so as not to drop or muddy the thick dot of crimson at the tip. He was ready to put on the stroke that would light her lips; but he would not risk doing that while something was tugging at his attention.

It was a knocking at the door. Here on the fourth floor his visitors usually arrived winded from the stairs and just said his name through the door.

He wiped his palms on his paint-stained jeans and buttoned the flannel work shirt to cover his undershirt, stepped barefoot off the heavy dropcloth that lay on the floor beneath his easel, crossed the scarred floorboards, and turned the doorknob.

She walked in.

"Rina." He announced, largely to himself. Like one naming a hurricane or identifying the suspect in a whodunnit.

His sister was a twisted little cinder of a person, although she looked attractive to the naked eye, standing there in a tasteful peach-colored skirt and sweater, little tasteful shoes. He had not seen her in six months.

These six months had been, it suddenly seemed to him, the most creative and profitable months of his life so far.

"Are you still painting?" she asked, without a preamble, as a person would ask, "are you still smoking?" or "do you still gamble?"

"Apparently so." He gazed at her, half-smiling, mostly out of bafflement that some trick of the universe had brought her here, as if she were drawn by a sixth sense, just when he was standing on a pinnacle of triumph: completing the best painting of his short artistic career.

"What brings you to this part of town?" It was his way of saying: You have no reason that I know of to be here. So how is it possible that you have appeared at this time?

She walked past him and looked his nearly-finished canvas over. She turned away and looked around at the clutter in his studio apartment: the undone dishes in the sink, the unmade bed, as if the painting and the clutter were all one to her.

If she had informed him that she was coming, he might have tidied up…

"Still don't make beds, do you?" she gave him a cockeyed, knowing smile. In the smile he saw how inadequate he still was. He was still someone who couldn't even make a bed. The triumphant portrait over there lighting up the room — that was negligible. He lived in squalor and clearly couldn't rise out of that.

She strolled to the window and looked out.

He breathed deeply, as quietly as he could. So as not to disturb the knife-thrower.

Joel was the guy strapped to a wooden disk at an old-time circus like the ones in the movies, with his limbs spraddled so they could be outlined by the knife-thrower's blades. The razor-sharp knives that had been thrown, to stick viciously into the meat of the wood at his waist, beside his neck and knees, at his groin — had come close enough to draw a little of his blood here and there, but none were deadly. Yet.

Now, the knife-thrower's assistant thought passionately, I'm finished with this. I need to get unstrapped, collect my pay, and quit the circus.

He repeated: "What brings you to this part of town?"

She sniffed, a single-syllable laugh, and turned toward him. "You, of course."

He gazed at her, waiting for the real answer.

"You haven't visited *me*, Joel. I thought maybe you didn't have the… means to." Another blade whispered through the air and bit deep into wood. It delicately nicked the tender skin below his left armpit. The greatest sin: having no money. "So I'm visiting *you*," she concluded.

"Well thank you." He stood looking at her face, still waiting for the real answer. He thought of his paint, the perfectly mixed color on the tip of the brush, also waiting.

"Would you like something to drink?" he was finally forced by custom to say.

"Thought you'd never ask," she said, and another lopsided smile said: You have forgotten your upbringing and such lapses mark you as a failure. Another knife whispered and thunked into wood, drawing blood at his right calf.

"May I sit down?" she added, her sarcasm delicate and very civilized-sounding. The sofa was covered with books and magazines, so she was indicating one of two chairs at the small kitchen table.

"Of course."

He began to make tea: filled the kettle, turned on the gas, found some tea bags, let her choose. He refrained from saying much, to encourage her to get on with whatever it was that she wanted. She didn't.

When the tea was ready he sat with her and waited for her to wave her teabag delicately through the mug of hot water a few more times, then press the water out of it carefully with her spoon, then look around for a saucer to put them both on, sigh, and put the spoon onto the tabletop with the teabag and the string wound around the bowl and neck of the spoon like sea-garbage strangling a gull.

He sipped when she did, thinking again of his brush with the drop of perfect paint on it. Waiting.

"How is Arthur?" he asked finally.

"Arthur? Oh, you know. Same as always."

Poor Arthur.

They sipped in silence again for a while.

The wait and the dismal anticipation of what she might have in mind were beginning to get to him, when she said:

"And you? Any girlfriends?" She looked away delicately at the end of her question, as if she knew the answer would not be admirable.

"Dozens," he answered carelessly. He had kept her out of this part of his life successfully for years — ever since they were adolescents.

She looked at him for a moment, letting him see her assume things. "Any paintings sold?" Again she looked away at the end of her question, again with that delicacy: she wouldn't pry for the world, she had no desire to see his dirty laundry or his failures...

"Yes," he said. "About...sixteen since I saw you last."

She smiled knowingly again, knowing that he was not telling the truth.

Although it was the truth.

Now he would either have to urge the truth on her and prove it to her — or let her go on with her certainty that no one would buy something he had created. She had him off-balance. Thunk, a knife bit the wood too near his ankle, and it vibrated there, stinging.

"Is there something that's on your mind?" He pushed back at her quietly. "You must have something that you came to talk about."

"Oh, this and that," she said. "Nothing in particular." She smiled innocently. He saw the cinder inside her twist, black and red, coruscating in the dark, eating itself.

He breathed shallowly. The wish to fight with her outright had always brought him trouble. Still, right now his desire to push her off a fire escape was vivid and huge.

It was just as huge as this feeling that she had him pinned here, strapped to the wooden wheel, waiting for the next knife.

He rose. He walked to his easel, feeling his heart swell as he saw his painting there. Still lighting up the room. Still full of all the joy he had painted into it. But with horror, when he looked at the mouth of the woman in the composition, he realized he could no longer see exactly what to do to finish it. He had descended from the heights. His mastery of the painting was gone.

Rather than let Rina rise and follow him here to the easel — where she might spoil things further — he was forced to return to the table.

But he sat facing her again with a new certainty: that it was time to be rid of her. Permanently.

"Would you like more hot water?" he asked. Breathing.

He could slap her. Satisfying, but useless.

He could kill her. Both would just infect him with her poison.

He could tell her to stay away. But she would make up ruses like this one — to come around anyway so she could draw more blood.

"No thanks," she said, sipping again innocently, looking at each feature of his kitchen with individual scorn.

He had no idea what to do. Fed by tributary years of the same stuff from her, a tide of desperation rose in him. But afloat on the tide he found a temporary remedy:

"I haven't eaten today and I have an evening out," he announced. "Would you like to join me at the local greasy spoon now for an early supper, before I take off for the night? I'll buy."

He rose, cleared his cup and spoon from the table, and stood waiting for hers. She looked surprised but she was compelled by custom to take her final sip and hand it over.

It was either join him for his greasy-spoon supper or part company downstairs at the street entrance, and she agreed to join him. With satisfaction he locked his apartment door as they left. Locking her out.

**

An easy block away, the café windows steamed and the place smelled of burgers and bacon, mac and cheese. He insisted that Rina would love the liver and onions, and ordered that for both of them. In fact, he himself loved it and ate heartily while she picked at hers.

And then, he abruptly pulled out his phone, poked at it a couple of times, and said, "The time was changed. I'm late! Must go, excuse me."

She caught up to him at the entrance where he was paying the cashier. She said, "I'm so sorry you have to rush. I was hoping we'd have time to *discuss the inheritance.*"

There it was, what she came for. As the oldest, she must recently have been named the executor of their parents' estate. She dangled this power now like that tempting little light a deep-sea fish holds out in front of its slashing knife-studded jaws.

He didn't take the bait. "Sorry, have to rush. Give me a call if you need me to sign papers."

He hastily caught a cab, ordered a ride through the park to give her time to go away, and returned home by a roundabout way, panting and sweating behind the cabby now that the danger was mostly over. Thinking.

Inheritance. She could be counted upon to use that to wrap him like a bug in spidery, sticky thread. Keep him dependent on her somehow. Then slash at him casually now and then with a spider's knife-like fangs. How could he paint with that going on?

Well, there were lawyers and accountants, and one of them could be his agent, right? He could have a new, undisclosed address with a post office box for legal papers.

Or just move to a new address and skip the rest.

To her, he could be politely, permanently, utterly unreachable. He sighed with huge relief just imagining it.

When he looked, her car was no longer visible anywhere.

He entered his building cautiously, locked his apartment door, watched a funny movie to empty his mind of her, and in a gush of renewed confidence he stood and finished the painting.

When it was done he stood back, in love with the portrait and the paint and the paint-stained hands with which he had created one from the other.

**

The moon was full and high. A nightingale sang in the shadows among the trees. As if he had just wakened, the knife-thrower's assistant noticed that the strap was undone at one wrist. He pulled his arm free and unfastened the other straps, stepping down the two steps from the wooden wheel onto the creaking wood of the knife-thrower's stage.

The lights of the circus were out; the performers slept in their tents. It was silent all around him except for the sounds of crickets, the wind in the trees...

With the air of a magician, he swept his pack from beneath the stage and checked to see that paints and brushes and rolls of canvas were inside.

Leaving his pay uncollected, he made a humorous bow and announced politely to the locked door that said Circus Office: "I hereby retire as the knife-thrower's assistant."

He walked across the dung-scented circus grounds, past the cages of dozing elephants, the pacing fanged tigers and cheetahs, past the prison-like bars of the circus railroad cars.

As his strides lengthened, moonlight washed the blood from his wounds; they were small, after all.

And he set off down the grassy path between the railroad tracks toward some other town.

Red Planet Blues

S MILE, KARIN." The women stood in the noonday light of Mars, suited against the deadly cold and cargoed with tools. First step: the mandatory photos in front of their landed vessel, for the press at home. Sol raised the special media-direct camera that was corded to her suit at the hip. Karin turned the visor, a twin of her own, to face Sol and grimaced hugely. With luck, the no-glare helmet window would show some of her kidlike face, light hair and white teeth. The headlines would say, "First Humans on Mars" and "All-Female Expedition Lands."

Karin turned away immediately to gaze out across the surface of Mars, her helmet reflecting the ruddy vista. It was stunning to be there at last, a long-awaited moment for both of them.

And Sol could tell that something was bothering her. Not that that was unusual.

She sighed a little and turned her head to scan around her, savoring this moment of triumph. She heard her breathing and Karin's, disliking the tiresome air supply and wishing she could try the real Mars air out there. The plain on which they stood stretched far on one side, to her left, broken only by the raised lip of a crater far away; but in the three other compass directions it was encircled by rising cliffs carved by unfamiliar light. She would look at the maps later to see how tall the cliffs were, but her eyes found it hard to tell; with so little atmosphere softening them, the cliffs probably looked nearer and smaller than they were.

Sol was commander of this expedition, "a born leader," the recommendation said. And no follower. And not much of a teammate either, she knew. She had already given Karin sufficient reason to dislike her, on the flight here, by being brusque and demanding.

This long, close-quarters partnership with another astronaut was a tough go. Partnerships were not her specialty. But if she wanted another such command, or a bigger one, she'd better succeed at this one.

"Now shoot one of me, and we can check this task off," she said. She gave Karin a toothy, wideyed grimace, as they had been trained, so that in the publicity photo her teeth and the light parts of her eyes might accent her cinnamon-tinted skin and closely braided dark hair.

Their prediction said that the peculiar Martian windstorms, recorded as regular occurrences on the last ten years of Mars meteorology reports, were not going to blow today, so they had scheduled an ambitious number of testing steps from their long program.

**

When they were almost done with today's list, they walked in tandem, gathering final samples for some on-site tests, with the direct channel open between them. Karin said, dourly, "Are you singing to me?"

Sol realized that she was. Her voice had just ceased; she heard her husky contralto replay in memory. What had got into her? "It's odd," she murmured. "Being here makes me want to sing."

"Not me," Karin said. "Makes me a little homesick, actually."

Well, you're tied to a suburban house and hubbie, Sol thought smugly. Not me. Born in Egypt, raised in Buenos Ares, and a citizen of the United States — really a citizen of the world. My home is wherever I am.

Without noticing, she began to sing again, then heard and stopped herself. Embarrassing.

**

Sol woke in her sleep cocoon, wet with sweat. Even her braids were soaked.

Across from her Karin was thrashing and groaning in her sleep. "Karin, you sick?"

Karin raised her head and groaned again. "What's going on? I keep having crazy dreams and I can't sleep for more than five minutes at a time."

Winds were buffeting their land lab. Although it was anchored tightly to the surface, it shuddered and moaned as the massive moving air shoved it hard on one side and then the other.

Sol unbelted and eased out of her berth, used handholds to move across the rocking cabin floor to the monitor panel. The instrument displays came on at her touch: wind-speed graph wildly erratic, electromagnetics hitting the ceiling of a chart "designed to show the full spectrum of conceivable electromagnetism on Mars." The winds had been predicted; they were ready for those. But the magnetic field—

"Why didn't this stuff show up on pilot instruments?" she muttered. "Karin, we have heavy magnetic force."

"Yow." Karin groaned again and shook her head to clear it, without succeeding. "I feel like my head is being crushed."

"You're the shielding expert; work on these shields, will you? See if we can protect ourselves better while I get some analysis going on this 'weather' we're having."

**

By the time dawn arrived the winds had dropped and so had the bars on the electromagnetics display. And by the time full sun hit the side of the lab, the turbulence of the night before was as gone as a bad dream. "Maybe a freak storm," Sol said, entering the statistics in the ship's log. They looked at each other.

"It's going to be a long day on so little sleep," Karin said. There were a lot more tests to do, and every day of the next fifty-six was scheduled full. Fifty-six — or now it was fifty-five — till takeoff for Earth again.

**

Sol woke tangled among her thermal covers, sweating. Karin was sitting up with her head in her hands. She groaned. The land lab shuddered and moaned as if it might break apart from stress. Sol leaped out of her berth, but even before she touched the displays, she knew what the graphs would look like.

They had plodded through yesterday's tests. If this means another night like last night, Sol thought, we'll have to worry about our ability to work without sleep. —Hell, another like last night and this lab may be splinters.

She sat at the displays, running through them again for correlations. Karin threw up twice into an elimination bag and then sat at her monitor, bringing up the shield data, moaning under her breath.

Sol's head hurt, and she was struggling to think.

"Lullabye?" Karin grimaced at her.

Sol realized she was singing again. She stopped, struggled to think, and heard her own voice start up automatically — a sort of tuneless tune, like humming while you cook. She stopped again, and tried hard to think but not sing. She couldn't think. She sang deliberately, then, a few random notes, found that the pain in her head lessened. Stopped singing, the pain returned. "Wait a minute..." she said to herself and Karin — as if Karin was actually paying attention.

She started singing deliberately, and feeling the pain diminish again, sang more: some wordless blues melody, and she rocked forward and back to the rhythm to ease her body a little.

She could think. The headache was dissolving. Beside her Karin sat silently monitoring and fiddling with the useless shields, no longer moaning or fidgeting. What about this singing thing?

She wasn't going to stop, though. It felt so good to sing. Odd, she thought. Like water when you're thirsty or a massage when you need one. It was that kind of feeling, deep in your bones and muscles. As she continued to do correlation testing, she sang the song over and over till she noticed she was sick of it, thought of another that didn't have too many high notes and started that one. An hour passed without a sound except the wind and her own crooning voice.

"This is amazing," she said to Karin. Silence. She turned to Karin and found she had dozed off in front of her monitor, chin in her hands, eyes shut.

"Lullabye, huh?" she muttered, and shrugged. One of us had better be able to think straight when dawn comes. Looks like you're it. She began a new song.

Her voice was getting husky, and she was still struggling with correlations, when the wind began to die away. Sol had a lot of reserve strength but the lack of sleep was making this harder. She was on the edge of finding something out when Karin abruptly woke, struggled up out of her seat and went aft to relieve herself.

Sol ignored Karin, she was concentrating so hard — until Karin's return trip from the lav when she stopped by the one small window. "What?" Karen said in a quarrelsome voice. "It's snowing?"

Both crowded the window like kids, then, forgetful of the separation of rank. Some kind of crystals, ones that looked like sparsely falling snowflakes, were descending in the glow of the outside lights, hitting the window, whirling off as winds took them. In the pre-dawn gray, not much else could be seen.

Nothing in their briefings had included this sort of phenomenon, either.

But their job was to observe and report. And survive it. Sol had forgotten to sing for five minutes, without a new onslaught of pain or witlessness, so she decided that the nightmare phenomena were over again — for now. She saved her calculations, gave Karin the tasks of sending a full report homeward to the space station and monitoring the "snow" for a few hours. Then she slept.

**

By sunrise, Karin later told her, the snow was nowhere to be seen. Not a hallucination though; both had seen it. Karin had gotten some shots of it, too, using the exterior cameras. Not great shots, maybe, but no hallucination.

There was a big stir back home about this. Why had no previous instruments picked up snow? The research lab was examining the shots, asking for samples, would get back to them soon with a collection protocol to follow in case it happened again.

Now it was full noon, and they were eating. They would be off to a late start on their list of tasks. But Karin announced, "I spent the morning doing inside research tasks that were scheduled for a couple of future days. The net of that being that so far we are not falling behind."

Sol nodded approval. "Smart move," she said, a little grudgingly. "Thanks."

Karin nodded back.

**

There were gusty winds today, intermittent. The two anchored themselves to the lab using the long cables that were designed for research in such weather. With their channel open so they could talk, they did air sampling, further soil samples, and their own wind measurements to correlate with the lab's automatic recordings of wind velocity and direction.

The work was fascinating. They were trained to work in tandem, like two circus acrobats who could do their synchronized moves rotely, dispassionately, even half-asleep. Neither thought of eating, but when their reminder signals went off they broke for squeezepak glop, something called "quiche," and then continued.

After hours had passed, and their sample containers were nearly full, Sol stopped to turn 360 degrees, feeling the gravelly surface under her shoes, looking at the dry crags nearby. Shadows were long; the distant sun was nearing the mountaintops. They were both fatigued after two bad nights. It was time to think of the next plan.

Sudden small gusts blew around them; they leaned into them to stay on their feet. Reddish dust and grit sprayed them.

"You're singing," Karin reported. Sol hadn't noticed.

"Weird," Sol mused. "My head doesn't hurt, I can think OK, but I still feel like I need to sing." She thought, It's like humming to keep noise from bothering you when you're trying to concentrate. "It seems to help me relax and withstand the disturbance."

"What disturbance?"

"Good question. Don't know what it is. Whatever kept us up at night is here in the day too, if you ask me."

"Maybe it's like belly-dancing," Karin said. Sol wondered what that was all about, but Karin didn't leave her guessing. "When I was pregnant it felt so good to belly-dance. I can't even remember why."

**

Sol predicted that more of whatever-it-was would happen again tonight. She asked Karin to stay awake and make "weather observations" of the violent Martian surface for another few hours. Sol would nap after the evening meal and then stand watch through the night researching while Karin got her first full night's sleep in two days. Karin raised her eyebrows at this breach of normal scheduling, but she didn't refuse the offer.

**

Sol woke when she heard Karin's moan. She struggled up out of dreams as deep and thick as quicksand, slick with sweat, and sat up in time to see Karin throw up into the bag. Her own head was pounding. The wind sucked and roared outside. "Hey! I told you to wake me!"

Karin pressed her hands to her temples. "I got absorbed. Sorry. It's only midnight, you didn't sleep much longer... That thing is happening again." She grimaced.

Sol's feet landed on the floor, hard. She dug her nails into her palms, struggling to keep an upwelling of boiling anger in check. In disobeying orders Karin probably thought she was being motherly and helping out. Sol gritted, "Give me your report."

She listened to the shielding figures, nodded.

"Now, sleep!" she ordered, pointing.

She slid into the seat at the monitors and began to sing, furiously.

The angry blues lasted for an hour before the song shifted to a soothing one, but that didn't seem to matter to Karin, who fell asleep quickly. Once it had dissipated, Sol was amazed at the intensity of the anger. *I've never been a goody-goody, but jeez. That was a real urge to kill, totally out of line. Scary.*

She entered Karin's shield adjustments, did some more calculations, and finally, two hours after Mars midnight, she stopped work abruptly, listening. A weird melody came to her, so intensely that she could almost hear each separate note: it was a bluesy sound with ululating parts something like the traditional music she remembered from Egypt. She realized the winds had stopped.

Sol followed the melody, crooning it. Then turned to look at Karin, out cold over there. A few hours ago she had wanted to roast that idiot. Now Karin's freckled kid-face, slack with sleep, made Sol want to tuck her in and whisper goodnight.

She didn't, of course.

Instead, she tucked herself in and crooned herself to sleep.

**

She woke before Karin, refreshed.

While she rolled in the sarcophagus-like shower chamber, letting its rubbery tentacles flush and suction her skin clean, her early-morning dream came back to her, startling her.

It was so vivid in recall, more vivid than the events of yesterday. In it a woman in a long dress or tunic, wearing a queenly headdress of some sort, sang. She had exotic features, oddly formed. Someone appeared at times beside her, singing with her, dressed in a kilt or half-tunic, wearing strange headgear of his own. Their harmony seemed perfect.

During the dream, her mind had been riveted on the song, which was mesmerizing, and one other thing: the changing scenery around the singers. The scene faded from a view that was verdant, with desert-like greenery and irrigation ditches like those near her home in Egypt, to the sere and dusty landscape outside their craft, and back to the green of tiered gardens and splashing waterfalls, over and over.

In the green views there were sounds of humming and creaking that might be insects, whispers of opening and closing plants and the rustling of dry palm-like trees; and when darkness fell in the dream, there was a startling sparkle of lighted and phosphorescent creatures flying and scurrying everywhere.

Each time that the scene changed back to the dust of real Mars, dry and barren dirt-sample Mars, Sol felt a pitiful loss. In the dream she was hungry for more of the green landscape and the song. She didn't want it to end.

But it did, she guessed. She was awake, wasn't she? Funny what your mind dreamed up to explain what was going on around you.

She climbed out of the shower tank and wiped herself down, watching the shower close and seal to sterilize itself. As she mopped off the last moisture she found that she was crooning the song.

She stopped, realizing that Karin's shield adjustments from the night before must have been what finally shut out the turbulent wind and electronics.

—Exposing what was left, this melody that was "playing" in the air somehow?

Out of nowhere, something strange struck her: right now she just plain loved being herself, for the first time in who-knows-how-long.

Also weird: she couldn't wait for her partner, kid-faced Karin, to wake up so they could plan their day together.

Martian Crepes

THERE WAS NO WAY TO EXPLAIN IT TO SURI. Jaarin couldn't imagine explaining.

"These crepes are phenomenal," she said. "You sure there are no other ingredients?"

Jaarin shrugged to hide a twinge of guilt and pointed at the recipe sheet sitting on the metal prep table in front of her. His shrug said, What else would be in them?

For him the dimly-lit hotel kitchen, in Hotel Mars Freeport Fantastique, was composed of only two categories of things at this hour: one was spotlessly clean vertical and horizontal metal, porcelain and tekryl surfaces, gleaming softly, and the other was the extraordinary fragrance of his crepes.

Well, make that three: there was Suri — the intent, goodhearted look on her face. Did he owe it to her to tell her everything? Suri sat on a stool, her elbows leaning on some of the polished steel, and closed her green-gray eyes, breathing it in. She delicately sliced another wedge from the crepe with a knife and folded it into her mouth with her fork, in the old traditional way, breathing some more as she chewed dreamily.

Her long light hair, straight as fine wires and tied up tightly in a knot, was the same color as his. Like him, she had come to Freeport from Finland on Earth to apprentice here; maybe to find a better life than disease-ravaged Northern Europe could offer. They had met on the transport to Mars, recruits of a cattle call from a job placement agency; she had befriended him because she was the only one on board who spoke Finnish and his English and Spanish were so poor. He was a student of classical art, and they both knew how little of *that* was likely to be happening on Mars right now. She had talked him into pursuing this career with her. For now, anyway. After all, they both needed to eat.

Sous-sous-sous-chefs: that's what they were, slaving by day in the kitchens to help the real chefs feed tourists and diplomats in the only high-class hotel on the planet. He was getting used to life on what used to be Mars Colony One, now ascended in status to Freeport, in the new nation of Knath_Biorin, Mars. The cold here didn't bother him, but the thin, half-rehabilitated air cover, the thin and struggling plant life, and the ubiquitous darting lizards made him long for home sometimes.

He washed up his kitchen tools while she ate. Suri had gone to cooking school in Finland, which until today hadn't seemed to matter to anyone at this hotel; she just slaved along with the rest of them.

"I know crepes enough to know these are perfect," she murmured in Finnish. "You've been practicing these nights, Jaarin! You should be careful — but you did a good job. Also there's something different about these. Better. What?"

She would not believe it if he told. Besides, his secret was one of the few things he had. He clung to it like a poor child with a single toy.

Several months ago, a new Spanish arrival, one of his 11 roommates in the hotel apprentice dormitory room for men, had offered him a small book on the history of Mars. Carlo was at least 40, a professor at University of Madrid who had lost his position. He was strongly built despite the white hair at his temples, with warm, sad eyes.

"You were a student, right? You might like this."

"Mars has a history?" Jaarin stared at the thin volume, intrigued. He borrowed a dictionary from one of Suri's roommates and struggled through the English, forcing himself to learn the language as he went. The book sounded like legend, dreamy stuff: violent wars, and some kind of leader, a goddess of freedom... But then, didn't most history emerge from legend, passed from one voice and memory to another? And finally it was put into writing by someone?

Doubting that any part of this history could be verified, he found, by asking around the hotel, that some of the place-names in the book actually had known locations: a cliffside with a drop of thousands of feet, and a mountainside with some ancient cliff-dwellings where bones had been found...chills crept up his arms to hear about them, and he was filled with the wish to go see these places.

Asking questions always seemed to be good luck for him: after more asking around, he found that the cliff dwellings could be visited with a local guide and transportation. He had saved his small pay for months until he could go.

Suri was still looking at him. A good friend, but he couldn't bring himself to tell her.

"Thank you for testing them. Hey, maybe I have a talent for good crepes," he grinned at her. "Since I'm so good, promote me if you have the power! But eat up, so I can clean the last dishes and you can sleep."

**

The basement dormitory room was cold and absolutely dark, but the bunks were locatable by soft breathing and snores. As he slid into his own bed, a quiet voice prodded, "So, you have a secret girlfriend!"

He chuckled back at the voice in locker-room fashion, then feigned immediate sleep.

His girlfriend: he had not seen her but he had heard her, up there at the cliffside, on the way to the cliff dwellings. High up the mountainside, so high they needed to use the breather tubes that were seldom necessary in Freeport. The guide had offered to play the music into his helmet sound system: a decades-old recording made by some visitors to Mars, of a singing legendary "ghost."

It had to be a woman's voice; it carried the presence of a woman. It nearly knocked the legs from beneath him. The song was impossibly beautiful: eerie, vibrating throughout his body like the wildness of body love raised to a higher pitch so it put fever into your mind and wringed waves of emotion from you. He felt the fever just now, hearing the song again in memory.

The words were not understandable — some other language. But it had affected him so much that day that even now he couldn't remember his return to Freeport at the end of that afternoon, or taking leave of the guide.

For days after that excursion he longed to hear the music again but couldn't remember any of it. A week or two later, though, bits of it began to come back to him, floating to the surface of his mind. As he hauled steel mixing bowls and crates of vegetables he softly sang each part that reappeared in his memory until he had learned all the words and music without understanding, like the verses of a childhood song.

"When did you learn to sing?" one of the kitchen-slaves had taunted.

"But didn't you know, Arlin? I'm a Finnish opera star," he grinned. "And you're a billionaire, aren't you?"

Today's notice on the display had made him want to show Suri the crepes. Today, the kitchen slaves had been informed that due to "hotel budget reductions," their pay would cease until further notice. No pay! They would be fed and housed and trained without cost to them, the notice said: "a tremendous value." As trained kitchen professionals they would one day have "limitless job opportunities on Mars and the Moon." Those who did not wish to continue under these terms were free to leave, with proper notice. And as soon as they had other lodgings, because Freeport vagrancy laws were strict. They could even return to Earth if they chose. At their own expense of course.

Today also, Suri had been promoted to the next rung up: given a tiny wage to work longer hours, managing all the supply orders and running all the lower help. She commiserated when he showed her the notice he and the others had received. He congratulated her on her promotion, but his teeth were on edge when he said, "Who can save for a ticket back to Earth, with no pay? I am truly a slave now."

**

"Why is your knife never dull? I've been to the sharpening tools twice this week, and you never seem to go there!" Arlin's tangled beard and hollowed eyes appeared at his side again.

Why *is* this knife so sharp? Jaarin considered the question as he chopped Martian greenhouse cabbage, pale green and fragrant, at what he hoped was professional speed. He sang softly to himself. To keep himself from the fury that slavery lit in his heart and lungs, his eyes were fixed on the gleaming edge of the knife, and the joy of cutting, the thin edge of steel in motion like the slice and scratch of a drawing pen making thin edges of ink.

Later Suri, mistress of the low-tier kitchen slaves, stopped as she walked by to watch him whip some eggs with cream by hand. The help was her request, although the task was thought to be above his skill level. The froth rose in creamy, cloudlike heaps as he sang quietly. "It's a blur! So quickly you mix them!" She grinned at his smile and his snort of derision — the shared moment of home-country humor. He saw the respect in her bafflement, though, as he handed her an enormous finished bowlful.

When she and the shining bowl had disappeared down the aisle between rows of worktables, he saw in memory the beginning of his wonderful crepes, the night when he had slid into the silent kitchen to make some food for himself. It was forbidden, but that night he had a tormenting hunger and the song of the voice on the cliffside, the woman he had never seen, seemed to ring in his ears. It had him in a fever of longing that would not let him sleep.

He sang her song as he mixed a batch of crepes in near-darkness, softly singing her music back to her like a love song, making the recipe exactly to the letter, folding in egg-whites and butter the size of his thumb. Singing delicious love to her, wherever she was, while he poured and turned thin skins of crepe on the hot griddle.

Was he delirious? He cut into a small folded stack of them, too hungry to let them cool any further, and filled his mouth.

They were good.

But to his wonder, they were more than that. These tasted like no crepes any of the chefs made here. He knew because he and Suri often pilfered and smuggled leftovers to sample. His crepes had flavors he never had tasted, on Earth or on Mars...

Now Arlin sidled up to Jaarin as he pulled forward a crate of lettuce to prepare. "I know you come down here to cook in the nighttime," he muttered in French-accented English. He dumped a gleaming bowl of onions onto the shining steel worktable next to Jaarin and slid a cutting sheet onto the surface before him, swiping an armload of onions onto his sheet.

"You think you know that, huh?" Jaarin said without looking at him.

"Yes, and I have told Suri. But it seems she protects you from punishment." Arlin grappled a dozen onions forward with thick fingers and hacked at them, taking off the ends.

Jaarin continued the appearance of nonchalance. But a doomed thought came to him: now that withholding their pay could not be used by the hotel to enforce behavior, what punishments might be leveraged against the unpaid? Against slaves?

He began to sing softly, to block Arlin out.

His fingers flew, releasing the lettuce from its central stem and breaking the leaves into pretty bite-size segments: one huge steel bowlful, retrieved by a runner and taken to the salad chefs. Then another and another: faster, faster.

It was against rules to move from one's work station. But sometimes you had to. To help the sweating runner and have a rest from this standing position, he took the last bowl himself to the salad table. On the way back to his station he accepted the thanks of the runner, Zund, who took his kindness as an opening to blurt desperately, "Don't know what to do, my friend. My family in Austria: I came so I could send them money. Now, no money, my father is sick…"

Jaarin nodded soberly. "Later. We can talk," he said.

He returned to his worktable, to the shock of Arlin's blood puddled on the slicing sheet around his onions. He had just cut himself badly. He clasped one hand with a red rag.

"Suri! Get her here, pass the word!" Jaarin urged the tomato-chopping Pakistani on his left, Alf. He used his own rag to tie the wound up tighter.

Suri arrived with a medic in a dingy jacket. To them Arlin confided that Jaarin's distracting behavior had caused him to slip. Jaarin shook his head, a flat denial sent back into her questioning eyes, as Suri took Arlin away.

Someone's idea of justice was to decree that Jaarin should complete both his work and Arlin's by the end of the day.

His teeth went on edge again. But he sang in defiance.

He completed the work by suppertime. He was in love, he decided. Maybe that made him invincible. At least it made slavery bearable.

**

"I have a plan," he told Suri two weeks later. The dark sky was dusted thickly with stars and the air was thin and cold. Although they both packed breather tubes on their backs, you rarely needed them in this valley, around Freeport, where the reviving atmosphere had recovered most because of returning plant life. They stood on the arched bridge over a flat-bottomed canal threaded with skeins of trickling, star-speckled water that someone told him was being bled from underground ice deposits. It flowed toward the greenhouse district — a beginning of good water for Mars, better than the manufactured stuff.

Here on the bridge he always seemed to hear the voice if he listened. Now it sang softly, thoughtfully. "Do you hear music?" he asked. Suri shook her head. It must be singing in his memory, then. But it seemed so real.

In violation of their hotel contracts — Jaarin had kept his stored safely in a secret place, so he knew what it said — the restaurant manager now permitted them only two evenings off a week. Most of the kitchen slaves slept off their exhaustion on those nights. Even Suri looked tired tonight. But she was waiting. "Yes?"

He told her quietly in Finnish, watching her eyes widen. "I have spent many evenings, and all of some nights, walking around the city," he said. "I talk to many people. My English is getting good. Plenty of people walking, but not much food."

"No wonder you have shadows below your eyes. Did you hear about the strike at the clothing factory? Most workers were returned to work — and punished."

"They had nowhere to go, so they were at the mercy of the factory. They were owned by their 'free' food and lodging."

"And you are not?"

"I will not be. We can all do this."

She sighed and shook her head, baffled. "If you leave, more work will fall on everyone else… What do you want from me?"

"If no one takes a chance we all will be slaves till we drop dead. I want nothing but your hope for me. And that you'll help when the time comes."

"Help what?"

"When it comes." He shrugged. He wasn't even sure what it was that he meant.

He walked her to the rear dormitory entrance, keeping them in the shadows and, because he had learned how, out of the scope of the security cams. She looked even wearier now than before. "Go in and rest. All will be well." On impulse, he cupped her face in his hands and kissed her forehead, then grinned at her surprise. "Go to bed, lazybones." He turned and left the dark side of the street by an alleyway.

**

The small cart was sturdy, made of tekryl. The wheels were new. He had traded for it, accumulating cash and goods the long way to exchange: two dozen bloody unopened onions recovered from Arlin's disaster, scrubbed clean, peeled and sold; a silver ring that he had found on the street; a Spanish-to-English translation service by Carlo that he brokered; and one long night's labor on a road crew, substituting for a man who wanted to go woo a woman somewhere.

His help had made a friend of the wooing man, who gave permission to store his cart temporarily in a fenced City of Freeport road-equipment yard, in the weeds and dust among the other machinery. With a sign that warned, "Public Roads employees: DANGER, KEEP OFF."

Now he took a deep breath and pushed his cart out the unlocked gate and by a winding route to a street corner near the spaceport downtown. He set up quickly. The Martian air, thickening month by month, seemed to pulse with some kind of energy, like music. Breathing deep drafts of it, he began to sing as he worked.

Twelve days ago he had splurged to try the menu of a small restaurant near the spaceport — operated by Kreenids, offering their native foods that were famed for roots and spices — and he had loved the stuff so much that he offered them his first business deal. When he cooked them a sample crepe in their own kitchen, they weren't stupid; they accepted. Loan of a battery-powered griddle, an apron and utensils, and a supply of ingredients, in exchange for 50% cut of the profits? He was as happy as they were.

Jaarin's cart was surrounded now with the beckoning aroma of the first little pile of crepes, loaded onto a disposable plate. A man drawing two large hovercases behind him jerked to a stop and took the plate, pouring the required coins into Jaarin's hand without even bargaining.

While Jaarin began the next set of crepes two more people formed a line. No one bargained; everyone bought. By midnight the line stretched for a block.

He cooked all night, like someone drunk and dancing merrily without any care about the next day.

**

"You have no right to lock me up!" he spat at them, struggling furiously. Behind them, Suri's eyes were horrified, and then her eyes were blocked from view by the blankness of the closing door. It was a storage room, glaringly lit, in a basement level below the kitchens. A lock turned, and he and the empty room were alone.

Someone must have reported him missing. Arlin maybe, the twisted freak.

Despite his fury, after the long night of mixing and pouring the silence of this room soon threw him heavily into sleep. In his slumber he dreamed of crepes and song and the heavy, coin-stuffed pockets of his apron as they had been at the moment when dawn broke over Freeport.

But when he woke at a noise, found himself propped limply in a corner like a seated rag doll, and looked down at his smeared apron, the pockets were empty.

He remembered: his cart had been called stolen goods, and taken from him. They must have called the money — his money — "stolen" too. The borrowed cooking utensils and the remaining eggs and butter of his business partners were now indeed stolen goods — stolen from him, with the cart. And with no 50% profit received by them, his friends the Kreenid restaurant owners would think he had run off and betrayed them.

He heard the voice now, singing as he remembered it, on the cliffside. That song.

The song that had somehow deluded him into believing that he was free to do what he wanted. Bitterness choked him. He passed out again.

He opened his eyes again to the glaring overhead light, hours or days later. Inside his head the song, which had lulled him to sleep and waked him again, was now loud and angry. He began to sing with it, as an enraged drunkard sings: every word and note a blow against something.

He rose and pounded on the door while he bellowed. The sound vibrated back to him as if the Martian earth were echoing. The doorframe vibrated. He pounded harder, singing violent anger and destruction. Singing furious revenge.

He realized his jailers were probably sleeping far above in their soft hotel beds. Only the dormitories and the kitchen storage were at this chill, windowless depth. No one would be listening. But he pounded for hours, it seemed, and his anger was tireless.

There was noise in the hallway, shushing him.

He paused to listen: Suri's voice. The door opened.

There were Suri, Zund, Alf, and three others. Their eyes were tired from overwork and little rest. "Ssshh, come," she said, turning to lead the way. She would help him escape!

But the others who were with her would make escape harder—

At her signal he shut his mouth and followed: up a metal staircase they went silently, two floors to a loading area with a people-door next to the large bay door that admitted vehicles. And out into an alleyway. "What is this?" he hissed. She quieted him and beckoned, and led them all in hasty silence through a labyrinth of alleyways and delivery-drives a kilometer or two deeper into the center of the city.

They stopped in a very narrow alley, with trash receptacles along the clifflike walls. Far above, stars showed in a half-lit sky, dawn or twilight, one or the other. She said, "This is the back of your friends' restaurant. I inquired last night till I found them — told them."

At his relieved sigh, she knocked on the rear door. "Your cart, Jaarin: we couldn't find it in the hotel anywhere, but until you get another the owners will loan a table for cooking out on the street."

"How can I thank you all?" He was astounded.

A light came on, attached to the concrete wall above the door.

"Do you hear singing?" Suri asked the others, turning her head to catch the sound better.

Two of the others nodded. Jaarin stared. The voice sang in the clear gray twilight, full of passion and longing. But now it wasn't singing only in his ears.

"Why are you all here?" he demanded.

A latch clicked inside. Suri turned to look at him, her mild green eyes no longer mild — lit with something he had never seen in them.

She said: "You're right, Jaarin: better danger than slavery." She gestured to include the others. "At the hotel we all have left our notice, and yours. We are joining your enterprise. The sun is setting, and night will come soon. So: show us how to make these Martian crepes."

The Trade

WE PLEDGE OUR LOYALTY to the sovereign nation of Knath Biorin, and to its Sacred Decree of Freedoms; one nation, under the gods of all creation unique, with liberty and justice for all.

This was the group induction ceremony for new citizens. They stood around Kit in the crowded Immigration Office public room, proudly wearing the banners of their countries of origin, hopefully holding the small Knath Biorin flags they had been issued for the ceremony, reciting the pledge paragraph from their tablets. They smelled of the familiar spicy chowder of Io, the intense garlic and algae paste that fed the workers on the asteroid greenhouses, and the complicated root-and-herb cookery of some of the newer Martian colonies.

Welcome to Knath Biorin, once Mars Colony One, thirty years ago launched as an independent nation. This was the place where Kit had been born, they told her. Not everyone who arrived was slated for citizenship, but she had been advised to take it, since her birth here made it hers for free.

Just returned to Mars by one-way charity transport from Io, Kitren Reed was 16: too old to be called an orphan, although her parents were probably dead, light-years away; too young to have anyone respect her wish to stay on Io; too alone to have any resources; too surrounded by people and noise right now to think.

And too bitter to pledge anything to anyone. No one noticed that she didn't.

Kit lifted her head from her arms and stuffed some thick copper-colored curls back into her silken headscarf. The scarf was her mother's, bought long ago in a marketplace in Egypt on Earth. Where her mother met her father, they had told her. Bedtime stories that seemed like long ago already.

A little knot of females her age were already shouldering their way out of the room, headed for the door. They signalled each other with their eyes as they went. Girl-gang. Kit was used to avoiding these types, especially on Io.

On Io she had more friends. There she could have gotten help, maybe to find out something about what her parents were trying to do. She sighed. Here, the few friends she had could be found — eventually. And she had some research she had done in transit from Io...

She rose to leave, and ran her fingers over the bulge in the small side pocket on her pack.

When they told her she had to come "home" to Mars to live she had fought it hard. Stodgy Io law said that if you were under 18 you couldn't live alone. Her travelling parents, on the rare occasions when they didn't take her with them, had left her with an Io boarding school that was full of kids like her — traders' kids. But the school stopped at sixteen, and by sixteen she was done with the school too.

Her parents never treated her like she didn't know anything. Her education had been the whole galaxy, and all the accessible trading ports in it, and her studies had been the words and books of centuries — so a dozen months of pour-and-stir knowledge from that boarding school were about all she could take. She had been packing up at the school, eager to rejoin her parents — to go learn from them and their friends again — when their trading ship had ceased to respond to Perimeter Guard tracking signals.

Her insides cramped hard now, as if she'd eaten something bad, when really her stomach was empty. She felt empty everywhere.

A large man brushed carelessly past her. She reached and felt for the little lump in her pack again.

On launch day for their flight her parents had left her with a tracker, one of the latest; the kind that permitted you to put a coded beam on a person or vessel and hold onto it without fail, showing its traveling image on the maps of your choice, orbit or system or galaxy. It would project on a wall or send to a tablet.

It was set to track their ship. So she could follow their course while they were away this time, they said.

She had pulled it out hastily when she heard the news. Her device must be slicker than the Perimeter Guard's because it showed their ship — but far away, out near Vega, moving outward fast. The next day, they were past Vega, going twice as fast. She signaled at them each time she checked, disbelieving. And again she signaled after the next tracking, when she saw their trading ship heading right into a wormhole or something. Then she had stopped looking.

The tracker had to be valuable. She could sell it if she needed to.

The little crowd was dispersing, carrying children and flags. They all seemed to have someone to meet, somewhere to go.

She was hungry. She had somewhere to go, but that might take a while. And no one to meet. All the dozens of times her father's trading ship had put into port here at Freeport, the capital city, they had landed at the trading docks, a few miles away, humbler and friendlier than this place. She might find an old friend or two there.

She had to get there first.

And very first: get out of here. Standing here alone she would be noticed as a homeless person and might be ordered around some more. Might be chased or tricked. She boosted one strap of the heavy pack onto her left shoulder, stuffed her flag into it, and followed the last of them out, trying to look as if she knew what she was doing. Trying not to look alone.

She pushed out the doorway, close behind the trailing family, and into a marketplace corridor filled with intense food smells, jewelry and clothing vendors, sellers of travel necessities, and noisy voices in many languages. The corridor was chilly. As always, they said, Mars was cold right now. It was still regaining its atmosphere. You had to watch where you were and use breathers in some places. She remembered, now, to reach up and loosen the breather tubes from the zipped pouch up above her right shoulder, so they would be handy.

Signs pointed the way to public transport, latrines, newsfeed screens...

Protected by the swirling crowd, she stopped to check her phone, standing by the one window in the corridor that framed a view of the surface of Mars. She slipped the holosheet from the slot behind the phone screen and slapped it onto the left side of the window, sheltering it with her body to avoid notice. In flat-screen mode she checked directions on the phone and read again the information:

Mars Search Services. Interplanetary Missing Persons. We find anyone, no matter how impossible. Followed by a number, an address. She sent the directions to a map on the holosheet because she liked maps. Her father's voice came back to her:

Use maps. They orient you. Find people who know. There's always someone who can help.

Well, maybe.

She peeled the holosheet from the window, folded and slid it into the slot, and stowed it in a cargo pocket, looking out through the glass. Outside the window even the multi-story buildings of Freeport couldn't hide the famous Martian rose-tinted soil. It seemed to call out for her attention everywhere. It was visible between buildings and among the sparse vegetation that struggled to reclaim Mars, 50 years after colonization: the small imported palmettos and native vining plants, not quite covering any part of the soil, but eagerly consuming minerals from it.

And native plants bursting with ferociously beautiful blossoms like these trap-flowers, in red and violent orange. Their thorny vines curled around this window, as if seeking to enter. Her mother had shown her pictures of them when she was little, promising that she could touch them someday. You had to be fast to touch them safely.

This thick window itself must be a souvenir from earlier days when the planetary atmosphere had to be held away, and atmosphere artificially created indoors, everywhere on Mars.

Besides English, Kit didn't recognize any of the other languages that she heard around her here. From reading books she knew Icelandic poetry and the words of Shakespeare, in the languages gifted to her by her parents. And she knew bits of the languages spoken in many of the ports. But of the popular Martian immigrant tongues she knew little Sereid, no Kreenid, and only a little Spanish.

Nonsensically, she followed someone speaking English out through a broad doorway into cold, vibrant sunlight. She stopped to pull off her pack and pull on her long-sleeved travelling cloak, hungrily feeling the comforting soft scratch of the Icelandic wool, looking around her and breathing deep the thin metallic air as she closed and re-shouldered her pack.

Before her, a long paved main street extended to the right and left, crowded with pedestrians and hovercars, lined with young trees trailing long finger-like leaves that were pale gray-green. In one of them nearby a shimmering flying thing, opalescent, lizard-like, and large as the ferrets on Io, boomed and hummed from a branch.

Across the thoroughfare was a dinner for travelers in need, spread on temporary tables by some religious organization. Kit felt the coins in her pocket that had to last.

**

They let her serve herself from the bowls and platters of spicy grains, meats and tubers, adding to that some crumbly slabs of sweet breadlike stuff, with fresh peas and lettuces (which were impossibly expensive on Io).

Words poured at her ear as she gazed around in a daylight sunnier than Io's — even now, at sunset. Fascinated in spite of herself, she listened to the babble around her.

When Kit came back out of the trance-like joy of relieving her hunger she saw that most of the guests had already finished. Many had gone. The rest were rising and leaving around her, without word or ceremony.

Well, she was not so badly raised that she didn't know how to thank her hosts. But when she looked for one to talk to, they were all engaged in clearing the tables and putting the leftovers neatly into containers. They moved quickly and no one seemed to notice her waiting there.

Eyeing the dark settling around her, she sighed, moved her pack to the door of the food tent where she could watch it, and began to help, imitating the nearest host. She would try to pay for her supper by cleaning up. Then she'd ask where to spend the night. These people would know.

**

Kit woke to the sound of explosions. She leaped from her saggy bed and ran, ducking low, to the clay wall of the room she shared with "three other young females," courtesy of the free-dinner people. Her hand on the rough frame of the window, she raised her head and peered outside to see the air lit with fireworks. Not that she was an expert, and Io never had them because of the composition of the air, but she had seen holovids of them going off on Earth. Home of fireworks, Earth.

"Why fireworks here? In the middle of the night?" she muttered.

"Change of government in Knath Biorin," a voice said in careful English. Kit's roommates were beside her now, too, peering out at the stuttering, blooming and fading lights. The voice chattered quickly to a third in an unfamiliar language. "If you go, better go soon," she added to Kit.

They had been asleep when she entered the dark room. Now she saw the light on their faces and recognized them: the girl gang from the port. Not going to be her choice of travelling companions.

Kit left the window to them and slipped out of the room unnoticed while they argued.

The city had many shadows. She traveled from one to the next. In a small parklike place, near a bridge, she saw that the water was sparse: thin braided streamlets reflected starlight in skeins that draped across sandy soil. She slid down the embankment and ducked under the bridge, feeling absently for the familiar lump of the tracker in her pack side-pocket. She squatted, looked around at the boulders and detritus in the darkness there, and satisfied, she pulled out her holophone and opened it up to see if it still had charge.

She hadn't shown her phone to her roommates because it signaled "rich Earth-person" to people who were just running around loose in places like this. Letting it show was stupid, like wearing diamonds in public when you are no-way rich. Now she "checked politics," as her father had always taught her, on the Martian worldweb. Should have checked on the incoming shuttle yesterday, before arrival, she knew. Mistake.

Mars Political bloomed on the screen: a midnight parliamentary vote had brought in the predicted new regime for Knath Biorin, a win of the Earth-Alliance Party. Which had sounded good to some people, but Earth was still a dragging anchor when it came to free trade and free exploration…News an hour ago: they were shutting the borders of Knath B. to incoming and outgoing traffic "to protect our citizens against insurgents."

It was all she needed to know. If they were restricting travel it was time to go.

"But I can't go!" she muttered. She had things to do here.

"Who *are* you?" The voice next to her made whirl toward it, dragging her pack behind her.

The voice was young, American-sounding. The dimmed light from her phone showed crudely chopped dark hair and wide dark eyes. Whoever-it-was wore some kind of tunic and cargoes like Kit's, only very ragged ones, and an equally ragged backpack.

"Who asked you to creep up on me?" Kit spat.

"On *you*? You sat down next to me!"

In the darkness Kit felt her face go hot. Great safety check she had done!

In the silence that followed, Kit remembered her mother saying: companions are valuable; they help each other. How likely that this ragged one was a decent companion? "You asked who I am. I'll tell you if you tell first."

"Why should I?"

"*Possibly* we could help each other."

"Who needs help?"

"So you live under bridges like a troll just because it's fun?"

Silence.

She had been schooled in courtesy and politic behavior by her trader parents. The rougher the situation, the more courtesy was required. She could do better than this. So she opened again with an admission:

"Stupid of me not to check better to see if this bridge was occupied."

"Yes. Stupid. I could have killed or robbed you."

"Thank you — for not killing or robbing me."

The dark-haired person sniffed disdainfully.

"Do you want me to leave?"

"Yes."

She shouldered one strap of her pack and prepared to rise. Even among beggars or castaways, she knew, there were rights. She was encroaching.

"...But not yet. Maybe I can help you get somewhere."

Her relief was huge.

**

Cary walked beside her in the morning sunshine now, down a dusty Freeport alleyway far from the spaceport where she had landed. Here it smelled of garbage and sunbaked walls. The walls were a funny kind of brick, probably made from Mars dirt, because who would want to pay for imported bricks? The air was warmer so Kit had taken off her cloak and strapped it to her pack again.

In the night's exchange of data she had learned: Cary came to Freeport from Earth as a tourist, a student on holiday, with a free-gift pass his parents had received and passed to him. Robbed and beaten a month ago, his phone and enoculars stolen, he spent a month without funds hiding and recovering, eating from discarded food-bags behind the restaurants, then working small jobs to earn food that wasn't scavenged... his adventures had been many. More like struggles — but he told them with relish. He didn't seem to have minded them much.

Last night when the telling of stories became wearying, they had both wrapped themselves in their cloaks and slept, with their backs to each other for defense and their weapons out, till dawn.

Now they walked on companionably, almost like friends. He breathed easily because he was accustomed to the air. She was still adapting so she puffed and gasped a little. Cary had small precise freckles sprinkled across the golden skin of his nose and his hair was glossy despite the ragged cut. His shoulders weren't very broad but they looked like they were going to be.

"Almost there," he said. He had agreed to take her to the trading port by a route that would not expose them to Freeport authorities. In return she had agreed to buy him some kind of breakfast there at the port. It was a trade.

"We both have to leave Freeport soon or be forced to stay in Bnath Biorin. What are you going to do?" she asked. Cary shrugged. He pointed: there was the wharf, visible ahead now at the end of their alleyway. She felt her pack pocket, as usual, for the tracker. She longed to check it again. Soon enough she could.

Something heavy landed on her pack from above. She whirled and pulled her knife out, in time to see a cat streak away down the alleyway after a rat. Cary turned a lopsided grin at her fright.

He looked up, down, all around and said, "the real danger is ahead."

She didn't think so. She might know some wharf people.

**

They sat on a pair of tool lockers next to gigantic coils of braided steel cable. Around them, for hundreds of yards, small craft occupied horizontal berths or stood balanced on their tails, and beyond there were enormous berths filled by vast freighters and tankers. Between the two kinds of craft were the smaller berths of the swift little trading ships, like her father's.

"They'll throw us out," Cary had warned when they walked onto the wharf from the mouth of the alley. He gasped when she walked directly toward one large, gangly person in a wharfmaster jacket and called, "Hello, Alf! That's you, isn't it?"

At the sight of her the man's tough face softened below the helmet. "Hey, girl-child. You OK? Heard about your parents… Bad job, sorry to hear. And who is this? Ho, I've chased *him* off a time or two—" He added a lowering look.

"This is Cary. A *friend.*" And she nudged him forward. Cary raised a hand hesitantly to touch palms with the wharfmaster's glove. The gesture was accepted without question, and Cary seemed to be struggling to keep his eyes neutral.

"You must be hungry—"

"We are," Kit said. "Where can we buy—"

"No buy. Plenty here." He led them among the rows of little craft to a guard house, and up some steps to its snug interior. There, when he displayed them, his cooler and cupboards seemed to be bristling with flexible tekryl containers of food.

Now they sat on the lockers and ate — dried fruit and salted seaweed, canned fish and thick, tough "crackers," watching the business of the wharf go on around them.

"Maybe Alf could help you get home to your parents," she suggested.

"Nope," he said, that American word that reminded her of her father. "This is my vacation and I'm not ending it early." When she looked at him unspeaking, he added: "Maybe you can send them a message for me so they don't worry."

She nodded and pulled out her phone. While they drank the liters of recycled water Alf had supplied, she helped him send the message.

Were her parents worried? she considered this wistfully. Absurd question. They were dead, probably.

How could they have let themselves go into that hole?

Now, out of years of bargaining, she instinctively brought forth a plan: "Cary, how would you like to make a trade?" She had already got them some food. What about another two months of adventure, provided for (somehow) by her, in trade for his help to find her parents?

He considered, and shrugged, then grinned and touched palms with her.

**

Her guess was right: Alf said the Knath Bioran edict about travel didn't apply to spaceport workers, who of course had to be free to come and go, take hitches to the asteroids or the outer planets for weeks and return to homes on Io or Earth or wherever between contracted months of work.

When she proposed it, Alf was willing to hire the two of them as "longshore help" for part-time work when certain cargoes came in: hard work, not too heavy but fussy, unloading delicate live cargo: plant starts from the lunar nurseries for the burgeoning greenhouses of Freeport.

She and Cary would work for food and for lodging in an unoccupied guard shack nearby. And for a small amount of cash. Alf could pocket the extra money the cargo ships paid him for their work as "skilled laborers," which of course they were! and no one seemed to argue.

As soon as the first cash came in they bought Cary a clean set of used clothes and a real haircut — so, she explained, he could help her by looking more professional.

"Less gutterbum, you mean?" He grinned at her.

On their first day off, they went to visit Mars Search Services. Without explaining much, she told Cary that her parents had gone missing, and she wanted a missing persons search to try to find them.

Cary navigated her there, again through the back alleys of Freeport, to a location that turned out to be close to the spaceport where she had landed a couple of weeks before.

In the Mars Search Services office on the fourth floor of an early-Freeport brick office building, an agent named Rance pulled a tekryl toothpick from his mouth, looked Kit and Cary over again, and shook his head. "Really. No off-Mars searches. Well, now and then there's one on Earth or Io if Mars figures into the picture, but for the usual MP searches — missing persons searches — they have their own pros."

Mars was a place where people tended to get lost, he said — maybe on purpose. People with pasts to leave behind, prospectors looking for rich mineral strikes, people with vague hopes and no resources — they arrived, changed their identities, disappeared and became new people. Or perished. So Search Services stayed busy doing missing persons traces "everywhere," but that meant everywhere on Mars, that's all.

It wasn't the first disappointment since she'd arrived, but it was the biggest.

No, there was no other Missing Persons agency on Mars, he said. In answer to her next question, he looked into the air and frowned. "People who are lost in space? Ha! I think they just stay lost!" He grinned at his own humor.

**

When they returned Alf was leaning against the metal railing that fenced off the unloading area. His large gaunt frame and craggy face seemed to make him the proper representative for what was behind him: a giant freighter, bristling with connectors and compartments built for strength and versatility rather than speed. The freighter was surrounded by the gaunt knees and elbows of cranes and by rusting containers that sat half-unloaded inside the heavy security fence amid stacks of emptied crates. Its hatches lay gaping while the day and night crews changed shifts.

"Alf?" she asked, as they neared him. "Do you know a way I might trace my parents?"

"Hey, haven't seen you all day! Got some starts in from Phobos and they can't wait much longer. I almost got those clumsy lunks from the big-haul team to try their hands at it, but those idiots scare me. Need you right now! Can do?"

Being a pro meant you delivered when you were needed. Kit nodded, looking sideways at Cary. They had just double-timed it here, all 15 kilometers, from Search Services. Cary gave a rueful grin and turned, without speaking, toward their dormitory shack. She knew he'd bring back some food.

"But Alf, did you hear me?"

He was preoccupied. "Hey, get moving!" he shouted at a line of entering longshore laborers, and strode away.

**

The tracker slapped against her thigh as she bounced down the gangway. It was still in her cargo pocket from the visit to Mars Search — where she had not shown it, once she understood the uselessness of revealing it there. If the Mars Search "agent" was less than honest it might also have been dangerous to show the thing.

She and Cary lifted the next temperature-sealed flats of tiny saplings onto a cart at the end of the gangway and stacked them perfectly, nub into hole, so none of the flats could slide. If they slid it would crush the saplings. These were future trees for Freeport and the surrounding farms, nursed from Martian seeds that had blown into crevices or hollows and freeze-dried through the many nearly-airless millenia since Mars had lost her atmosphere.

She told Cary what she had read: that the germinating of the native seeds, and breeding of more, was a delicate process that had become the specialty of a colony of patient Phobos farmers, emigrants from the Kreenid planets.

When the cart was full she and Cary would drive it the hundred meters or so to the ground transport loading dock and reload the flats

219

of trees onto a truck owned by the nursery that had ordered them. They kept count; they'd have to make sure the nursery truck driver signed for every one of the flats they delivered.

"Looks like this is a whole greenhouse-load of stuff!" Cary took her box and lifted it further than she could reach, upward to the top of one stack. "My turn to drive."

She stopped for a long inhale from her breathers and looked around. It was full dark now. She didn't say it, but there was at least this much more left, still to be walked out of the hold. Maybe he knew it and wasn't mentioning it either, to keep her from getting discouraged.

They were becoming friends: the kind who know and take care of each other a little. The time between her parents' trading flights had never been long enough for her to make such friends her own age.

She walked up the gangway behind him into the hold, and out of the hold again down the gangway with another flat, wondering if she'd be walking in her sleep by morning.

In the space between thought and blank weariness, it came to her: Alf would not know how to find her parents. He had given them up for dead, hadn't he? They would have to find them on their own.

Cary put up his flat and reached out to take hers for the top tier. Then they turned and tramped back up the gangway out of the glare of the port-lights and into the dark of the hold.

"Wait." She said. In the dim port-light he turned toward her from the nearest stack of flats.

She tugged the closure on one cargo pocket and pulled out the tracker, springing the lid. The display lit, and his eyes widened with interest. "What's *this*?"

"Know anything about electronics?"

"You kidding? That's what I do. When I'm not homeless on Mars, I mean. That looks like one of those hot new trackers. Is it?"

There's always someone who can help. This might be better than she could have hoped.

He had about six weeks before someone expected him. They had made a trade for adventure, right? Well, she could deliver more adventure than this wharf job without half trying.

"Hey." She said. "How would you like to up the stakes and the action level on this trade?"

Bracelet

U P HERE ON THE CLIFFSIDE the starlight was enough to read by. There was no such starlight on Earth, was there? Kit couldn't remember now; she had spent so little time there. On Io, there was certainly nothing like it.

The silence and cold seemed holy. Weird for her to think that, but it did. If it was holy, the scratch of this heat-patched rented suit and the smell of the uncomfortable breathers were not. Who knew what microbes the prior users had left living in the nosepiece, and she could only hope they both would last long enough to get her back to Freeport.

Far out on the horizon, there was the city of Freeport: until recent years the capital of Mars Colony One, it was a thick cluster of lights that radiated slender luminous streams, making it half an asterisk spread from the horizon across the valley toward her. Those radiating lines of light faded out long before they came near, so here the darkness of the landforms would have been deep — if it had not been for the starlight that backlit and sculpted the dry mountains, valleys and foothills.

Maybe this idea was crazy. She only had a few hours to find out. She had heard her mother say that sometimes a dream might come when you were not watchful, slipping out to inform you, from between the scenery in your life, of things that were non sequitur but always vital.

She looked toward the rocky jutting hills upslope from her cliff perch. And saw instead her parents — as the tracking device had last showed them — the tiny dot of their trading ship about to disappear into some kind of hole in space, an impossible distance away. Impossible not to think of that now, when she was on the spot where they had stood.

How real was it to think that maybe this craziness would help her locate them?

The kitten hissed, pinched by the waistband of her suit. She nudged it upward, above the tight part, with one gloved hand.

[I was quiet while we flew,] the kitten announced.

[Thank you. It was necessary.] She refused to soften on this point till they were safely back. Strictly speaking, animal life sharing a spacesuit was prohibited. Probably illegal, even on Mars. What if her driver was friends with the suit-rental company?

She began to walk uphill toward a rock-strewn ravine.

She had traded expertly, as sixteen years on a trading ship had taught her: promised a favor to get her workmate to agree to watch her things, left her top-quality sleep sack at the shop as collateral for rental of the suit and breathers, with full payment to be made in coin when she returned safely; earned enough extra coin selling castoff merch on the waterfront to pay for the costly transport to this cliff from Freeport. Good trades, all of them.

It was two months since she had arrived on Mars by one-way charity transport. At 16 Kitrin Reed was too old to be called an orphan, although her parents, they said, must have died light-years away. But she was too young to have anyone respect her wish to stay on Io. And too alone to have any resources worth talking about. She had accepted the offer of citizenship from Knath Biorin, once Mars Colony 1, since her birth here made citizenship hers for free.

Although she had seen it said on the WorldWeb that occasional scientists or curious travelers came to this cliffside spot, there were no amenities and no sign of other people now.

"No tour, thank you," she had repeated politely, in her bare-minimum Universal Spanish, to the Spanish-speaking Kreenid driver as she tied and stuffed her copper-colored curls into the helmet, then paid him a fourth of the fare. "The remainder and a tip when you return for me at dawn."

That was not many hours from now, but the breathers only lasted so long... He took the kite off the cliff-edge as lightly as a sparrow takes wing and disappeared in the distance against the lights of Freeport. It was a bargain that could work: she needed him to return for her on time, without fail, and he wanted to make sure he got the rest of his pay.

She looked out toward the city, once the only spaceport on the planet, now capital of Knath Biorin. There the atmosphere was thicker, and sparse plant-life grew in the native soil because of the water that was manufactured there. Helped by natural water slowly being recovered from underground ice. Gradually Mars was coming back to life, but here in the lonely hills it was still dead.

In spite of that something here spoke to her.

[Upward here.] the kitten said.

To any sensible person it would be preposterous to take directions from a kitten. But she had heard all her father's stories — and yes, her parents had nodded, they were true: the cats of Mars were no fairy tale. They were formidable, crafty, and real, and they meant business. Listen to them at your peril, but you'd better listen regardless.

In her dream two weeks ago Kit had seen this cliffside, long ago described by her mother, who had once found here a mysterious

Singer sleeping in the bones of an ancient race. In Kit's dream, vivid as a holovid, she had traveled upward into the mountainside above to find cliff dwellings still housing the skeletons of a people killed and preserved by bitter, airless cold many millenia ago.

And in the dream, in one pathetic tableau, there was a beautiful bracelet that she immediately knew she must get to recover her parents.

Preposterous. The nonsense of it woke her from the dream. And in the darkness, when she shook the sleep from her head, she found a kitten curled beside her in the hammock.

A kitten? Right here in the waterfront shack where she and her workmate Cary were housed. How it had entered was easy: the shack probably had enough holes for more than kittens to use as doorways. But why?

"Not much food for you here," she had whispered at the little gray thing, petting it gently. It shrank from her touch, then leaned into it.

[Not here for food] was what she heard. Was she dreaming again? Sleepily she accepted the answer and succumbed to the heat and the whirring noise that the kitten radiated.

**

Right now she thought she heard music, faintly. Odd music. It must be in her memory, something coming back to her now as she walked and scrambled among the boulders uphill — there was a song or chant the kitten had sung to her as she slept that night:

Air sweet with blossoms and full of insect songs,

boom and hiss of flying creatures, music everywhere,

small lighted dragon insects, singing in the night...

But again now, she thought she heard music. Live music, this time.

What nonsense! she suddenly protested. Just because her mother followed cats didn't mean it was a good idea. Where had such stuff gotten her parents? Never any wealthier.

And now it had got them lost in a wormhole or imploded by negative matter or something. She shuddered, not wanting that to be true.

But their life! She had grown up loving it: life on a trading ship, light and fleet as the ancient clippers. She had learned from the markets and ports and the precious collection of books they carried onboard, every day something new.

She could do the math: the worth of the riches and treasures they had bought and sold, found and lost, was staggering. But their real riches? Their friends, all over the galaxy, mourned them and sent her funny stories about adventures that "maybe she never knew about." She knew the adventures she herself had shared with them. Who could say their life wasn't worth that?

And if it were possible, which it probably wasn't, who could say that saving them and restoring them to their lives would not be treasure enough for her whole life? It was a thought she had not allowed into her mind before now.

Such nonsense. Still, you had to try. She sighed and stood still at a place where the ravine stopped against a near-vertical cliff. [Where now?] she asked.

[Up.] the kitten said, matter-of-factly.

[But I have no jet-pack!]

[You can do it. Just don't crush me against the rock.]

She felt the kitten scramble, digging into her skin with needle claws, to lie spraddled on the top of her left shoulder. She surveyed the cliff and found a foothold for one boot, spread her arms wide to hug the rock, and dug her fingers into the gaps between layers. At least a fall would weigh less here.

**

She stood panting in the last dark chamber, sure that she could smell the ancient dust of the earthen walls in spite of her helmet and breathers. She gasped as the cold of this hidden place seemed to pass through her suit. She would have to hurry.

The only warmth lay on her left shoulder, where the kitten stretched tiny legs and flexed now, digging his claws into her sweater. She shrugged to tell him to stop.

Shreds of starlight somehow entered under the overhang, onto the ledge, reflected through the doorway. As her eyes adjusted, there was the sad tableau from her dream: the bones of a long-dead trio huddled together, mummified in the dry air, with bits of cloth and jewelry still glued to them by thin layers of flesh. They were not exactly human-looking, but close: two adults, maybe a man and woman, who held a child pressed between them — giving their last warmth to it in a vain hope that now was long-dead too.

So far from the other dwellings. No wonder no one else had found this place.

She knelt on the cold earthen floor in front of the ancient family. There on the nearest wrist was the bracelet that was vivid in her dream: lapis in silver, with tiny silver vines and leaves spiralling around and around the stones. It was knockout beautiful. She stared at the exquisite thing, hesitating to disturb a grave site.

Then, knowing that the dream had told her to take it, with clumsy gloved fingers she felt for the hook to unfasten it from its place around the bone.

The kitten dug its claws into her shoulder. "Ow!" she shrugged crossly, then breathed deeply and stretched her fingers again toward the lapis bracelet, struggling to make her muscles work precisely in the cold.

The claws dug at her shoulder again. "WHAT?" she exploded. [What is it???]

[Look.]

When Kit looked, the magnetism of the pretty treasure ebbed and she saw the whole scene: the three skeletons, joined in this sad group hug, all wore bracelets of silver, or something like it, at their wrists. Wealthy people, probably. Or maybe mama or papa was an artist who made such things.

That might be the father, on the right, wearing the rope of heavy silver links around his wrist. It seemed odd that his braceleted hand also held a small carved slice of glossy black, nearly invisible in the darkness. His hand resolutely held it ready, as a person waiting in line for a show would hold his phone display ready to show that he had paid. Without his gleaming bracelet, she never would have seen it.

She pulled at its top edge. The rectangular slice of black stone slid easily from his hand into Kit's.

It was carved on both sides with rows and rows of tiny runes or symbols of some kind, unreadable. Trying very hard to say something. And maybe it was something she needed to know. But still, totally unreadable. Kit's shoulders ached from the climb. She sighed, feeling tired. She should put the little tablet back.

Despite the helmet and breathers, her sigh must have disturbed some arrangement of the dust that remained in this cold, silent place. So little had touched this room for so long.

The child's elbow abruptly went lax and its forearm lolled downward, allowing the smallest bracelet to slip, with the faintest of rattles, over the bones of its hand and onto the earthen floor.

Kit started and shuddered. The kitten froze.

Scolding herself for being so easily frightened, Kit picked up the bracelet between two stiff fingers and hung it in the air at a place where there seemed to be the most reflected starlight. She saw that it was a procession of little carved jet bugs, like the scarab beetles of Egypt, on silver backings that were each connected to the next by a silver link. They marched in three columns of ten, side by side and head to tail, round and round. So clever and tiny! Kit knew what price this treasure could bring a trader.

But she was also too proud to give in to greed. It was wrong to take burial treasure just to make yourself rich. She had been drawn here for the tablet only, she decided. It seemed intended to be read. By someone, anyway. Maybe not by her.

Before she laid the bracelet to rest beside the child-bones of its owner she took a final curious look at the scarabs and the silver backings so artfully fitted around each one.

She stared and held the treasure closer. Each smooth oval backing had carvings, a tiny symbol and a finely etched pictograph: an insect, a leaf...

Seconds passed while she gazed without breathing. Something about it was familiar, but she didn't know why until a memory came back to her from the days before she could read: A is for apple, B is for bird... In memory she saw the letters, each letter with a pictograph, in a simple infant's book.

This might be an alphabet bracelet, Mars style. She smiled to think so, and then was flooded with pity for these ancient people with the strangely-shaped skulls. Pitied them for their loss, millennia ago.

Wait. What if this bracelet was the Rosetta Stone that would let you translate the jet tablet? She exhaled an awe-struck hope.

[Is this what you were trying to show me?] she thought at the kitten suddenly, without intending to.

On her shoulder, he only dozed and purred.

**

The lights of Freeport were winking out as day began again on this part of Mars. The driver was talkative, happy to be near landing and paytime, she imagined. Everyone liked to be paid.

Cary, her workmate, had looked at her funny, then laughed at her when she told about her dream. He would be amazed when she returned with the bracelet and tablet.

Only then did it really hit her. She had been so dazzled by the beautiful baubles — and then fascinated by the mysterious symbols — that she had lost sight of her purpose. She went to the cliffs with the idea that the search would lead to a map, or toward an ancient piece of technology, that would give some clue to her parents' disappearance out near Vega.

These treasures were nothing like that. Maybe the tablet would end up saying something important, if she could figure it out. Or maybe not. More likely the tablet was covered with the guy's will or religious quotes.

She paid the driver generously, for luck, and shook his hand when he offered it.

The kitten was demanding exit. A block from the rental office, just inside an alleyway where she would not be seen, she let him out of her suit. He ran off after something, maybe a large Mars-bug, and disappeared. He didn't answer when she called after him.

At the rental office, with the gloves and helmet on the battered counter, she felt the weight of the treasures in her cargo pockets while she sat and took off the suit, paying the clerk, collecting back her collateral — her sleepsack in its sheath.

She would have a story to tell Cary. But she knew she had missed the mark. He would have every right to laugh at her again.

She put on her cloak, looked around for the city airbus, then decided to save money and walk the mile of alley shortcuts to the port where Cary would be getting off work.

The alley here was lined with trash receptacles and greasy-looking back steps. Leading into the kitchens of restaurants, probably. An ugly place.

She had never been a believing sort of person, like her mother. But in going to the cliffs she had tried out her mother's way of doing things.

Without a whole lot of success so far.

Thoughts paraded through Kit's mind as she walked onward: ways to try to translate the black tablet. What to do if the tablet was useless to her (take it and the bracelet back to the burial site?). Things to ask if another cat ever showed up. Trades to make to fund the next search idea.

As she went on, she also strode deeper and deeper into things that were not plans or trades, but some kind of labyrinth within her that she suddenly she knew she was walking. Trying to find her way.

She stopped, smelling the stinging odor of the ugly bins of chemicals in this alley. Puddles of black gleamed below a few of the battered bins. She was four or five blocks from the trading port now; its huge cranes were visible out ahead.

Gazing around her, she saw that the labyrinth wasn't about cliffs or legends, maps, devices, treasures, or cats. About beautiful or ugly. Or even about what shouldn't be, like most of her life right now. It was about her, herself.

Right now she had only a little more than she had left with yesterday. But the labyrinth had changed, almost without her knowing it.

Now, although Kit couldn't say why, contained in it there was hope, and a future.

It Might Be Today

RILL WOKE with the polished stones of the turret floor pressing freezing angles into her back. Under the brim of her hat, between the notches in the crenellated wall, she saw thick stars. *In the daytime?*

The last she remembered was sunlight here on the hotel roof, the sound of a gust of wind rising, her dark hair blowing into her eyes, and holding her hat to keep it on. Damned hat; floppy-rimmed, styleless marsh-fiber, the proper local cowl for newcomers: that is, those not living under the Law of Swathil. For her protection, she had been assured. So far it had not protected her.

She pulled the hat off and threw it aside. The heavy air — enough like the air of her birthplace for breathing — was cold but sweeter now, not as it had been in the fetid daylight earlier when it was thick with the nasty smell of souring vegetation.

She lay sluggishly, still half-out, listening idly to the small scratching sound that had wakened her. It was nearly drowned by the drone of insects coming from somewhere in the greenery far below. Some of the stars dusting the dark were gold or red, instead of silver; they were colored silver almost always on Paris, her home planet, but these were the proper colors of the Ares starscape, she had read — when? — sometime during her journey here...

Power of thought returned abruptly. After years of self-defense training, had she stupidly let herself be ambushed? Alone on the roof of an ancient fortress made over into a hotel, on a violent planet. Not a place to be unguarded, ever.

Maybe she had forgotten! she recognized it bitterly: here, and professionally, she was just a little person, subject to the orders and sometimes the violent whims of those who hired her. She shook her head to wake herself fully, also awakening the bruise at the back of her skull.

She rose abruptly to sit looking down along the length of her body, massaging arms that were bumpy from the chill. Her undyed tunic hung rumpled and creased over her brown leather leggings, but nothing else seemed amiss except her boots. She started when she saw them beside her feet rather than on them.

Against the hasty sliding of her feet, the freezing flagstones finished waking her. She reached to snatch her boots and plunged a hand into the left one, seeking the holstered knife, a fine Bindi blade from her twin brother Solen. Who languished in prison on Bindare. Her heart twisted.

Then it rose into her throat: not there. Solen's knife was gone.

Looking all around her stupidly as a belated act of self-defense, she plunged her hand into the other boot. And withdrew it hastily, with a hissing furry beast following just behind it. As it leaped out of the boot, it spat fierce threats at her in some beast-language.

"*My* boot," she said to the small thing steadily, forcing her heart to slow. "*You* are the one who was trespassing." Many times she had been accosted or even threatened by a client who was fearful of being cheated, angry about property rights, or shifting the truth due to greed. She had learned to hold her own fear in check.

[My napping-place!] The creature's defiance echoed in her mind.

A telepath! As a translator, sensitive to language since birth, she had worked for a few telepaths. But in all her travels to translate contracts, sales, treaties and talks, she had not seen a creature like this on any planet. Its black fur was lustrous in the starlight, covering triangular ears and a long smooth tail. It had golden snake eyes and pale foxxenish whiskers, and a white comet like a comma on its forehead.

And holy starlight! a telepath, too.

It sat obstinately between her and the boot, staring at her. Its next hiss bared a set of needle-sharp white teeth. Was its bite poisonous?

She had no time for this. If it was truly evening, trading would start sometime soon; she should prepare and she should be properly rested.

She had worked a long year to earn the money for defense so her brother could be freed: another foolish little person, wrongfully jailed... Of course she would do this, and more, for him; it just had been a long year without rest or Solen or the company of old friends, and the next 38 hours would be the last work day of the religious year on this planet: for her, this one translation might pay her all she needed — with her saved funds, this might be all it would take to bribe the bitterly grasping Bindare court system on Solen's behalf.

She was not a trader, but she had sat at table with them and translated for them for years; she had assisted the delicate art of trade-making well enough to know how to begin a peaceable agreement. She sent the thought as clearly as she could to this creature:

[Although it is my boot, and therefore a thing over which I have primary rights, I see that you have been occupying it in my absence and therefore you would like to have a right acknowledged.]

The creature gazed at her, very attentive now.

Her next move came to her mind out of the air because she had watched it so often: the play for information. She asked: [Did you notice who removed the boots from my feet?]

Silence. Despite the cold stones and the late hour, both of which made her anxious to rise, she composed herself to sit and gaze blandly at the creature. Its eyes never blinked and never left hers, for long minutes. Then it said:

[Human. Man.]

When the creature offered no more she said, [Thank you. Are you able to recall enough to describe the human?]

She saw that her questioning the creature's ability had irked the black furry thing. It sniffed and began licking a paw with leisurely indifference.

She waited. In ten years of translating for chieftains and legislators, scientists and pirates, she had seen how the ability to wait was everything. An impatient translator could harm negotiations or break a trade. Translators with excellent timing won praise — and sometimes rewards — from tense bargainers.

At last the creature lifted its head, licked one more leisurely time with its eyes fixed on hers, and sent her the image of the man: [light hair, braided at the sides; light eyes, aquiline nose; strong hands with fingertips dyed red.]

It was not a description of the typical denizen of Ares, a planet where teeming spaceports, spacers and hot-blooded humans from everywhere rested heavily atop an ancient civilization ruled by strict religious rules and fitful intrigues. But she had met a man of this description on entry to her hotel; someone of the native Swathil culture, who had remarked that he would be sitting at the table with her this evening.

She groaned inwardly at the thought. But she slid her feet smoothly into the boots, while she made her thanks gracious and smooth as well: full of extravagant expressions of respect because these seemed to be what the creature would accept.

It watched her, then began to make a soft snoring sound while it chewed daintily between wickedly-curved claws. In grooming them, it displayed them lavishly to her, like a vain woman or man showing off finely laquered nails. It made Rill glance at her own. For the meeting to come she would need to repair them, quickly.

She rose. [So the man took my knife?] she asked. It was a bonus question; maybe she could learn more from this furry thing...

And where could she obtain a replacement knife? Going to a meeting without such minimum protection would be so foolish that her guild manual listed it as a primary warning.

The creature only sheathed its claws and looked at her. Then it turned and walked to the open doorway that led to the spiraling staircase downward.

After a short glance above her head at the gold and red stars, and a deep breath of the cold air, Rill followed.

**

Her eyes searched each door as she passed down the dim, lamplit hallway, looking for her symbol: she had been given the room with the leaping fish. The hall smelled of cloth and the damp of stones, which radiated cold. When she relocated the door with the fish she found to her surprise that the black-furred creature was at her feet in front it, sitting on the thick green of the carpet with its tail wrapped around it, apparently awaiting her. Surprise again: when she keyed the wooden slab with her card and pushed it inward, the black thing entered, without hesitation, before her.

By the time it occurred to her that this hissing thing might be a risk in her room, she found it had taken up residence under the sleeping frame, out of reach.

No time for this now.

She quickly checked the information wall slot: as she feared, little more than an hour remained before the scheduled meeting time. The location would be the Ibis meeting room, this hotel. Meal service hours displayed: all long past. She groaned aloud and checked her own hand-sized relay, finding confirmation of the meeting time, followed by a wise, character-building quote sent by another translator. And a message from an old friend, lightyears from here. *How is everything going?*

She sighed. When she shook her head it ached from the bruise.

New information now displayed on the wall-slot with a quiet gong: An invitation to dinner by one Paran Kaan, whoever that was, sent hours ago, and how did he get her room number? Too late for dinner anyway. She was glad to have missed the need to make excuses for not accepting; she never dined with anyone before a translation meeting. This offer made her edgy. She rechecked the lock on the door.

But she pushed the communicator button, and when the voice came on, thick with that unpleasant Ares-Swathil patois, she ordered some hard sheep cheese and the local tree-fruit and "a very sharp paring knife to prepare them." The patois answered, without any doubt or suspicion, that her order would arrive in minutes.

She inspected her slender arms and hands. No time to bathe fully; she could only wash to get the roof-soot off her skin. As she wound her hair and fastened it high on her head, and as she scrubbed her face, hands, arms and legs, she sighed at how much her skin missed the people she knew, male and female, all ages. Missed arms around her, friendly hands to clasp. Solen most of all: his rough hugs. It had been a lonely year.

Rill wrapped herself in the soft drying cloth, pulled a small clear sack of nuts and dried fruits from her travel case, and sat chewing fast while she opened the little bottle of pale retouch laquer for her manicure.

While she brushed the stuff on meticulously a small platter arrived through the service slot, carrying a wedge of ochre-colored cheese, two small green fruits and a little, heavy-handled knife. The hotel would charge her a high price for these, she knew, but what choice did she have? Little people pay.

Pointed and very sharp: she tested the knife on an edge of her fingernail and the hem of her towel. She sighed again, this time with relief; it looked as if she would go into this meeting prepared after all.

She continued eating, chewing busily while the laquer dried. And while she pulled on her gray professional leggings and tunic and wove her hair into the tall, stylish look that was considered proper by young interstellar professionals.

Fifteen minutes to meeting time. She booted, sheathing the knife again; she gathered up her relay and tablet and a folder of printed information on the case involved. She checked to see that the extra copy of the case information was still hidden within the lining of her travel case behind her money and private papers. She would arrive early, as always, to take possession of the room before the others arrived. It was her personal policy.

Then she remembered the black creature. "Pssst, Comet-Person. Ho, Comma. Come now, I have to leave the room."

There was no sound. She was perfectly dressed and coiffed and she wasn't going down on her knees to look under the bed. "Psst, last chance or you get locked in here."

What if the worst happened? "If you mess on my floor the maid may not treat you with much dignity. Hey?"

No answer. She opened the door to the adjacent room that contained the bidet, to provide an alternative, and left the rest in the hands of the gods. She opened the door to the hallway.

The creature Comma flew by into the hallway ahead of her.

**

She entered the Ibis Room through double doors, heavy wood like the door to her hotel room — only to find that one person had arrived before her and was already seated at the large round table. His white hair was braided in front of his ears.

She made a show of shutting the door completely. This man was the one whose image she had seen in telepathy from Comma: the one who had unshod her. Mr. Knife-Thief. And worse: also the one who had spoken to her early this morning in Swathil as she arrived at the hotel.

She nodded politely as she reached the table; he bowed his head slightly in turn. Was it her imagination, or was he disappointed to see her? "Your pardon," she said in Swathil, with a gracious smile. "We met earlier but I don't believe you gave me your name."

"P.D. Kaan," he answered. As in Paran Kaan, who had asked for dinner with her? He was certainly a busy man, wasn't he? She gave her professional name: "Diana Rillan Su," and touched hands with him barely, according to custom here. She looked around for her place marker.

Her turn to be disappointed: she was seated next to Mr. Kaan.

To signal that she was not inviting a chat with him, she opened the woven-reed folder and her tablet to review her materials on this case.

Had she been so starstruck by the idea of reaching her goal, freeing Solen, that she had carelessly studied these before? The information seemed hopelessly unfamiliar, even confusing, now.

When she looked up Kaan was watching her as if he read her thoughts. And when he raised an eyebrow triumphantly, she felt that she was again unprepared — at an unexpected disadvantage already, without knowing why. This was a like a small social duel; well, better to attack than defend, then. She challenged: "Perhaps you will tell me what your role is in tonight's meeting?"

He was silent a moment but then he seemed to decide it would do no harm to say. "I am one of the two negotiating parties," he shrugged.

Her mind sped up. "Ah," she smiled pleasantly at him, showing teeth. "Then the lands in question are yours?" she said, deliberately mistaking the information of the case to force him to correct her.

His eyelids dropped halfway down. "Yes, I believe so," he nodded.

If he had been selling her something she would have taken those eyes as signals that he was lying. She glanced at her papers again. Even these complex paragraphs unmistakably said that eons-old rights to the Lysantr mountainside and a full, well-watered valley called Pathanar were the recorded property of someone else, some huge ancient family, and that the present Mr. Kaan wanted to take ownership of these lands, based on his current use of them for grazing and farming.

He underestimated her. But how had the information that she studied for hours on the flight become so changed? The document in front of her was full of Swathil terms and complicated legal pronouncements.

"Very odd," she said. "The description of this case that I studied seemed simpler than this document shows." She looked into his eyes, mildly.

She saw the ripple of self-consciousness inside those eyes, which were so blonde a shade of brown that they almost looked white. So this Kaan had access to her room and her papers? A shiver ran down her arms, inside her tunic sleeves.

To disguise the moment she added, "Would you be so kind as to restate the facts of the case simply for me now, before we begin?"

He dropped his lids again and bowed his head graciously. "Of course." His voice was smooth and light as sheep-cheese, like his eyes.

**

By the time he had finished describing the land, the parties involved, and their rights, the table was nearly full and they were surrounded by a gabble of mixed languages. A waiter was circling the table, pouring coffees and preparing the rich local teas that were served with mint and butter.

All eight seats were occupied but one. The social introductions that accompanied coffee and tea showed that someone had rearranged the placemarkers. The party that claimed ownership of Lysantr mountainside and Pathanar valley held three seats, one of them unoccupied, grouped opposite Kaan and his two legal associates. The moderator, gray-haired Dr. Tsu, sat singly, in a space between the two parties, but Rill's seat was incorrectly placed at Kaan's side of the table.

Busy Mr. Kaan had probably done that. Did he think she was a beginner who would allow it? Or so small and helpless he could force this on her?

"There seems to have been an error in seating," she said clearly during a quiet moment. "If you all will excuse me, I will place myself correctly, opposite the moderator." She rose, which forced Kaan and his people to rise too and shift to new positions, grouped opposite the Lysantr pair who bookended the single empty chair.

When Rill's seat and the moderator's were comfortably separate from the negotiating parties, set in open spaces facing each other, Dr. Tsu asked the two Lysantr representatives, "Where is the third of your group?"

Both rose. The Lysantr pair were both curly-haired, dark-eyed and rotund, the man a little taller than the woman. Both wore outlandish black business suits that looked like they originated from another planet entirely, but unusual looks seemed to be usual on Ares. Both looked uncomfortable. "Soon to arrive," Rould NilArun said in Ari, and he bowed politely.

His accent Rill had never heard before. It had been clear in her contract, though, that the mountain group would need translation to Swathil from Ari-Swathil patois, commercial Ari, and "possibly even Universal Language or others." And Kaan would need translation from

Swathil to whichever language might be in use.

Kaan's two companions, probably attorneys, wore traditional Swathil long tunics with feathers sewed to the lapels of their robes. The robes might mimic those of thinkers or philosophers but the men inside them had scheming looks.

Fortunately this moderator was well-known for correctness and fairness; in such a case it was a condition that the contending participants be willing to be ruled, in case they could not agree, by the final judgment of the moderator.

Tsu was one of the reasons Rill had accepted this case, on a squabble-ridden planet out here at the far frontier of the solar system. Tsu and the pay, of course. She knew he thought highly of her, possibly because she was a rarity, like him: one who could translate telepathic speech and a number of other curious, dwindling tongues.

"But," the woman added in Ari after a pause, "As you can see on the case sheet, Mr. NilArun and I have permission to establish the facts of our case in advance of the arrival of our client, Ms. Hrenn. I suggest we begin."

**

Rill smiled and nodded at the latest speaker in spite of her headache. Kaan's voice began again, grating on her ears. It was after the midnight hour. The curved silver wall-lights in the meeting room wore haloes, her eyes were so tired. And she was beyond hungry. It seemed likely that Mr. Kaan would win this negotiation, but that didn't seem fair.

Maybe she should be grateful that she had been unconscious for hours on the turret today. Her head swam with the complexity of the concepts she had been translating: legal rights, documents, traditional rights, monetary exchanges, family feuds... It wasn't that the complexity of ownership was so unusual, but the level of tension was, and the languages involved made it more difficult still.

And Kaan's maze-like substitute document, which he seemed to have slipped into everyone's possession, muddied the facts and required that each issue be redefined by the curly-haired pair laboriously — in the face of hot and haughty Swathil rebuttals from Kaan's two legal experts. The static in the room had been thick as stormclouds all evening.

She had done all she could to translate so clarity resulted. She had not succeeded. Kaan's complicated nonsense had held them all hostage for five hours, with no result.

The two parties at the table weren't the only ones who wanted a conclusion to be reached; if the result were not satisfactory within the allowed time, and the case had to be dropped for the holy days, she would be here as a hotel guest at her own expense until they resumed, or lose the work and the cost of her ticket by dropping the case — which would injure her reputation as well.

Now that midnight had passed, and with no appearance from Ms. Hrenn, Dr. Tzu regretfully recessed the meeting until next morning. He might have debts to pay or places to go too, poor man.

**

The silence of the hallway, when she reached it, was a huge relief to her. She stood on the thick green carpet and thumbed through her small purse for the room card.

A hand touched her elbow from behind. She whirled, and that wound her into the firm hold of a thick arm, eye to eye with Kaan.

She pushed against his chest with her free hand, and to her horror saw his own free hand go to his waist. Would he kill for this case?

A hiss and yowl landed on his chest, claws going into his hair, and he recoiled from Rill to drag and push at the black furry thing that screamed in his face.

Rill didn't hesitate. While Kaan struggled blindly she pulled the card, keyed the door, and stepped in; she hated to leave the creature to its own defense, but after a quick look at Comma's fiercely waving claws, she shut the door hard and locked it.

She called room service to say that a man had harassed her on her way into her room; would they send a guard? And when the scuffling outside was replaced by the sound of voices, she stood behind the door and opened it a few inches. The creature flew in and shot under the bedframe. She turned the bolt.

"Thank you, Comma," she said into the silence.

**

A moon. What was its name? Through heavy-lidded eyes Rill could see its white light shining between the pairs of slats on her windows, patterning the floor.

The weariness that had submerged her in sleep instantly, hours ago, had relaxed its grip enough that now she lay awake remembering too much and thinking too much. Seeing Kaan's face, merciless and eager to overwhelm her. Seeing Solen telling her stories, up in a tree when they were seven. She shuddered at how much she feared for him in Bindare prison, a brutal stew of misery. His puckish grin and his love of stories: what help could they be to him there?

She had to finish tomorrow, had to get Solen out; but would Kaan permit a settlement, or insist on contention? The back of her head ached.

Something shifted beside her. With minute noises, the creature Comma was arriving on her pillow, dark as a shadow in the moonlight. It began to make that soft snoring noise, as it had on the turret.

The sound was irresistible, like a small rippling stream or the coming and going of waves.

Rill slept.

**

When the room display clock woke her, sunlight had replaced the moonlit patterns on the floor, lying in long, buttery bars.

Her confusion seemed to have gone. Everything seemed perfectly clear; about Solen, about the case. It wasn't up to her to solve or judge the case. The facts had become simple to her though, and seeing them simply made her confident enough to do her job.

Rill's tired worry had been replaced with some kind of certainty, too. She would do all she could. What more was there?

Right now Comma sat beside her head on the pillow, rumbling and grooming its claws. When she rose on one elbow to look, the creature ceased its manicure and said, [You're welcome.]

[For what?] The puzzled thought escaped her before she could stop it.

Comma froze and looked levelly at her. The black tail swung back and forth warningly.

Only then did she recall the story she had heard in the night, while she slept: a dream that seemed like fantasy as it passed, but as simple as any true account always is: about the native people of the mountainside and valley, how they belonged to the land there and were its owners from the beginning...

She politely extended her palm to the creature. It nuzzled, then licked her palm. Then sat and gazed at her, its eyes as still as golden pools.

She smiled and went to bathe.

Afterward she would eat and be there in time for the meeting to resume. While she bathed she wondered if Comma, who had defended and befriended her, had a human owner or companion. Would the creature want to travel on with her? She liked the thought.

While she bathed she remembered the second copy of the case summary that she had brought and hidden in the lining of her travel case. During breakfast she ordered copies of it at the hotel business center to give to all the attendees. They would understand her suggestion to a change of the information to the "original, simpler form," which was the truth, and they would recognize that this version was what they had read before. Only Kaan might protest, but what could he say that would not expose his trickery?

When they all joined at the meeting table again, Kaan wore a matched set of red scratches down one cheek. He emphatically did not look at her. The attendees from last night had arrived and all were seated; she paused before she sat to nod a greeting at all of them.

But she noted with disappointment that one seat remained empty. How could they complete this without Ms. Hrenn, the main representative of the Lysantr group? Fear arose again in her: here was opportunity for Kaan to play more tricks and cause delays.

"An incident of harassment, inappropriate to these proceedings, has been reported," Dr. Tzu began. "There was no damage — " he looked blandly at Kaan's scratches— "so I mention it only to give warning to you all that any such activity could result in penalties. All attendees are warned.

"And will Ms. Hrenn be arriving soon?" Dr. Tzu asked the two curly-haired people seated a quarter of the table to his right. Everyone in the room moved restlessly at this, even the weary-looking meeting guard behind Tzu.

[I have arrived.] Ms. Hrenn rose to an upright position in her chair between the two curly-haired people, her head above the tablecloth.

Rill's mouth fell open. Ms. Hrenn's black fur was lustrous in the white meeting lights and her eyes were calm like gold pools. How almost-comical Comma looked sitting there! Yet the presence surrounding the creature was so...human.

"Get that vicious thing out of here!" Kaan leaped to his feet. His two legal assistants rose hastily after him, hands reaching for weapons.

Wide-eyed Dr. Tzu signaled furiously to the guards to bring order, scowling a warning at Kaan and his shouting men. He turned to Ms.

Hrenn.

She nodded slightly and her gaze met his. [Pardon my seeming absence yesterday evening, Dr. Tzu,] she said. [I wish now to tell, to all who are here, the story of my people.]

Her people.

Their valley.

At the first words Rill breathed deep, full of some unexpected pride. And full of new hope for Solen, for Ms. Hrenn and her triangle-eared race, and all the other little people.

Hope for herself too. It might be that today the little people would win.

She shook the astonishment from her face, raised her voice above the din to call for attention, and began to translate.

***

Also by J.K. Stephens

If you liked this story collection, you'll also enjoy

The Ibis Door, Dreamers Book 1

Readers say:

"I loved this story. It was a perfect read." GCH

"Hard to put down." PG

The Singer, Dreamers Book 2

Readers say:

"Whimsical, challenging, and a whole lot of fun." JM

"It has everything a good book needs." C

In the Ring, Dreamers Book 3

Readers say:

"A great story with a perfect ending!" VS

"You know you have found a good read when you finish the first book in a series and find yourself looking forward to the next, and the same for the third…I am looking forward to reading more…" JC

Connect

Join the author's own mailing list for access to the latest stories and news.

I like staying in touch with readers, who after all are the people I write for. To join my mailing list for blogs and periodic updates, just email permission to:

JKStephens@daybreakcreate.com

… and to welcome you I'll send you another story.

Your opinion helps other readers

Your reviews help readers like you to find books they will like—including this one, I hope.

If you enjoyed *The Emperor's Golden Carp and Other Stories*, you can leave a short review on the page where you bought this book, or at

JKStephens@daybreakcreate.com

ACKNOWLEDGEMENTS

Grateful thanks to the many people who have helped me to create and publish this collection of short stories — especially Dean, Marcia, Maggy, Kathy, Torsten, Janice and Cheri. And thanks to my readers for joining me in imagining these tales.

J.K. Stephens

ABOUT THE AUTHOR

J.K. Stephens lives and writes near Tampa, Florida.

A fan of funny movies, dancing, long walks and bike rides, the author is as crazy about mountains as beaches, and travels at any opportunity—not only to gather ideas for further writing, but also to enjoy the remarkable people, places, foods and dreams that make the world the way it is.